cut off from sky and earth

cut off from sky and earth

Melissa F. Miller

Cover design by Jack Miller
Creative director David Miller
Cover image Michele Jackson/Jackson Stock Photography

ISBN 9781961427297 (ebook)
ISBN 9781961427303 (paperback)
ISBN 9781961427310 (hardcover)

The author wishes to clarify that this book was written by a human being.

To me, for finally leaving my tower. And to my therapist and escitalopram, for lighting the way.

<h1 style="text-align: right">part i. the princess</h1>

There was once a King who had a son who asked in marriage the daughter of a mighty King; she was called Maid Maleen, and was very beautiful. As her father wished to give her to another, the prince was rejected; but as they both loved each other with all their hearts, they would not give each other up, and Maid Maleen said to her father, "I can and will take no other for my husband."

—*Maid Maleen,* as retold by the Brothers Grimm

Maleen bit down on her lip, then implored her friend, "I'm right, aren't I? I love him, and I can't marry anyone but him."

Ruth hesitated, torn between Maleen's needs

and her own. *Of course*, the princess should follow her heart and marry for love. Every woman—every *person*—deserved the freedom to do so. But. But what about Ruth's freedom? What about Ruth's agency?

Maleen knew as well as Ruth did that her refusal would enrage her father. But what Ruth suspected, and Maleen would never admit, is that her choice would have disastrous consequences for them both.

Ruth knew, and yet, as Maleen waited, her clear blue eyes anxious and unblinking, she sighed. "You make terrible decisions." Then she grinned, "But you should do it."

— *The Tower,* by Emily Rose

one

`Tristan`

I'm parked behind the organic market located halfway between work and home, waiting for seven o'clock to roll around so I can pop open the video conferencing app on the tablet my wife doesn't know I own to log in for my semiannual visit with the psychotherapist my wife doesn't know I see.

Around the corner, the church bells at St. Agnes chime the hour, and I hit the meeting button. Right on cue, Dr. Wilde's face fills my screen.

"Tate," he says, "good to see you."

Even though I've been using my brother's name for these appointments for more than six years now, a frisson of shock runs through me every time the psychiatrist calls me Tate. I have to stop myself from looking over my shoulder to make sure my older brother isn't looming in my back seat.

"The beard suits you, Doc," I tell him.

He strokes his chin, pleased I've noticed. "I grew it during my last work retreat. I highly recommend it. I booked myself a cabin and managed to crank out three articles to submit for peer review, and I made progress on a new project. Something groundbreaking—really cutting edge stuff."

I stifle a yawn and hurry to derail any discussion of his academic papers. "Take up any new interests since our last session?"

Mind-numbing academia averted. He gestures to the room behind him and says, "I've got a drum kit. I'm going to start hitting the sticks."

Is hitting the sticks really slang for drumming? I have no idea, and I bet he doesn't either, but I nod enthusiastically. He has a hip new hobby just about every time we meet, and he loves to recommend them to me. Over the years, he's suggested I try Tai Chi, rock-tumbling, candle-making, and beekeeping, to name just a handful.

"Cool. I hope you have a soundproofed room," I say, because he's clearly waiting for me to respond.

He nods seriously. "I do. After I gave up my office space in town during the pandemic, I upgraded my home office to meet all the requirements for patient confidentiality—

secure, encrypted file server, soundproof room, all the goodies. It wouldn't do for Mrs. Appel in the unit next door to overhear someone's session. So my treatment room doubles as a kickass music room."

"Great."

His concern about patient confidentiality and following the rules cracks me up but I keep a straight face. It was trivially easy to book my first appointment with him using a fake name. Apparently, if you walk into a psychiatrist's office and say you plan to self-pay and not submit to insurance, they don't ask a lot of questions. When I agreed to Venmo him the money for my sessions, he became even less interested in verifying my identity. I highly doubt he reports my payments as income to the IRS. In fact, I hope he doesn't. If he ever finds out I'm not Tate, we'll have a handy mutually assured destruction situation.

"How have things been, Tate?"

"Good. Work's going well."

"And your personal life? Seeing anybody special?"

"No, I'm not dating anyone," I tell him.

It's true. I'm not. Emily and I have been married for five years. We're definitely well past dating. But our marriage is yet another secret I have to keep from Dr. Wilde. He's also Emily's psychotherapist, and neither he nor she knows I'm his patient, too. I'm pretty sure even Dr. Venmo would find it a conflict of interest to treat us both individually.

And I can't risk having him cut one or both of us loose. It would be too disorienting, too upsetting, for Em. My singular goal is to shield her from harm, not subject her to it. Besides, I find my twice-a-year sessions a comforting ritual. It's odd to admit that. After all, these are psychotherapy sessions based on a series of lies.

I don't enjoy lying to my therapist. Assuming Tate's identity just happened. I blurted his name, not my own, at the first session. The reason I started seeing Dr. Wilde was to understand the trauma that shaped my brother and, to a lesser extent, me. So I was nervous, and I guess Tate was top of mind.

Then, once I started dating Emily, I realized using Tate's name had been a stroke of genius. When she mentions Tristan, her boyfriend/fiancé/husband, to her psychotherapist, it sets off no alarm bells with the good doctor.

He makes some noises about me putting myself out there romantically and gives me the assignment of asking someone out for coffee before our next session. I nod earnestly as I assure him that I'll try.

He moves on briskly, checks his notes, and asks if I'm still having night terrors. I know lying to him is counter-productive, but I'm not ready to talk about my latest nightmare fodder, so I tell him no.

He doesn't even blink, just breezes on to the next item on his checklist: Have I talked about the past with my mother since my last appointment?

"God no. I'm still not ready."

This answer happens to be true. I talk to my mom fairly regularly, but never about what happened. At least she and I talk. Tate and my mom have had no contact for well over a decade. I've been estranged from him for nearly as long.

I take advantage of his disapproving silence to ask the question that weighs on me. "Do you think a child can inherit an evil nature from a parent?"

He twists his mouth into a sour bow. "You know I don't find *'evil'* to be a useful descriptor." He draws air quotes with his fingers when he says the word.

I manage not to roll my eyes. "Fine, then. Substitute cruelty, criminality, or depravity."

He seems to ponder the question, but I catch him checking his watch. In the beginning, our sessions were one hour each week, then an hour every other week, then an hour a month. Eventually, I weaned down to half an hour once a month, then once a quarter. And now I get a thirty-minute session twice a year so he can check some box that allows him to keep me on as a current patient. He's a safety net at this point. But I'm on a tightrope, so a safety net's advisable.

He meets my gaze through the device. "I'm not certain those states of being are any better. We've discussed how people aren't bad simply because they do bad—even criminal, cruel, or depraved—things."

This time, I can't suppress the eye roll. He gives me a

disappointed look and a small sigh. "We've also discussed that people can overcome their upbringing. That neither nature nor nurture has the final say."

"The individual does."

"Precisely. Some people who were abused go on to become abusers. But others go on to become advocates and helpers. The human spirit is resilient and pliable."

I've asked this question before, but I ask it again. "What about killers? Do you think a propensity for murder runs in families? Not as learned behavior. Genetically?"

He frowns, which isn't a surprise. Despite what movies and books would have us believe, science hasn't definitively determined whether a "murder gene" exists. But I keep hoping Dr. Wilde will stake out a position.

"You have genes from two parents, don't you?" he answers my question with his own. "Have you asked your mother her views on this issue?"

I cock my head at him. "What do you think?"

"I think, Tate, that you're a good man, and you're not responsible for the sins of your father—or anyone else."

Even though he finally takes a position with this answer, it feels like a copout. "You don't think people can be complicit?"

By people I mean me, but also my mother. He's not stupid, and he catches it.

"I think that's a conversation you and your mother need to have. Sooner rather than later."

I grunt. The sound could be an assent. Or it could be heartburn.

But it doesn't matter, because just then the digits on my watch flip from 29 to 30, and the session's over.

He smiles warmly and says, "You're making a lot of good progress, Tate. I look forward to speaking to you in six months. Don't forget about your coffee date. And consider talking to your mom about your worries."

"Thanks, doc. Next time, you'll have to do a drum solo for me. What are you learning?"

He chortles but doesn't tell me. He likes to be personable with his patients, but not personal. I don't know if he has a partner, a child, or a pet, and I respect his boundaries. Apparently drum solos fall on the other side of that line, too.

Instead, he says, "You should consider a solo retreat of your own. Spending some time in a quiet cabin at the end of the world might do wonders for your productivity."

I make a noncommittal noise. *I don't need a productivity boost. But I know someone who does.* I make a mental note to search "quiet cabin remote retreat" as I power off the tablet, slip it into the side pocket of my gym bag, and tuck the towel around it.

I always tell Emily not to worry about washing my gym clothes with her stuff because they're sweaty and gross. Still, out of an abundance of caution, I keep the bag in the garage. As far as I know, she's never opened the duffle, and even if she did find the tablet, I doubt she'd think anything of it. Still, it's easy enough to be careful. So I am.

I Venmo Dr. Wilde a hundred and twenty-five bucks, then pop the locks and walk across the lot to the grocery store. I did the shopping yesterday, but I'm here, and the market's mango tart is one of Emily's favorite desserts. I step up to the bakery counter and wait my turn.

Em could use a treat. Stressed-out is her default setting. She wrestles with generalized anxiety disorder, panic attacks, and PTSD. But right now, her primary source of stress is a looming deadline on a book. And, apparently, her writer's block is worse than all her mental health conditions combined.

After dinner and a slice of mango tart, I'll suggest she have a soak in the bathtub and turn in to sleep early to get some rest. After all, she'll be wrenched from sleep before five o'clock in the morning, gasping, trembling, and trying to hide the fact.

two

Emily

The Grief Hour

I know before I open my eyes and seek out the illuminated face of the bedside clock what time it is. 4:51 AM. Or, as I call it, the grief hour.

My psychiatrist has patiently (and sometimes not-so-patiently) explained the concepts of circadian rhythms and habituated wake-up times and their effect on the human body. He insists this is why I jolt awake at precisely 4:51 each morning with a dry mouth, racing pulse, and tight chest. The fact that 4:51 is the exact moment that I unlocked the door to a tired rental unit to find my blood-covered roommate half-naked and fully dead is, according to Dr. Wilde, a coincidence.

He's utterly wrong. But I need him.

Need may sound like a strong verb to describe our useless twice-a-year talk therapy sessions. But, at the end of the forty-five minutes, he writes me a six-month prescription for Lexapro. And that, I do need.

My brother has suggested I trade my biannual appointment for a medical marijuana card. Joey says it'd be a piece of cake to get one, seeing as how I suffer from severe anxiety and a panic disorder. He's not wrong, but that feels too easy. Like cheating. Like I'm not paying the price for being alive when Cassie is dead.

Dr. Wilde would say this train of thought is unhealthy and punitive. He'd want me to reframe it. Easy for him to say. Don't get me wrong, I try. I tell myself I'm grateful for every new day. I pay attention to sunsets and songs that make my chest swell and the heady scent of honeysuckle on a hot summer day.

But the story in my head is indelible. I know it could have been me, should have been me, bleeding out on a stained and dirty carpet that early March morning seven years ago. And this unshakable truth has guided my behavior in what Dr. Wilde and Joey would both call unfortunate ways if they knew.

After Cassie's murder—still unsolved after all this

time—I left school. Fled home. But I didn't withdraw or take a leave of absence. I just ran. And when the mumbling administrator tracked me down to tell me I needed to request a leave, which she assured me would be granted, or risk failing the semester and losing my scholarship, I didn't ask for the leave.

Instead, I dragged myself back to Ohio and gutted my way through the last six weeks of class while working extra hours for the catering company to cover my new, higher rent in an apartment without bloodstains on the floor. When faced with a chance to give myself grace or grit my teeth, I always choose grit. I owe Cassie that much. I get to live, but I don't get to forget. And I don't indulge myself.

The one exception to this admittedly monastic rule against indulgence shifts in the bed beside me. "Em?"

"Mmm?" I murmur, trying to sound as if I'm half-asleep, too.

"What time is it?"

Tristan asks the question but doesn't care about the answer. This is clear when he rolls toward me and runs his warm hands along the length of my body before nuzzling my neck.

I take one of the long breaths Dr. Wilde is so fond of and relax into Tristan's touch. Tristan doesn't know. About Cassie, I mean. Or the grief hour. Or even Dr. Wilde. It's not like I set out to keep these parts of my life a secret from my husband. Or, if I'm being honest, maybe I did. I have to live with the story; that doesn't mean I have to tell it.

I melt into the dark, uninhibited and free, and give myself over fully to the experience of making love. Or try to. But Cassie's damaged and gouged face, the copper smell of blood, and the wind and rain whipping in through the smashed window—the killer's means of access—are as visceral and real as Tristan's low-pitched moans, the weight of his hips grinding into mine, and the taste of his salty skin. I shove the memories away and push on his chest, signaling for him to flip over. I ride him with a frenzied, urgent rhythm. I'm desperate to chase the shadows from our bed.

Afterward, I collapse onto the bed beside him. I push my hair, damp with sweat, out of my eyes and place one hand on my bare chest to feel the thrum of my heart under my skin. Tristan reaches for my free hand and laces his fingers through mine. We lay, spent and in silent communion, for a few moments. When I feel his weight shift toward me, I push myself up onto my elbows and drop a light kiss on his lips.

"Don't even try it."

"Try what?" His full mouth curves into a lazy grin.

"Try to seduce me into curling up and going back to sleep for a few hours. I know your tricks. And I have a deadline, remember?"

He chuckles. "I thought I just finished the seduction part. I must be losing my touch."

I laugh, too, and trace my fingers along his collarbone. "Never. But I do have to get up. You go back to sleep, though."

As I slide over him and roll toward the edge of the bed, he catches my arm.

"I love you, Emily."

His voice is tinged with sleep and passion, and it sends a frisson of tenderness through me.

"I love you, too, baby. I'm gonna hit the shower. Go back to sleep."

He doesn't.

When I step out of the shower, legs red from the as-hot-as-I-can-stand water, he's leaning against the vanity with my towel in one hand and a mug of steaming coffee in the other. He hands me the thick, oversized towel first.

"Thanks."

After I dry off and wrap a smaller towel around my wet hair, he presses the mug into my eager hands. As the warmth spreads from the ceramic to my palms, I smile down at the melting heart he's created from milk foam and cinnamon. Tristan took up latte art a few years ago, during the lockdown, and even now, every so often, a cat, a heart, or a bird taking flight greets me with my morning caffeine delivery. I take a sip and feel an inexplicable pang when the heart breaks, dissolving into the hot drink.

"I have an idea," he tells me while he watches me comb out my hair.

I meet his eyes in the partially fogged-up mirror. "What kind of idea?"

"This deadline's really starting to stress you out," he begins.

I open my mouth to protest. I'm preparing to lie and insist it's fine. Manageable. But he shakes his head and keeps talking.

"You can pretend it's not, but I can see it, Em. You're barely eating. You haven't been running. You put the milk away in the pantry yesterday. You're a million miles away all the time."

He's not wrong—although the milk in the pantry is news to me. I've been living in my story world, trying to immerse myself to make the words come faster. It isn't working.

I frown. "I guess I *am* distracted."

"So I was thinking. Why don't you actually go a million miles away?" He laughs. "Well, five hundred."

"What?"

He pulls his phone from the pocket of his pajama pants and reads, "Get away from it all in a quiet cabin at the end of the world. Wooded mountain retreat perfect for escaping the grind and returning to nature. No cable, no cell phone coverage, no distractions. Quaint, well-kept cottage-style cabin with views. On-site owner available if needed. Otherwise, you'll commune with nature and recharge in solitude. Message Alex for details." Tristan's eyes meet mine. "There's a photo gallery if you want to check it out. But I'm thinking this place is perfect. I'll bet you can whip out the rest of a draft in one week."

He wouldn't make that bet if he knew how little I've actually written. But the idea is tantalizing. No Internet. No barrage of notifications. Just me, the mountains, and Maid Maleen. The deadline for my retelling of the German fairytale looms, and I'm blocked. Completely and utterly blocked. This has never happened before. And the timing sucks.

Last year, Jillian James reached out to me through our mutual agent. Sam was practically vibrating with excitement when he told me about the opportunity. "She's putting together something like an anthology, but not exactly. Twelve writers, each of you choose a fairytale to retell. Any one you want. She'll pay for themed covers, editing, and printing costs. The group will release one book each month, and they'll all draft off each other. You'll cross-promote and share your audiences."

I was interested but cautious. "But, there's no publisher? No advance?"

Sam deflated and stared down into his bourbon. "No. It's a self-published thing. Royalty share, but no advance. Look, Emily, Jillian is the real deal. She's made the bestseller list more than a dozen times. She has a head for business, too. Frankly, she doesn't need me. She can negotiate her own deals almost as well as I can. Don't tell her that." He pointed at me and winked.

I laughed. "I won't. I know Jillian is a force to be reckoned with. It's not that. It's ..."

He sighed. "You're worried about the visibility."

I nodded because my throat was too tight to speak. It's been a longstanding issue between us. I turn down good offers if they include personal appearances, refuse to do signings or interviews, and generally aspire to be a cipher. I claim I want my words on the page to speak for me. Sam thinks it's some artsy affectation. But it's simpler than any of that: I'm terrified that if I make it big, Cassie's killer will come for me. I can hardly tell Sam that, though. And it *is* a plum opportunity.

So, here I am, eight months later, with a manuscript due to Jillian's editor in two-and-a-half weeks, and I'm quickly approaching the point where I'm not going to make the deadline. In addition to screwing myself over, I'll be letting down eleven other authors, which only makes the acid that's taken up residence in my gut churn more.

Tristan's idea could work. With no distractions, I might be able to write this book. I *want* to write it. I know my story idea is fantastic. Sam and Tristan agree. I owe it to myself and to Jillian's group of authors to at least try to execute it.

I nod to Tristan in the mirror. "Send me the listing when you get a chance. I'll think about it."

He wraps his arm around me from behind and presses his lips to my ear.

I lean back against him. "What did I do to deserve you?" I murmur, more to myself than to him.

three

I'm prepared to have to convince my wife that a writing retreat is a good idea. But the ease with which she agrees to consider the trip proves how much she needs it. She must be in serious trouble on her manuscript to even entertain the idea of spending a week apart from me.

I'm not saying Emily is clingy. Although, in truth, she is. She tries not to be. She takes the train into the city alone to have the occasional lunch with Sam, her agent. And she visits her brother in Colorado once or twice a year, now.

These independent steps are encouraging. Early in our

marriage, she wouldn't fly to see Joey without me. But now, while she definitely prefers if we travel together, she's willing—able—to go by herself. And, of course, she makes her annual pilgrimage to Cassie Baughman's grave alone.

But I'm not supposed to know about that tradition. I'm not supposed to know anything about Cassie, including the fact that she ever lived and died.

I watch Emily comb her wet hair. Her hair is her most distinctive feature. It's long, reaching the bottom of her shoulder blades, thick, and a luminous light red, almost pink, color—strawberry blonde, my mom calls it, marveling at the way it catches the Arizona sunlight whenever we visit Scottsdale to see her. Before he died, my mother's second husband, Jon, used to tell Emily she looked like Ann-Margret. She'd laugh and assure him she could neither sing nor act.

Although Emily's gorgeous, she either doesn't know it or doesn't care. She'll dry her hair and twist it up in a bun at the back of her head. Then she'll moisturize her fair skin and swipe on a tinted lip balm, but that's the extent of her beauty routine. No makeup to cover the constellation of freckles dotting her high cheekbones or to draw attention to her clear, startling blue eyes. I told her once that she's literally one in a million. Fewer than 0.2 percent of the population has the combination of genes that produces a blue-eyed redhead. She blushed furiously and called me a genetics nerd in a fond, laughing tone.

Now those bright blue eyes lock on me in the mirror. "You could come, too. To the cabin, I mean."

She makes the suggestion lightly, but I hear the anxiety beneath it.

I keep my voice gentle when I reject the idea. "We're backed up at the lab. I can't get the time off. Besides, the whole point is for you to work without interruption."

And for me to work without interruption, I think.

She nods and drops her gaze, hurt. Or maybe just disappointed. I caress her cheek, and she turns slightly to press her face into my palm.

"And trust me," I growl, "if I were there, you'd be interrupted. A lot."

It's not a lie. My appetite for her is damn near insatiable, even after five-and-a-half years of marriage. She mewls, and the small, soft sound of her desire is like a magnet, pulling me towards her.

It's always been this way with us, ever since I purposely arranged to meet her by accident outside Dr. Wilde's office—another secret.

Emily doesn't know I'm his patient, and she also doesn't know I know *she* is. These secrets are easier to protect, now that he's moved to a teletherapy model and we don't both have to find excuses to vanish for half a day twice a year to travel back to Ohio to see him.

I wonder if we have time for an encore performance. Then I glance at my phone to check the time and groan. "I gotta go."

The lab truly is backed up. I have piles of cases waiting for me. Crime is always a growth business, I guess.

In larger crime labs, forensic geneticists specialize in DNA analysis. But in a small community like Little Sweetwater, everybody's a generalist. Crime scene technicians gather all the evidence, and we analyze it. All of it. Everything from DNA samples to blood spatter to toxicology to ballistics makes its way across my laboratory bench. The saying 'jack of all trades, master of none' loops through my mind when I'm at work.

While I do have a heavy case load, the real reason I want her to leave town is this homicide I'm working. I rarely talk to her about my work under any circumstances, but the Giselle Ward murder is definitely off-limits for several very good reasons.

She stretches up on her toes to drop a kiss near the corner of my mouth and murmurs her standard goodbye. "Be safe."

I caress her shoulders and give her my standard response before I head out of the room. "Always. Write all the words."

As soon as I close the bathroom door behind me, I hear the telltale rattle of the pill bottle from the other side as she digs it out of her toiletry bag. She'll swallow her anxiety meds with a gulp of lukewarm coffee. It's probably not a great idea to store SSRI medication in the bathroom —too much moisture. But since I'm not supposed to know she takes them, I can't exactly point this out.

Her meds seem to be working okay despite her storage choices. Aside from her daily panicked wake-up just before five a.m., she's been doing pretty well. Keeping to a schedule, eating well, staying hydrated. These simple routines help her immensely, along with her yoga practice, meditation, and medication.

The book deadline is a problem, though. She's fraying at the edges, falling out of her good habits as her writer's block persists. And we're coming up on the anniversary of Cassie's murder, which throws her off-balance every spring. I see the telltale signs that she's about to start a downward spiral. All the more reason to get her up to that cabin, and soon.

four

Emily

The small house is quiet after Tristan leaves. He hits the gym before work most mornings, then showers there, ceding our bathroom to me and my morning routine.

I putter around, taking my time. Dry my hair and pull it back. Moisturize my face and apply sunscreen, although odds are, I won't set foot outside today. I perch on the edge of the bathtub to rub thick lotion into my feet, paying particular attention to my dry, cracked heels.

Then it's into the bedroom, where I paw through my dresser drawers to find just the right pair of soft yoga pants and an oversized long-sleeved top. I select a pair of fuzzy socks to complete the day's writing uniform and, finally, head downstairs with my empty coffee mug to start my pre-writing ritual.

A seated meditation in front of the living room windows to center myself in the story. A series of stretches. A few minutes spent writing in my journal, keeping my pen moving across the page even as my hand cramps. By the time I pour a fresh cup of coffee, light my grapefruit-rosemary scented candle (said to improve focus), and cue up my playlist of writing music (for this book, it's instrumental pieces from the soundtrack to a fantasy video game), I've somehow frittered away two hours before I set foot in the cozy sunroom in the back of the house that serves as my workspace.

Time to get serious about writing all the words. I raise my desk to standing height, roll my neck, and open my manuscript document. The cursor blinks at me in expectant anticipation. I blink back at it, summoning the story. The story doesn't come. My fingers hover over the keyboard. My mind is blank.

After an endless moment of suspended animation, I sigh, close the file, and plunk myself down on the armchair near the window with my story notebook and a pen. I scan my notes, chew on the end of the pen, stare out the window. Then I repeat the process. Scan, chew, stare. Nothing. Frustrated, I toss the pen onto the side table with a loud clatter.

I've been stuck like this for weeks, and I don't know

why. The source material is rich and full of promise. In the Brothers Grimm version, Maleen and her lady-in-waiting are locked in a tower for seven years by Maleen's father, the king, after Maleen defies him. She's in love with a prince who wants to marry her, but the king refuses. He's chosen another prince for Maleen, but she digs in her heels. So it's off to the tower with her and her unfortunate handmaiden. Eventually, the two escape the tower and make their way to the kingdom where Maleen's true love lives. Through cunning and luck, Maleen gets her happily ever after with her prince. It's a riches to rags to riches, entombed princess story. A contemporary romance would be the logical choice for my version.

Instead, my story focuses on the seven-year imprisonment, the friendship between Maleen and her lady-in-waiting, and their dramatic escape. When I told Jillian and Sam about my idea, they both squealed with excitement. Jillian assured me that even though most of the writers involved in A Year of Fairytales are romance writers like her, not everyone is. There's going to be at least one mystery, a space opera, and a historical fiction book.

She encouraged me to write what I wanted, declaring, "All that matters is the story."

I say the words aloud to myself now as a reminder. "All that matters is the story."

As I make this quiet pronouncement to my reflection in the window, there's a flash of movement behind the hedge of scarlet firethorns that screen our backyard from the Simmons' yard next door. A deer, maybe? I jump up for a better look.

Nobody's home over there. Tyrone and Lashina Simmons are snowbirds—retirees who spend the winters at their place in Lakeland, Florida. Every winter while they're away, Tristan goes over and starts their car a few times, checks on their water softener and alarm system, and shovels their walk if it snows. This year, though, Lashina specifically asked me to keep an eye out for deer in their garden because I'm home all day.

Before they left, right after the new year, she came over with a bag full of perishable food–eggs, bread, milk, a fruit and cheese tray from the game night they'd hosted–and pressed it into my hands. She leaned in so close that I could see the individual specks of glitter in her shimmery face tint and stage whispered, "Ty keeps complaining about the deer. The bushes are all trampled, but none of the leaves are eaten. Something's gallivanting around in the garden, but it's no deer."

My pulse ticked up. For days, I'd had the unshakeable feeling that someone was watching me. I'd pushed it away, tried to convince myself it was my imagination. But Lashina's whispers opened the floodgates, and panic crashed over me in a cold wave.

"A person?" I croaked.

She gave me an odd look. "I was thinking more like a bear."

It probably says something about my mental state that

the prospect of a bear standing ten feet from my house came as a relief.

Now, I race to the back door, Maleen forgotten. My heart hammers against my breastbone as I pull on my running shoes and fly outside. No coat, no phone, no plan.

I sprint to the hedgerow and peer over into the Simmons' yard. My pounding feet and loud breathing will certainly have frightened off a deer or a person. I guess all I have to worry about now is a bear. When I reach the bright red bushes, I almost wish a black bear were there to greet me. What I find is far more terrifying.

A set of boot prints is sunk into the soft earth of the Simmons' mostly dormant vegetable garden. Men's boots, large. I whirl around, searching the row of backyards and the alley that runs behind them. Whoever was here is long gone.

I wriggle between the tall firethorns, line my feet up with the prints, and stare straight ahead. My throat closes when I process the view from this vantage point. The man who stood here had a clear view of the sunroom. I can see my glazed coffee mug on the side table and the chair I'd been sitting in moments ago. He was watching me.

Chilling as that is, it's not the worst of it. A familiar scent lingers on the still, cold air. Sandalwood. I'd know it anywhere. My stomach lurches and then turns over completely.

I lean over the garden fence and vomit into my bushes.

January 2017

I was already running late for my Modernism in American and British Literature class when I walked through the kitchen and spotted yet another mouse.

"Thank God Cassie's not here," I muttered.

The mice freaked me out—a lot—but Cassie's reaction was over the top. Lots of screaming and standing on chairs while ordering me to catch the spotted rodent without harming it and take it somewhere else, preferably across a body of water, so it wouldn't find its way back.

I didn't have time to catch the rodent and, truthfully, didn't want to deal with the implications of trapping it and going on a field trip with it. But I could take out the overflowing trash and pull the bedroom doors shut. Finding mouse poop in your dresser drawers is not a fun experience.

I grabbed the trash bag, pushed down the gross contents to compress them enough to tie off the bag, and headed down the hallway to the apartment building's back door. A row of trash, recycling, and composting receptacles lined the rear wall of the apartment building. I tossed the bag into the nearest bin and wiped my hands on my jeans.

That's when I smelled it for the first time. Cologne. Woodsy, warm, a bit earthy. The distinctive scent mingled with the fetid garbage odors in a gross, stomach-turning combination, but I bet it was really nice on its own.

After that, I seemed to smell it everywhere I went. In the apartment building hallways, elevators, classrooms. The stacks in the library. The mailroom. A few times, even in my own bedroom.

Cassie, a psych major, told me I was experiencing something called frequency illusion.

"It's not an illusion, Cass," I insisted one day after the scent wafted from her car. "You can't smell that?"

She took a big sniff, then shrugged. "Sorry."

I couldn't believe she didn't smell it. "Is there even such a thing as an olfactory illusion?" I wondered.

I wasn't imagining it. Was I?

"Illusion makes it sound like it's not real," she explained. "But it's not the thing that's the illusion. It's the frequency. Another name for it is Baader-Meinhof Phenomenon. Basically, you're holding the smell in your mind and that draws your attention to it. You notice it when someone else wouldn't."

I frowned. "It's still weird."

"Yeah, well, you're weird. So that tracks."

We both laughed, and I more or less forgot about it. For a while.

Six weeks later, Cassie was dead. And the smell was stronger than ever.

Tristan

'm in line at the deli, trying to decide between turkey and Swiss on rye or onion soup for lunch when my phone buzzes in my pocket. I fish it out. Emily's texting.

I frown down at the notification as I shuffle forward in the queue. She rarely tries to reach me during the work day. Usually, she's caught up in the flow of her writing. Or at least she used to be. But even now, wrestling with writer's block, she doesn't interrupt me at work. In an emergency, she'll call. And if she wants to share something she's read or remind me to pick something up at the store, she schedules a text or email to hit my phone right around six PM, when I'm typically leaving for the day. Emily's considerate that way.

So, the text pricks at me. But it's my turn to order. I opt for the sandwich and a bag of jalapeño chips, grab a bottled water from the cooler, and pay the cashier without engaging in our usual Sixers basketball chitchat. Then I join the cluster of people gathered near the pickup counter waiting for takeout orders.

I unlock the messaging app with the print on my index finger and read:

> There was someone in Lashina and Ty's yard.

> Something? A deer? Rabbit maybe?

> SomeONE. Watching our house.

My pulse quickens and the moisture dissipates from my mouth. I try to work up enough saliva to swallow, but my throat's a desert. I twist open the water and take a long swig of cold liquid. I scan the cramped sandwich shop in search of a quiet corner. There is none.

I thumb out a reply:

> Are you okay? Are they gone?

I want to tell her to call the police. But that call could set off a cascade of consequences that will complicate my plans. I twitch my lips as worry and practicality battle it out. Her response gives pragmatism the advantage:

I'm fine. Just rattled. Yeah, he's gone.
TBH, I didn't actually see anyone.

You heard him?

Not exactly. I thought I saw movement
behind the hedge row. Went to check
it out.

...

He was gone. But he left boot prints in
the mud.

"Turkey and Swiss for Tristan," the sandwich guy calls.

I edge through the sea of people to grab my brown bag and a handful of napkins then rush outside. I turn my collar up against the blast of cold air and lower my head until I round the corner and the wind dies. Then I pull out my phone and call Emily.

She answers before the first ring finishes.

"I'm sorry. I shouldn't have texted. I'm just freaking—"

I cut off her apology and explanation. "I can come home."

She manages a shaky laugh. "That's stupid. I'm fine. Besides you have that big murder..."

When she trails off, I bite down on my lower lip hard enough to draw blood. Damn. I've been careful not to share any details with her, and the media has been surprisingly circumspect about Giselle Ward's death—most likely because the victim is the daughter of a local pastor. But from the tremble in Emily's voice, it's clear she's heard enough to know the twenty-year-old victim was stabbed.

If she also heard that Giselle's roommate found her body, that's all it would take to whip up her anxiety. It's understandable, given the similarities to the Cassie Baughman murder, and it's probably why she thinks someone was watching her from the Simmons' garden. Avoiding this exact scenario is part of the reason I wanted her to leave town.

"Are you sure?" I ask now. I'll leave work early if she says she needs me, but I really shouldn't.

"I'm positive," she says in an uncertain voice. "I'm packing up my laptop to leave anyway. Maybe working at the coffee shop will help me break through my block. Shake some words loose."

"That's a good idea."

"Speaking of good ideas, the thought of doing a writing retreat at that cabin is starting to grow on me."

"Really? That's great."

"I ran the idea by a friend, and he thinks the change of scenery will help."

A friend? I pause. "Sam?"

Now she pauses. "Yeah, Sam. So, will you forward me the owner's contact info? I'll send an email."

I can tell from her voice she's lying. She didn't call her

agent. I'll bet anything she called her psychotherapist. If she's running her daily decisions by Dr. Wilde, she's in worse shape than I thought. But the upside is the good doctor certainly would've endorsed this plan—after all, it was his suggestion.

"I'll take care of it for you. There's a messaging feature through the booking site, and I already set up an account. Just in case." I falter, considering how best to phrase this next bit. "Listen, you should go to the coffee shop. But ..."

"But you don't think anyone was there. You think I imagined it. I *saw* footprints, Tristan." Her voice shakes harder.

I hurry to soothe her. "I don't think you imagined footprints. I believe you saw them, but there may be an innocent explanation. A neighbor kid chasing a loose football or something. Footprints don't necessarily mean someone was watching you."

She inhales a ragged breath then explodes, "It wasn't a kid getting his football, Tristan. Someone was watching me."

She's definitely spiraling, which is bad. But there's a silver lining—this incident, real or imagined, may convince her to leave town.

"Okay, Em. I'm sorry if it sounds like I'm doubting you."

"I smelled something," she insists.

My heart skips. I have to ask, even though I know what the answer will be.

I force the words out. "What did you smell?"

"Sandalwood."

March 2018

I was nervous, even more nervous than I thought I'd be. I must've told myself to forget it and walk away a dozen times during Emily's forty-five-minute session with Dr. Wilde. But I didn't.

Instead, I paced back and forth inside the crystal and candle store across the street from the psychiatrist's office. The one-year anniversary of Cassie's murder was approaching, and I knew this would be a vulnerable time for Emily. It was important that I meet her now.

So I ignored the dirty looks of the wild-haired proprietor of Insight, Scents, and Sense and continued to keep one eye on the glassed-in lobby across the street and one eye on the time. Finally, the owner approached me.

"Sir, your energy is unsettling. Please either buy something or leave." She met my gaze with clear hazel eyes.

I peeked at the time—four more minutes until Emily's session would end—and grabbed a candle at random from a skirted table. I caught a whiff of a familiar scent that reminded me of aftershave as I crossed the cramped shop and plunked the candle down beside the cash register.

"Mmm. Sandalwood and amber. Excellent choice. Sandalwood is known for relaxing, calming qualities and is believed to bring positivity and purity of thought," she told me as she carefully wrapped the glass candle container in brown paper.

"Yeah, that's great," I responded absently.

She reached out and wrapped her bony fingers around my wrist. I started.

"Your pulse is quite high, and your energy is agitated. The candle should help regulate your nervous system."

I didn't want to get snarky with her. And I definitely didn't want to miss my chance to meet Emily by getting sucked into a conversation with this woman. She was woo-woo but well-intentioned. So I managed a smile.

"That's good to know. I hope it works."

She smiled back and slid a pack of wood matches with colorful tips into the bag alongside the candle. "It will. I know it."

She rang up the purchase, and I handed over two twenties. Apparently, relaxation and positivity didn't come cheap. Another glance at my watch. T minus 90 seconds.

I practically ran out of the shop. Then I jaywalked across the street and positioned myself to bump into Emily. I waited with my hand on the building's entrance door and stared through the glass at the lights above the elevator bank inside. When a light and a faint ding announced the arrival of the elevator from a higher floor, I rushed inside the small lobby.

Emily stepped off the elevator, her head down. I knew from past encounters that she lowered her gaze to hide her red-rimmed eyes and puffy face after her sessions. I walked directly into her path.

A middle-aged mom-type shook her head and skirted us as Emily bounced off my chest.

"Oh, I'm sorry!" Emily exclaimed, raising her head.

"Don't be. It was my fault. Are you okay?" I caught her elbow with a light touch and guided her over to the wall, out of the flow of foot traffic.

"I'm fine. I wasn't looking where I was going," she confessed.

I smiled my understanding. "I get it. I get lost in thought, too. Sometimes what's going on up here,"—I tapped a finger against my temple—"is way more appealing than what's going on out there." I waved my hand at our surroundings to indicate the outside world.

She eyed me more closely. "Yeah, sometimes it is."

After that, it was easy enough. I walked her back to her apartment, invited her for coffee the next day. We fell into a casual friendship. Started hiking on the weekends. Our first kiss. Some Netflix and chill, as we used to say. A few parties. Eventually, we started having sex, always at her place. But I never spent the night.

Then, at the end of March, I had her over to my place

for a dinner date and a sleepover. Decidedly not casual. I wanted to signal my readiness to take our relationship to the next level.

She stopped on the porch to stomp the snow off her boots. I yanked the door open, and she hurried inside, her cheeks red from the cold and her long hair windblown. She thrust a bottle of red wine into my hands.

"Here. I hope this goes with what you're making."

"Lasagna. So, yeah. Thanks." I kissed her, and literal sparks flew from the static electricity.

We both laughed.

"Lasagna, huh? Do I smell garlic bread, too?" She inhaled deeply, sniffing the air. Her blue eyes went saucer-wide and the color drained from her face. She wobbled on her feet.

"Em, are you okay?"

She looked like she might puke or maybe pass out, so I led her to a kitchen chair and got her to lower her head below her knees. Then I uncorked the wine she'd brought and poured her a splash.

She waved it off. "Could I get some water, instead? Please?"

I filled a glass from the faucet and watched the color return to her cheeks as she slipped slowly.

"Feeling better?" I was torn between concern about her and not wanting to burn the meal.

A small nod. "Yeah, thanks."

She wrinkled her nose and cast a glance toward the

coffee table in the living room, where the overpriced candle from the crystal shop crackled and burned.

I followed her gaze. "What?"

"What's that scent?"

"The candle? Sandalwood. Doesn't it smell great?"

She mustered up a weak smile. "Yeah, I guess. I smelled it everywhere I went for a while, then, out of the blue, it disappeared. But now it's back."

Her fixation on the candle confused me, but she seemed to expect a response. "Well, it's a very popular scent. Has been for years. I can remember my stepdad wearing it as aftershave when I was growing up." And, before him, my dad. But I don't talk about him. Ever.

"Really? I never smelled it until ... last winter."

Last winter was her oblique way of referencing her roommate's murder. And while she didn't seem to make the connection—at least not consciously—between the aroma and the killer, I sure did. I covered the candle with its lid to extinguish the scent, then pulled her into the dining room and got her settled in the chair.

As she draped her napkin over her lap, she murmured, "Such a strange coincidence."

"What is?"

"That scented candle."

I hurried to the kitchen and grabbed the wine and two glasses. I poured her a generous portion. As I handed her the glass, I said, "Not really. It's a phenomenon called frequency illusion."

She smiled an odd, sad smile. "Yeah. Baader-Meinhof Phenomenon."

"That's right." I clinked my glass against hers. "Cheers."

She brightened, visibly shrugging off her sorrow like it was a coat. "Cheers. I'm so excited to try your cooking."

Neither of us brought up her reaction to the sandalwood candle for the rest of the evening. The next morning, before sunrise, I left her sleeping in my bed, crept out to the trash can in the backyard, and tossed the thing in the bin.

six

Alex

The tea kettle whistles, and I jump. I'm not easily startled anymore—at least not usually. But I slept poorly last night, and my nerves are frayed. I woke with the vague feeling that I'd had the nightmare again. Seems I only have this particular dream when Robert's traveling for work. Unfortunately for me, he's a linguist with the Air Force, so he's pretty much always traveling for work.

"Two more years," I say aloud to my empty kitchen as I cross the room to turn off the burner under the kettle and prepare yet another mug of fragrant jasmine tea.

Two more years of service and then Robert can retire with full benefits and a stellar pension. And I won't spend most of my time alone and isolated on this mountain.

I stir sugar into my tea and watch the granules swirl in an eddy until they dissolve in the hot liquid. I wonder if Cicero coined the phrase that loosely translates to 'tempest in a teapot' or 'storm in a teacup' while fixing a beverage. Then I wonder if the ancient Romans drank tea.

And I'm off, chasing one shiny thought after another down Internet rabbit holes courtesy of my slow, unreliable connection. By the time I learn about a restaurant in Rome whose chef recreates recipes from *De Re Coquinaria,* a cookbook that has somehow survived since the first century AD, I've managed to drink an entire kettle's worth of tea. I add the name of the restaurant to the notebook where Robert and I scribble bucket list ideas for travel and adventure after he separates from the military.

"Two more years," I remind myself again.

I rinse my mug and turn it upside down on the drying rack. No reason to wash it yet. I'll probably make another pot of tea tonight. I glance at the clock and have to laugh.

I've frittered away more than an hour reading about how Virgil used to make cheese. This is not unusual for me, but it's still funny. My nephew Douglas, the oldest son of Robert's eldest sister, is the school psychologist for a sprawling suburban district in Oregon. Doug tells me that if I were a school kid today, I'd be diagnosed with ADHD–

Attentive Type and would learn skills and tools to harness and channel my curiosity. I'd probably also be medicated.

But in the late 80s and 90s in a speck of a town in rural Maine, I was just a quiet, flighty girl who couldn't concentrate on what the teachers wanted me to pay attention to. Off in my own world. Spacey. Flaky. They'd render these judgments on report card after report card. And eventually, I stopped trying to focus and embraced my role as ditzy Lexi Lincoln.

I managed to graduate high school, but with my grades, getting into a four-year college was a pipe dream. Besides, my family didn't have that kind of money.

I did take some classes at the community college, and I've often thought about going back to get a degree. Robert's all for it. The son of first-generation Chinese immigrants, education is his religion. Maybe I will; we'll see. He wants me to add it to the bucket list, but the idea's too daunting to commit to paper just yet.

For now, I have the farm, my online language-learning communities, my virtual sewing circle, the garden, my soap-making hobby, and the vacation rental business to keep me busy while Robert's away.

Do I get lonely? Sure. Doesn't everybody, sometimes?

But I tried moving around with Robert from posting to posting, and that, somehow, felt lonelier. Being the new face, having to break into established groups, and, in the back of my mind, always, *always,* wondering when someone from my past would turn up in one of these new towns. This is better. Safer.

And I keep busy. I spent this morning doing chores around the farm, not taking a break until late morning, when it was time to make my lunch. There's always something that needs fixing, trimming, or painting when you have a farm. Between the manual labor and the internet research, I barely notice my isolation.

The notification bar at the top of my browser is blinking at me when I settle back in front of the old laptop. For all I know, it was there the entire time I researched the diet of the ancient Romans. When I do focus on something, I get tunnel vision. I'm like a racehorse wearing blinkers. But this notification is one I shouldn't ignore. The icon with the red numeral '1' popping out is for Stay Your Way, the vacation site where I list the cabin for rental.

I log into my Stay Your Way account. There are other, bigger vacation home sites. There are sites that take a smaller percentage of the booking fees. And there are sites that advertise more widely, bringing in more prospective renters. But this site checks all the important boxes: privacy is their, and my, priority. Guests and prospective guests and the owners communicate solely through the website's messaging, voice, and texting app. Exchanging personal contact information with a client gets you banned from the site permanently. The listings aren't indexed, so they don't show up in Internet search results.

And the vacationers don't get the exact address of the house until forty-eight hours before check-in. It's not the perfect system, but it's as close as I can find. And the vacation rentals pay the monthly mortgage for the entire farm, with plenty left over to add to our travel fund. It's a good source of income with a low likelihood of exposure.

I open the Stay Your Way email client and click on the new message, which is time-stamped just minutes ago:

To: Alex Liu
From: T.C. Rose
Re: Cabin availability ASAP?

I saw the listing for your quiet cabin and it sounds perfect for my wife. Emily is an author with a deadline coming up and is looking for a place where she can write without distraction. It seems you don't list your available dates on the Stay Your Way calendar, so I'm reaching out to see when the cabin might be free to rent in the near term. Emily's schedule is flexible. Any seven-day, six-night stretch would work for her. The sooner, the better.

Looking forward to hearing from you,
Tristan (and Emily) Rose

I leave the message up on the screen and open another browser tab. Mr. Rose is right that I don't mark available dates on the convenient, integrated calendar that Stay Your Way provides. This undoubtedly costs me some bookings, but it gives me an extra layer of security. Because once I get an inquiry like this one, I do rudimentary research into the prospective guest(s) before I decide whether to let them book the cabin. And it's much easier to say, 'sorry, we're fully booked' than to find out after the fact—as happened once—that a prominent national reporter has booked the spot and make up a reason to cancel their reservation and refund their deposit.

Stay Your Way provides basic information about guests. You know those reviews of properties/hosts that all the sites publish for everyone to see? Stay Your Way has similar reviews of you, the guest. They're only visible to the hosts. But if you have a wild party, steal something, fail to take out the trash before you check out and leave it to fester, we know. I read these reviews, of course, but whether you're a good houseguest isn't my primary concern.

My background check is more wide-ranging. Do you have a social media footprint? Have you ever been arrested? Do you have a connection of any kind to Windy Rock, Maine? Does anything about your presence in the world set off an alarm bell, no matter how faint?

I search the wife first, since she's the one who'll actually be here if I book her. At first, I think Emily Rose must be a pen name because the only information I can find about the woman is related to her books. She's published four. They all appear to be what I think of as book club fiction. Not quite genre, not quite literary. Those thick women's fiction books that talk show hosts and movie stars push on their followers. The books that are impossible to check out from the library because the waitlist is endless. I study the covers. I've never read any Emily Rose, but a few of these intrigue me. I write the titles on the notepad at my elbow.

There are no photos of Emily Rose on her author social media accounts. She uses book covers as her avatar. As a rule, I don't trust people who aren't on social media. It's a red flag. I realize that's pretty rich, coming from me. You could scour the web for the rest of eternity and not find a profile for Alex Liu. In any case, I'm inclined to give Emily Rose a pass here. I mean, I've seen *Misery*. Readers can cross the line into stalkers more easily than ever, thanks to the interconnectedness of the Internet. I do find a handful of pictures where she's been tagged by other authors at signings and conventions. She's younger than I imagined, but she definitely looks the part of an author. Long light red hair pulled up in a bun, hipster glasses, fringy scarves, flowy kimono-style sweaters. I stare at her freckled face for several moments and decide she looks harmless enough.

I click through to her website. There's a professional headshot that gives the same vibe as the pictures she's tagged in. She comes across as dreamy and ethereal. Lithe and long-limbed, I peg her as a yoga devotee. Maybe a

Pilates addict. I'm neither. I'm all about functional strength. I can split firewood, haul my oil from the pickup to the basement, and carry a twenty-five-pound bag of rice over each shoulder. With Robert away so much, I need to be self-sufficient and capable. I'm sturdy. Emily Rose, on the other hand, looks like a stiff breeze could blow her over.

I nod my approval and move on to her biography. She grew up in Illinois, attended a small liberal arts college in Hope Falls, Ohio, and resides in Little Sweetwater, Pennsylvania, with her husband—all very far from Maine. No mention of pets, children, or hobbies. But that's all okay by me.

Time to check out the husband. I search his name. Like his wife, Tristan Charles Rose's social media footprint is unusually sparse. He does have a BizConnect profile, though. He graduated from a high school in Arizona, went to a university in Kansas where he earned a degree in genetics, and then onto Ohio to get a graduate degree in forensics. He attended a different college than Emily, but their schools are in the same town. That must be where they met. Now, according to his resume, he works for the county crime lab in his hometown.

I open one final tab, plug my address into the map site, and set Little Sweetwater as my destination. It's a bedroom community five hundred and fifty miles from here, an hour outside Philadelphia. I stare at the route snaking south and west as I ponder. There's no reason not to take the booking. And there's not a lot of interest in vacationing in a rustic cabin in the North Carolina mountains in late winter/early spring. It's either rent to Ms. Rose or let it sit empty. I push down the uneasy feeling that rises in my gut and return to the first tab to type out a reply inviting Tristan to book any six-night span in the next two weeks.

seven

Emily

After I call Tristan at work, things move quickly. So quickly that I can't quite catch my breath. Although he's been working late most evenings, tonight he beats me home.

When I open the front door, I'm greeted by the unmistakable scent of sautéed garlic. I dump my laptop on the table and follow my nose to the kitchen, where I find my husband, wearing a Kiss the Cook apron and stirring something in our large sauce pot. I do as the apron instructs, then peek into the pot. I spy a whole peeled carrot in the sea of tomato sauce. Tristan's secret to a low-acid sauce.

"Homemade pasta sauce? It's not Sunday. What's the occasion?"

He grins at me. "Two occasions. One, if you're only now getting home from the coffee shop, I assume that means you got some words down. That calls for my lasagna." He pauses and paints me with an expectant look.

I reach for one of the glasses of red wine he's already poured and take a sip before answering.

"Yeah, I actually did."

"I knew it. Tell me all about it."

The words bubble up from my throat like the roiling tomatoes and spices in his pot. Tristan's excitement about my writing process fills my heart, as always. He's unfailingly supportive of my work. And, believe me, I've heard enough horror stories from my writer friends to know this is not a universal trait.

"I wrote a scene exploring the dynamic between Maleen and Ruth," I tell him.

"And Ruth is ...?"

"Her lady-in-waiting. They're friends, but Maleen's a princess, remember? So there's a bit of a power imbalance."

"Okay." He waves his hand through the steam coming off the pot, directing it toward his nostrils, inhales deeply, and gives a satisfied nod. Then he places the mesh splatter guard over the top of the pot and picks up his wine glass. "Do they have an argument?"

"Not exactly—or at least not yet. Ruth's conflicted. She

knows Maleen is in love with Prince Manfred, but Maleen's father has refused to bless their union. She wants to support Maleen, but defying the king? That's a bold move. She has a decision to make, and Maleen isn't being particularly understanding."

"So a fight's brewing?"

I don't realize it until Tristan says the words, but he's right. "Yes. They're going to have it out in the next scene." I sip my wine. "What's the second reason?"

It takes him a moment. "Oh, right. The second reason is this is your last supper before you leave for your retreat. Alex, the owner of the cabin, got back to me. It's all yours for the next week. You can check in tomorrow any time after noon."

"Wait. Tomorrow?" It's so soon. Too soon.

He reads the frantic note in my voice and answers soothingly. "I stopped at the grocery store on the way home and bought all your favorite, low-effort foods. I got your tea, your kombucha, your favorite snacks. We'll pack up the leftovers from tonight's dinner—Alex says there's a microwave in the cabin. It's small and low-powered, but it can reheat lasagna."

I frown. "I need to do laundry."

Another smile. "I already washed everything in the hamper. It's drying now. All you have to do is eat your meal, drink your wine, and then pack a bag. I'll drive you out to the cabin in the morning. We'll need to get an early start. I'd like to leave by six if we can. It's an eight-hour drive."

"You can't do that round-trip in one day. It's too much. I'll drive myself."

"That won't work. I need the car. I've got field visits to do next week on this murder I caught."

Tristan doesn't like to talk about his work, so I don't ask any questions. But my frown deepens. If he drops me off, that leaves me without transportation while I'm at the cabin. I consider suggesting I rent a car. But, then I shrug. Where do I think I'm going to go in the mountains? The whole idea is to hole up and do nothing but write this book. And he's making it frictionless, easy.

"Still, that's a long drive for you. Too long. And then you have to turn around and do it again in a week."

He waves off my objections. "I'll be fine. I'll stop halfway back for dinner. And if I get too tired, I'll catch a nap at a rest area."

"I don't know. Sixteen hours—maybe more?"

"You worry too much. Tell you what. When I pick you up next week, we'll stop for the night in Charlottesville. You love that place."

It's true, I do. Charlottesville reminds me a lot of the little college town where Tristan and I met, only without all the blood-soaked trauma and grief. And if I use an overnight in Charlottesville as a carrot, my reward for getting the book done, maybe I'll actually finish the thing. Hope blooms in my chest.

I lean across the counter, drop a kiss on the corner of his mouth, and repeat the question I asked this morning in the bathroom. "What did I do to deserve you?"

It's a real question, one I ask myself daily. My life would be so different without Tristan taking care of me, looking out for me, loving me.

In answer, he pulls me closer and says what he always says in response, "I'm the lucky one in this relationship, Em. Don't think I ever forget that because I don't. Not even for a moment."

"I'm going to miss you like nobody's business," I tell him around the lump in my throat.

"I'll miss you more," he whispers, his breath riffling my hair.

I give myself a beat to savor this moment, then I say, "Did you text Tyrone or Lashina to let them know about the person in their garden?"

He stiffens, and I pull back, pressing my palms flat against his chest, and look up at him. "We need to tell them."

He clears his throat. "I didn't, but I will. Tonight."

"Do you promise?"

"I promise," he says, handing me my wine glass.

eight

I glance at Emily's relaxed face, so soft and trusting in sleep, before I turn off the windy, narrow, paved road that curves up the mountainside and onto the gravel lane that Alex's instructions specify I must take no matter how much my GPS-guided map app might protest. As if on cue, the polished robotic voice with the inexplicable Australian accent scolds me for turning off the county road.

"Make a U-turn."

I ignore the bossy Aussie and continue to bump along the unpaved road. We jostle over a deep rut and Emily jolts awake.

"How long have I been out?" Her voice is froggy with sleep.

We're going around a hairpin turn, so I answer without turning my eyes away from the road ahead. "Not long. Just after we stopped for gas in that little town."

I didn't catch the name of the blink-and-you'll-miss-it town. All I know is it's in Tennessee, a state that we passed through for a heartbeat before crossing back into North Carolina, and it did not have a charming used bookstore. Emily checked with the cashier while I filled the gas tank and she used the facilities.

The road—which is a generous description for this ribbon of earth—appears to drop off the side of the mountain up ahead. *Optical illusion,* I assure myself. I realize I'm white-knuckling the steering wheel and try to relax my grip.

Em glances at the map display. "It says you need to turn around. We're off the route." Then she peers through the windshield. "Is this even a road?"

I chuckle. "Alex said the apps don't work properly up here. See that printout on the console?"

"Yeah."

"Now that you're awake, you can be my navigator."

She picks up the sheet and scans the directions. "This place really is remote, huh?" Her quavering voice is tinged with fear.

I wrack my brain in search of a subject that's guaranteed to distract her before that seed of worry has a chance to blossom into anxiety and take root. Her current work-in-progress is my usual go-to for this purpose, but she's under deadline pressure, and I'm not sure bringing up the book is the best strategy right now. I settle on her brother.

"How's Joey doing?"

She lifts her bowed head from the page, and I glance at her, making brief eye contact. She furrows her brow.

"Okay, I guess. I mean, he's great. He and Rick are ready to start a family. They're working with an adoption agency."

"That's awesome," I enthuse. "Aunt Em and Uncle Tristan can spoil the heck out of a baby."

"Mmm, yeah. I guess. They're so far away, though. I always imagined our kids would grow up together. You know, in and out of each other's houses, the way some cousins are more like siblings." She falls silent.

I don't know, actually. I don't have any cousins. I have one much older brother. Our nine-year age gap is one of the myriad reasons we're not close. I smother a snort. That's the understatement of a lifetime. We're estranged. I haven't spoken to him in over a decade. As far as I know, neither has my mom. We never mention him. Emily doesn't even know he exists. But this topic is guaranteed to ratchet up *my* anxiety, so I don't go there.

Instead, I ask in a hopeful tone, "Our kids? Does this mean you're ready?"

It's no secret I want kids. Emily insists she does, too. Just not yet. But our fifth anniversary is coming up this summer, and I've wondered if the milestone might prompt her. To be honest, I've always suspected she's waiting for Cassie's killer to be caught before she brings a child into the world. Does a change of heart mean she's given up on that? It's times like this when I wish we could talk about the murder. But we're too far down this path now.

"I don't know," she muses. "Maybe."

I flash her a grin. Before I can say anything corny, she points at the road.

"After that big tree trunk up ahead, you're supposed to make a very sharp left."

I slow the car from a crawl to an even more deliberate pace. At this speed, we're barely making forward progress up the incline. But Alex's directions don't overstate the sharpness of the turn. Even at a plodding ten miles per hour, I hold my breath as we curve close to the mountain's edge. The GPS app gives up and falls silent.

"Jeez." Em lets out a long, shaky breath.

I nod and remove my left hand from the steering wheel to wipe the sweat from my palm on the thigh of my jeans. Then I replace that hand and repeat the motion with my right.

"We should be almost there."

She peers at the directions. "The good news is there are no more turns. We just follow this heart-stopping road straight uphill for another two miles."

"Is there bad news?"

"Nope." She beams at me. "I mean, not aside from the fact that your wife's going to miss you like hell for the next week."

"That cuts both ways, believe me. But finishing this book is important to you," I remind her. What I think but don't say is, *And getting you out of town for a while is important to me.*

Her smile widens. "And if I finish the book, we'll definitely spend the night in Charlottesville to celebrate."

I smile back at the lively note in her voice. This trip could be exactly what we both need.

nine

The winding uphill climb ends at a wide gravel driveway. A rustic wooden sign staked into the grass welcomes us to "The Farm at the End of the World." I raise my eyebrow at the name, but it's apt.

The driveway continues for about the equivalent of a city block before it forks. To the left, it leads to a large white farmhouse with blue gabled roofs and a gracefully curved wraparound porch. A barn behind the house matches the structure. A dirty black pickup truck is parked beside the farmhouse. Tristan takes the right branch, which meanders downhill and ends at a tiny, adorable cottage-style cabin. It's a squat box of stacked white stone covered with a faded red slate roof. A tall, skinny chimney protrudes from the roof. Flower boxes hang from the shuttered windows. The online photo gallery on the rental website could never capture the charm this place oozes.

"It looks like something out of a fairytale!" I exclaim, delighted.

Tristan parks the car and gives me an indulgent smile. "So long as it's not a fairytale tower."

My grin falters. Fairytales *do* have a way of transforming enchanting enclaves into dark dangers.

After a beat, I shake off the whisper of foreboding. "It's perfect."

I hurry out of the car and approach the little structure with a mixture of joy and disbelief. It's too freaking cute. I almost expect it to dissolve right there in front of me, revealing that this whole thing has been an elaborate hoax, an illusion, or maybe a dream. If *this* setting doesn't shake my story loose, I'm a broken writer.

Tristan joins me on the porch, my laptop bag slung over his chest and my weekend duffle bag in his right hand.

"I could've carried that," I protest.

"Your toiletries and the groceries are still in the trunk," he tells me.

I jog around the car to grab the two remaining bags. As I slam the hatchback closed, the black pickup truck bounces into view. The driver parks parallel, across the mouth of the driveway, blocking Tristan in, which is fine, I guess.

A broad-shouldered woman with close-cropped flaming red hair, several shades darker and brighter than mine, hops out of the cab. She's a few inches shorter than I am, but muscular. It's obvious even though she's wearing a heavy field jacket and jeans. As if to prove the point, she reaches into the truck's bed and hefts out a large bundle of firewood one-handed. She carries it past me, nodding a greeting, and drops it into a holder near the cabin's front door. Then she smacks her gloved hands together, knocking up a small cloud of wood dust.

"You must be Emily and Tristan. Have any trouble finding us?"

"Nope," Tristan says cheerfully. "Alex's directions were spot on."

"Glad to hear it." She fishes a key out of her jacket pocket and extends it toward me. "Let's get you settled. I'll give you the VIP tour."

"Do you work for Alex? I thought he was going to meet us," Tristan asks as I shift the grocery bag to my other hand and take the key.

She laughs. "I am Alex."

Tristan does a double take. I guess he assumed Alex Liu was an Asian man, not a White woman. I know I did.

"Oh, right. Sorry. I didn't–"

Alex waves off the apology. "No worries. I don't have a profile picture on the rental site. You're not the first person to make that mistake, and believe me, you won't be the last."

I frown. Why doesn't she just put up a photo, then, and avoid the issue? Instantly, I chide myself. She might live here alone. A single woman residing in an extremely remote location might not want to advertise the fact to the entire Internet.

I unlock the door and push it open. Alex gestures for me to go inside first. I walk through the living room to the galley kitchen and dump the insulated grocery bags on the small butcher block island.

"The bedrooms are upstairs, right?" Tristan asks.

"Right. The stairs are behind the kitchen. I only made up the bigger of the two rooms. But there's extra bedding in the trunk by the foot of the bed if you want to use the other bedroom for some reason."

"I'm sure the big one's fine," I tell her as Tristan trades me my laptop bag for the toiletries case and heads upstairs.

I swivel my head around. "Where are the outlets?"

"Your best bet is the little table between the two windows in the living room. There's an outlet under the table. But, you do know you won't get cell coverage up here, right?"

"Yeah, I know. It's one of the reasons I'm here. I just need to keep my laptop charged."

I walk into the living room and check out the burled wood table. It's actually a small writing desk. I take it as another sign that this is the place where I'm meant to write *The Tower,* my version of *Maid Maleen.* I run my hand over the smooth surface, feeling the decades of stories pulsing up from the furniture's memory.

I feel Alex's eyes on my back. I turn and smile at her. "I'm here to write."

"That's right. Your husband mentioned you're a writer. Have you written anything I've read?"

I will never understand this question. How could I possibly know? But people ask it all the time. They must mean something else by it. But I don't know how to answer it. So I give her my stock response.

"Maybe?"

She chuckles. "That's a dumb question, I guess. I did look you up after I got the booking inquiry. I didn't recognize any of your covers, but I read *a lot.* Like, a lot. Sometimes I get three-quarters of the way through a book and suddenly realize I've read it before."

"That's the lot of the voracious reader, I think." I smile. "Have you read anything good lately?"

I'm always happy to bond with strangers over book recommendations, and this question is usually a winner. Not with Alex.

Her mouth thins. "A biography." She says it flatly and without elaboration—no details, no title, no enthusiastic explanation of why I should read it.

I twitch my lips to the side and search for a different

topic of conversation, silently urging Tristan to hurry up and come back downstairs already.

"So, have you always lived up here, in the mountains?"

"No. My husband's in the military. I used to move around with him, but a few years ago we bought this place as a home base for when he retires. It suits me, so I stay here now."

"You don't find it … isolated?" The nearest community is at least a thirty-minute drive down the mountain, and it didn't seem like much of a town.

She shrugs. "No. I grew up in a very small town in rural Maine. This isn't all that different."

"Wow, really? Tristan did, too. Grow up in a small rural town in Maine, I mean."

"Huh."

"Where in Maine? The coastline is gorgeous. So wild and undeveloped."

"You wouldn't have heard of it," Alex tells me. "It's a little place on a peninsula—Windy Rock."

My jaw hinges open. "That's where Tristan's from! What are the odds?"

"The odds of what?" Tristan asks as he clomps into the room.

"Alex is from Windy Rock, too. Can you believe it?"

My husband draws his eyebrows together and frowns. Not exactly the reaction I'm expecting. I turn to Alex. Her face is pale, almost translucent. Her freckles stand out, stark against her white skin. Her pulse throbs in her neck.

She clasps her hands tightly in front of her. The two of them stand there in heavy silence for a long, awkward moment.

Finally, Tristan coughs. "We moved away when I was pretty young. My mom remarried a guy from Arizona. I haven't been back in a long time, decades."

This is true. We've vacationed in Maine, but never on the peninsula. He's never shown any interest in stopping there. He says there's nothing there to make the long detour worth it.

Alex finds her voice. "I think I'm probably a good bit older than you, too. So our paths wouldn't have crossed."

"But, isn't it a really small, insular community?" I insist. "Wouldn't your families know each other?"

"No," Tristan says in a firm voice.

Alex shakes her head. "Nope." Then she shifts her weight as if she's ready to spring. "I should get back to the house. There's a landline in the bedroom, Emily. Local calls only, I'm afraid. And there's a notepad on the night-stand with my number if you need me."

Before I can respond, she rushes from the cabin as if she's being chased. The door slams shut, and she runs down the driveway to her truck. The engine roars to life, and the truck speeds off, sending up a spray of gravel in its wake.

I give Tristan a puzzled look. "That was weird, right?"

He doesn't answer. He's gazing out the window, gnawing on his bottom lip.

"Tristan?" I prompt him.

He blinks and turns away from the window. "Sorry, what?"

"Are you okay?"

"Yeah. Fine. What were you saying?" He shakes his head like a wet dog.

"Nothing important. Just ... don't you think it's odd that Alex didn't want to talk about Windy Rock?"

"You wouldn't think it's odd if you'd been to Windy Rock."

He laughs. I join in, but my laughter is forced. There's definitely something off about Alex's reaction. Can he really not see that?

He crosses the room and wraps his arms around me. I lean into him and try to push aside all the questions tumbling around in my mind. He kisses the crown of my head.

I tip my chin up and study him. Something about his eyes feels wrong—distant and shaded. Like he's keeping something from me. I shake the thought away. Tristan doesn't keep secrets. That's my specialty.

He strokes my hair, tucking a stray tendril behind my ear, then says, "I have to get on the road."

"Already? Don't you want to stretch your legs? We can take a walk around the property before you get back in the car."

He gives me a sad little smile. "Wish I could. But—"

"I know." I shouldn't try to guilt him into sticking

around. I already feel terrible that he's making the ridiculous round-trip drive.

I stand on the tiny porch and watch him back the car down the driveway. He pauses, gives the horn a short beep, and waves goodbye. I blow him a kiss even though I doubt he can see me from this distance. Then his hand shoots up, and he makes a quick fist—as if he's caught the kiss. Guess he saw me after all.

I stand there until the car vanishes behind a curve in the road. Then I reach back through the open door and grab my coat from the hook on the wall. I'm going to take that walk anyway. The crisp mountain air is sure to get my creative juices flowing, and maybe it'll clear away the weird knot of uneasiness in my gut about the way Alex reacted to Tristan.

ten

Tristan

omehow—don't ask me how—I manage to steer the car down the steep hill with shaking hands. But there's no way I'm going to attempt that hairpin turn until I steady my nerves. I coast to the edge of the road at the bottom of the hill and put the car in park. Then I crack my knuckles, one by one, pulling on each joint until I hear that satisfying crunch of synovial fluid bubbles popping. By the time I'm working on the ring finger of my right hand, my pulse has slowed some, and my breathing, while still fast, isn't quite as shallow. I run a hand through my hair and sort through my jumbled thoughts.

Crossing paths with Lexi Lincoln has thrown me for a loop. I pound the steering wheel, pissed at myself for my carelessness. Then Dr. Wilde's gravelly voice sounds in my mind, asking me if it's loving or even reasonable to fault myself for expecting Alex Liu, owner of a farm located outside a remote North Carolina mountain town, to be an Asian man and not a White woman from the same accursed coastal town as me. Maine is a long way from North Carolina. And the names Alex Liu and Lexi Lincoln conjure up two very different mental images.

"No, of course it's not," I say aloud trying to absolve myself.

There's no way I could have known. Not really.

But that doesn't change the fact that my grand plan to get Emily safely out of town may backfire spectacularly. Although I haven't seen Lexi since I was nine years old, I placed her the second Em said she was from Windy Rock.

I spend a few minutes doing the deep box breathing Dr. Wilde is so fond of. Breathe in for a four-count. Hold for a four-count. Breathe out for a four-count. Hold for a four-count. Repeat. The rhythmic pattern helps more than I expect it to. I think I have a chance of making it down the mountain without running myself off the road.

Then a thought stops me cold. What if Lexi/Alex confides in Emily—or pumps her for information? Now I have to worry about Emily having a panic attack, and the stabbing back home, *and* Alex telling Emily about the past. Two decades of lying, running, and hiding are about to catch up with me, possibly putting my wife in the crosshairs. My pulse jumps again, and I work to regain control of my fear.

I just have to hope Alex gives Emily a wide berth. After all, we'd expressly booked the cabin so Emily could work without interruption. And given the way the woman bolted from the cottage, she's as intent on running from the past as I am. There's no way she'll drop by to regale her guest with the story of the time someone tried to kill her. Right?

I give the steering wheel another heavy thump for no reason other than it's a satisfying way to take out my frustration. I have to get down this blasted mountain and back to Pennsylvania. I'll deal with Alex when I return to pick Emily up. She has to be at least as rattled as I am—if not more.

I can almost convince myself that everything will work out.

I blow out a long breath and shift the car into gear to resume the painfully slow crawl off this mountain and back to civilization.

After I negotiate the heart-stopping turn, my shoulders drop down from my ears. I didn't plunge over the side. My constant checking of the rearview mirror has convinced me Alex isn't pursuing me. And the drive will be easier from here on out. I'll compartmentalize what happened in the cabin and forge ahead with my plan.

If there's one thing I'm a pro at, it's compartmentalizing. I bark out a bitter laugh at the thought and switch on the radio. I'm sure the stations here are going to be staticky and crappy, but I didn't take the time this morning to download episodes of the true-crime and unsolved murder podcasts I subscribe to, so whatever FM station has the strongest signal will have to do until I get to the interstate.

As the road rolls out in front of me like a ribbon, my scattered thoughts ping-pong from the evidence waiting for me at the lab to Alex and back to the recent stabbing. My mouth tastes sour and my gut roils. Queasy and wired, there's no way I'm going to make it to the highway without stopping.

I pull into the first tired-looking gas station I see to grab a can of cold brew and a protein bar. The clerk, a bird-like woman in her sixties or seventies, rings up my purchases without tearing her eyes away from the weather map on the television hanging over the counter. As I tap my card to pay, I follow her gaze. She's fixated on a graphic of what looks like a blob in the middle of the Gulf of Mexico.

"Bag?"

I turn away from the screen. "No, thanks."

"They're saying this could be a big one."

"What?"

"The storm that's forming." She jerks a thumb at the TV. "Saying it could be as big as the Storm of the Century."

I give her a blank look.

"The Superstorm of 1993." She squints. "You old enough to remember that?"

"I was born in '94," I tell her.

She scoffs. "It was one helluva storm. It hit in the middle of March. Hurricanes and tornadoes and even a dusting of snow down in Florida. They got fifty inches of snow over in Mt. Mitchell. More than that in Tennessee. The whole East Coast got hit, all the way up to Canada."

I don't care about a storm that's older than I am, not even a little. But she's waiting for a response, so I say, "Wow."

Satisfied, she hands me my receipt, and I jog back to the car.

I steer one-handed through the lot while I devour the bar and wash it down with the canned coffee. The caffeine and dense bar won't do my stomach any favors but it should help me focus. I pull out and get stuck behind a logging truck chugging along at twenty miles an hour with its heavy load. There's not a passing zone on this stretch of road, and I've seen the aftermath of too many head-on collisions to do anything risky. I settle in for a slow ride.

My thoughts return to the latest stabbing—less than a mile from the house that I vowed Emily would feel safe in. I need to camp out in the lab until I find the evidence that connects this new victim—a twenty-one-year-old ballet dancer named Giselle Ward—to Cassie's murder. They're connected, there's no doubt about that. The only question is whether the evidence will show it.

What about the attack on Alex?

Should I try to get the cold case files from her attempted murder, too? I know without having to check any databases that the case is unsolved. I wonder for the first time how much evidence the Windy Rock police actually collected, and what state it will be in now—twenty-one years later.

The logging truck's right turn signal blinks and I mutter a thank you to the Universe. The trucker comes to a complete stop before turning. I bite back an oath, but then he's gone. I accelerate to seven miles over the speed limit when I see the sign for the interstate on-ramp.

As I merge onto I-81, the radio signal strengthens and a whiskey-voiced deejay repeats the gas station cashier's warning about the storm system that's forming:

Could be a big one, folks. We'll know more in another day or two. Meteorologist Chaz Thunder will have more at the top of the hour.

I'm doubly glad now that Emily doesn't have a cell signal or internet access. Storms freak her out—especially this time of year. Hearing that a major storm is forming while she's alone in the cabin would send her into a tailspin.

I don't know if she's ever made the connection: The

night she found Cassie's body, there'd been violent storms —rain, not snow—but enough to flood the side roads and knock out a power station or two. This line of thought leads me to wonder if Alex Liu has a PTSD response to storms. I know for a fact that a huge nor'easter hit the coast of Maine the night she was attacked.

A buzz in my brain tells me that I've just had an important insight. What, though? I concentrate harder, but no clarity comes. After a long moment, I shrug. Must've been the coffee, not an epiphany.

eleven

I make it back to the farmhouse without crashing the truck into a tree or passing out behind the wheel. No small feat, I assure you. My heart is palpitating, my palms are sweating and I can barely breathe. If I wasn't sure this is a stress response, I'd be convinced I'm having a heart attack. But I'm not. My past has finally caught up with me.

I kill the engine and slump in the driver's seat. How could I have been so stupid? I should have listened to the whispered warning my brain gave me when my search revealed the Roses as social media ciphers. Who are they, really? It can't be a coincidence that someone from Windy Rock rented my cabin, out of all of the cabins in the world.

I scrub my hands over my face and drop my forehead into the heels of my palms, trying to think of a way out of this. Nothing comes to mind, and it's getting cold in the cab with the heat turned off. So I drop the key into my pocket and hop out of the truck. I land on the hard ground with a thud that jars my teeth. The sensation knocks me out of my rumination and back into the real, present world. It's a welcome intrusion, and, as I jog to the porch, I promise myself I'll figure something out. Don't I always?

Safely inside, I lock the door and secure the deadbolt. Then, I do a full circuit of every floor of the house, including the basement and the attic. I check the locks on every window, the kitchen door, and the bulkhead door that leads from the back porch to the cellar. Once I'm satisfied that nobody's getting in, I put the kettle on. But before the water can even get hot, I switch off the burner. I need coffee, not tea. Strong coffee that will help me stay awake to ward off the nightmares that the topic of Windy Rock always brings.

While the coffee percolates, I turn on the radio. Maybe music will drive the dark thoughts out of my mind. Then I head into the spare bedroom behind the living room. It's drafty and sparsely furnished. I don't often have overnight guests in the main house. The last time someone slept in here was three Easters ago, when Robert's sister and her husband came East for a visit. The room smells like camphor and dust.

I flick on the lamp that sits on the dresser and cross the room to the closet. There's a light in here, too. A bare bulb screwed into the ceiling. I pull the chain and blink at the brightness. Once my eyes adjust, I stretch up onto my tiptoes and feel around beneath the neat pile of quilts stacked on the shelf above the hanging rack until my hand connects with the cold metal of the crowbar. I heft it down then drag the old footlocker out of the closet so I can pry up the loose floorboard underneath—the one Robert doesn't know about. I ease the plank aside and remove the metal lockbox that's been nestled under the floor undisturbed since the weekend we moved in.

I leave the closet in a state of disarray and carry the box out to the kitchen. After I deposit it on the kitchen table, I pour a cup of coffee and roll my neck from side to side, staring at the damned thing like I'm waiting for it to jump off the table.

"Pull it together," I say aloud, cringing at the harshness of my own voice against the forgettable pop music playing in the background.

I take a big gulp of coffee, scalding my tongue in the process, and square my shoulders. Then I dig my keys out of my jeans pocket and flip through the ring until I find the small silver key that unlocks the box. I pretend my hands aren't shaking as I insert the key and unlock my memories.

First out of the box is the 1998 Windy Rock School

yearbook. In a town the size of Windy Rock, back then, there was one school for kindergarten through twelfth grade. Two hundred and twenty kids ranging in age from five to eighteen in one building. Average class size of eighteen students, one class per grade. It was as suffocating as it sounds. But it also means the yearbook contains the photograph of every school-aged kid on the peninsula. If Tristan Rose lived there the year I graduated, he'll be in the yearbook. If he's old enough. I frown. I'm not sure of his age, but he looks to be around thirty. He might be just a hair too young.

I shrug and open the book, turning to a page in the front where a gaggle of gap-toothed kindergarteners smile at me. A quick scan of the three rows of six names confirms there's no Tristan. I close the book with a loud snap and take another, more cautious sip of coffee. I set the yearbook aside and lift a yellow-orange Kraft envelope out of the box. I pry open the metal clasp with my fingernail and remove the bundle of yellowing newspaper clippings. They're held together with a rotting rubber band that snaps apart when I unwind it. I toss it in the trash and stare down at the reports of my attempted murder.

The local press coverage was surprisingly circumspect. The first three articles referred to me only as the "unnamed victim who fought off her attacker." Later, someone in the police department leaked my name, but the truth is they didn't need to: everyone already knew who'd been attacked. The whisper network spread my name all over town before I even regained consciousness. I was life-flighted to the medical center in Bangor, one county over, and Bangor's newspaper took a more sensational angle. Headlines like "Terror in a Small Town," "Stabbing Victim Fights for Her Life," and "Killer at Large in Coastal Community" flash by as I flip through the reports and force back the bile rising in my throat.

The scar that runs on a jagged diagonal from my sternum to my belly button throbs. I know my mind has created the sensation: the scar tissue is over twenty years old. It's not throbbing. But the phantom feeling tells me this was a bad idea. I shove the articles back into the box and grab the yearbook. I'm about to toss it on top when I think to check the alphabetical index of student names in the back of the book, just in case Tristan is older than he looks. **Roberts, Roman, Russell.** No Rose. I close the book, return it to the box, and lock it up.

After I return it to its spot under the loose floor board and put the closet back together, I head back to the kitchen to refill my mug. I should eat something. The acid from the coffee and the acid already swirling in my gut are guaranteed to give me a stomachache if I don't. I grab a box of crackers and the tomato jelly I canned last fall and boot up the computer.

While the ancient desktop wheezes to life, I wander over to the window to peer out into the rapidly falling darkness. I can't see the cabin from here, so I can only imagine what Emily Rose is doing. Did my poorly concealed freakout rattle her? Or is she one of those artsy types who live in their own heads? Maybe she didn't even notice.

Her husband did, though. Tristan Rose looked as sick as I felt when she announced we both came from the same Godforsaken town. And that makes me curious. I know why *I* want to forget Windy Rock exists. Why does *he*?

I scroll back through the snippets of the conversation that managed to permeate my panic. Tristan said he moved away when he was young. Something about his mother remarrying a man from Arizona. Of course. His last name probably wasn't Rose when he lived in Maine.

I poke around on the internet for a while, smearing the tart jam on crackers, one by one, and shoving them into my mouth while I search for any reference to the name "Tristan" in connection to "Windy Rock." Nothing. Bupkis. Zilch.

I try all my tricks—real estate deeds, tax rolls, church directories, and alumni listings. But he was just a kid when they moved away. By the time I reach the end of my very long dead end, I've polished off an entire sleeve of crackers, my lap is covered in a fine dusting of crumbs, and my coffee is cold.

I open my email client and send off a quick note to Robert. I'm not sure when he'll see it—or when he'll have a chance to respond. But the message is a touchstone or a talisman. A reminder of my new life. My safe life. My normal existence. And the act of sending it calms me, and I'm able to think more clearly.

My frenetic, swirling mind quiets just enough for me to realize that the kids and grandkids of the deceased almost always merit a mention in obituaries. Two minutes and twelve seconds later, I've found him in the online obituary archive for the largest of Hancock County, Maine's three funeral homes. Most of Windy Rock's residents seemed to prefer Zemansky Brothers, but Tristan's father was laid out at Timothy Lewis Funeral Home over in Fort Bradford. The obituaries stay up in the funeral home's guest book forever, but the individual archive results aren't indexed for internet searches. I guess funeral homes aren't overly worried about the SEO results seeing as how they have a captive audience.

The death notice was short, not particularly sweet, and dated three days after I was attacked. While I was fighting for my life in the ICU, Tristan's dad took a header off the cliffs outside town:

Thomas "Tom" Weakes, age 41, of Windy Rock, passed away on Tuesday, March 4, 2003, as the result of a fall from the cliffs into Penobscot Bay. Tom is survived by his wife, Tara (Fulton) Weakes, and his two sons, Tate and Tristan. Visitation will be private.

Tristan Rose's name didn't trigger any alarms because he was Tristan Weakes when he lived in Windy Rock, and I was right—he is considerably younger than me. He couldn't have been any older than eight or nine when Tara packed up and left town with him. She wasted no time after Tom's death. She and her young son had already moved away by the time I was released from the hospital three weeks after the attack.

Tristan barely registered in my consciousness back then. But I knew Tate. He'd been just a few years behind me in school. He was finishing up his senior year at Windy Rock and didn't move out with his mother and brother. He stayed behind, ostensibly to graduate, but as far as I knew, all he did was get drunk and pick fights in the parking lot of Nate's Burgers and Brews.

Not that I paid much attention. I was preoccupied with surgeries, physical therapy, trying to regain my footing in the world of the living. And I didn't waste any time getting the hell out of Windy Rock, either. By the beginning of May, I'd moved down to Connecticut, where I met Robert. When he was stationed in San Diego, I tagged along without a second thought. The more distance I could put between me and Maine, the better.

I never regretted the decision to leave. But I did wonder sometimes, on rainy nights when I couldn't sleep, if my departure had led the police to give up on finding my attacker more quickly than if I'd stayed in town as a reminder of what happened. If I hadn't moved three thousand miles across the country, would they have bothered to run down the rumors that Tom Weakes had attacked me and, then, racked with guilt or fear of being caught, thrown himself to his death in the bay?

I tell myself it might not have mattered if I'd stuck around. Probably wouldn't have. Because if the police had asked me, I couldn't have said one way or the other whether he'd done it. I don't know my attacker's age, ethnicity, or build. I am sure he was male, but I don't know why I'm so certain. I lost the hours immediately before, during, and after the attack, and my memory from that period never returned. Not that I'm overly broken up about that. I'm sure I don't want to remember the details. My mind is probably protecting me, according to the psychiatrists. And I'm happy to let it.

But, sometimes, those blank hours terrify me. My attacker could walk right up to me in the grocery store or rent my cabin, and I'd have no clue. And now Tom Weakes' son knows where I live.

My hands shake as I drop the crackers and run for the bathroom. As I crouch over the toilet, hurling crackers and blood-red jelly into the bowl, I'm gripped by a cold fear worse than any I've ever known.

twelve

Emily

The farm is still and silent—as are the woods that abut it. I don't see another person, a fox, or even a bird during my brisk walk. Of course, it's technically not yet spring, and I have no idea what—if any—wildlife overwinters here. It's eerie all the same.

Eerie or not, the sky is vast, the mountains are gorgeous, and the quiet must be good for my blocked writer's brain. As I hike along the narrow frozen path, part of my mind is focused on stepping carefully so as not to turn an ankle in a rut, but the rest is zooming ahead in my manuscript. The cold air has jarred loose the details of

Maleen and Ruth's confrontation about standing up to the king.

Or, I allow, the unsettling interaction between my husband and my host has inspired a scene. As the late great Nora Ephron famously said, *'Everything is copy.'* So I'm not inclined to question my muse. I am very much not a writer who follows the *'write what you know'* edict. If I were, I'd be known for gritty thrillers, not women's fiction. Even so, I manage to weave parts of my life into my work. And the thick tension between Tristan and Alex has inspired a scene where more is left unsaid than said when Maleen asks Ruth to help her defy her father.

Like Alex, Ruth will attempt to run from the situation. And it will be during this pivotal scene, I decide, that the king will send his guards to take the princess and her friend to the tower to begin their captivity. When they are locked in, the air will be thick with silent incrimination and fear, just as it was in the cabin.

I break into a jog, hurrying back to the cabin and my laptop while the dialogue and the sensory details are fresh in my mind. As I race over the hard earth, a stray thought intrudes on my mental story-building. Not about Tristan and Alex this time, but about me. Maleen and her lady-in-waiting were imprisoned for seven years in a dark tower without light. It's been almost exactly seven years since Cassie was murdered, and I've been trapped in my own sunless tower, a captive of fear.

The idea smacks me in the face. It's blindingly obvious. And yet, I've never considered it before. Am I drawn to *Maid Maleen* because I identify with her? Or, maybe, with her lady-in-waiting? I stop in my tracks, breathing heavily, and stare at the cabin, wondering. If I'm Maleen, then Cassie was my Ruth—an innocent victim swept up in my mess. It's what I've always believed, what I've always known, but somehow it feels viscerally true in this moment.

When I push open the door, I'm shaking and sweating. Capturing the scene is now the furthest thing from my mind. I kick the door closed with a booted foot and turn to engage the lock, then I beeline to the kitchen and the bags of groceries to unearth a bottle of wine.

It takes most of a glass of table red to steady my nerves. I make my way to the big window near the writing desk and peer out into the woods as I finish the drink. The long shadows of the trees encroach on the clearing as if they're marching toward the cabin. I shiver and turn away from the view.

It'll be dark soon, I reassure myself, as I grab the wine bottle by its neck and head to the small bathroom. I'm not entirely sure trading shadows for pitch-black night is an improvement, but at least in here, the only window is small and set high in the wall. I eye the old clawfoot tub that barely fits in the space.

A bath. That's what I need. A hot bath, another glass of

vino, and then my mind will be calm and I'll be able to write. I'll reheat the lasagna, turn on some music, and let the words flow. But first, a bath.

I pour the wine and set the bottle on the vanity, then lean over to fill the tub. Alex has left a little basket of toiletries on the tray—shampoos, fancy soaps, lotion. There's a small vial of scented bath oil. While the water runs, I uncap the oil and take a sniff. Lavender tickles my nose. Perfect. I dump the contents into the hot water, place a fluffy white towel within arm's reach, and strip off my clothes.

I lower myself into the steaming water and exhale deeply. I close my eyes, sip the wine, and trail a hand through the water cutting a lazy ribbon, back and forth in a slow rhythm. The combination of heat, booze, and water works its magic, and my near-panic and guilt over Cassie's murder begin to dissipate like the steam rising to fog the mirror. I tilt my head back and float, my hair streaming behind me.

If I were to tell anyone that I'm responsible for Cassie's death, they'd tell me I was being ridiculous. They'd insist I'm not culpable. Her murder wasn't my fault. I'm a victim, too. Survivor's guilt is common after a trauma. They'd say all these things.

But that's because they don't have all the facts.

Fact: Cassie was sleeping in my room, not hers, the night she was stabbed.

When it rained hard, like it did that night, the water came in through a crack in the corner of the wall up near the ceiling and leaked onto her bed. The apartment management company had been promising to fix it for months. So when the forecast called for rain, we pushed her bed against her dresser to keep it dry, and she crashed in my bed. It was plenty big for both of us.

Fact: The killer came in through my bedroom window, even though Cassie's room was in the back of the building —less visible from the street and an easier access point thanks to the ledge under her window.

When the crime scene investigators arrived, I heard them talking about it. They said it was poor planning on the killer's part. An unnecessary, wholly avoidable risk to take for no real reward. They couldn't understand why he'd chosen my window, not Cassie's. From my spot at the kitchen table, wrapped up in a thin, scratchy blanket, sipping the too-hot tea one of the first responders had pressed into my hands, I understood why: He wanted to be sure he'd have time to kill me before she woke up and heard him. He just hadn't expected me to be out and her to be in my bed.

But the most compelling fact was this: he'd told me. Two days after Cassie's murder, I returned to the apartment to grab some more clothes and books. A uniformed officer accompanied me, lifted the crime scene tape for me to duck under, and stood guard at the door while I shoved clean underpants and bras into a duffle bag. When I swept the stack of books and notebooks from my desk into the open bag, a sheet of paper fluttered out of my copy of *Their Eyes Were Watching God* and floated to the floor. I gasped when I read the words—loud enough to draw the police officer in from the front door.

"Everything okay?" she asked.

I nodded, not trusting my voice, as I shoved the page into my jeans pocket with shaking hands. I could've sworn the paper gave off the faint scent of sandalwood.

Back at my friends' place, I locked myself in the bathroom, smoothed the sheet and reread the message, printed in careful block letters: IT SHOULD HAVE BEEN YOU. Two hours later my mom had booked me a ticket, no questions asked, and I was at the airport waiting for my flight home.

Now, in a different bathroom, hundreds of miles away, my eyes pop open and my heart thumps wildly at the memory. I never told a soul about the message. Not the police, not my parents, and not Cassie's. Later, I didn't tell Tristan or Dr. Wilde. I haven't thought about that note in years.

Not since the fifth anniversary of Cassie's death, when I'd burned it at her gravesite and watched the ashes scatter in the wind. I'd had the notion that symbolic act would free me, bring me some measure of peace, and, maybe, for a while it had. But whatever solace I'd gained is gone now. Far from feeling relaxed, I feel vulnerable and exposed.

I stand up and grab the towel, wrapping it tightly around my body. While the tub drains, I hurriedly dress and go through the small cabin, room by room. I check the locks on each window and confirm that both the front and back doors are locked. The ritual does nothing to ease my fear.

Coming here was a mistake. I should know better than to think I can outrun my anxiety. No, correction—Dr. Wilde should know better. He's the professional. I lied to Tristan when I said I ran the writing retreat idea by Sam. I didn't call my agent, I called my psychiatrist.

Tristan doesn't know—can't know—exactly how badly this time of year affects me. The anniversary of Cassie's murder always messes me up, so Dr. Wilde is gracious enough to be on standby for quick check-ins throughout the month of March. Every year, he patiently listens as I relive finding her body, the details as vivid as they were when it happened. He must know them as well as I do by now. He says it's his privilege to hold the memories with me so I don't have to bear them alone.

Only now, I'm in this isolated cabin at the end of the world with no cell phone service, no internet connection, and a phone that makes local calls only. No check-ins. No support. No Dr. Wilde.

Alone with my memories, left to grapple with the narrative that defines me, the one that traps me as surely as any princess in a tower. Was it hubris or foolishness that made me think changing my setting would change my story? Ghosts don't haunt places, after all; they haunt people. And mine has come with me, taken up residence in my heart right here in this charming fairytale cottage. I sink down into the couch and try, with limited success, not to hyperventilate.

thirteen

It's late when I get back to Little Sweetwater. Later than I'd hoped, thanks to a four-car pile-up that closed the northbound lanes for nearly an hour and caused a slowdown for hours after that. Despite the time and my fatigue, I drive straight to the crime lab. The entire point of taking Emily to the cabin was to give myself the space and time to do what I need to do. I might as well do it.

I navigate the empty lot and park as close to the building as I can, directly under a light. Little Sweetwater is incredibly safe, the recent murder notwithstanding, and the county crime lab is an unlikely place to commit a crime. Even so, there's no reason not to take precautions. Especially now.

I kill the engine and grab my messenger bag from the back seat. Then I pop the locks and exit the car, slinging the bag across my chest in one smooth motion, as I hurry to the entrance. During the short trip between the two pools of light, my pulse hammers and my throat goes dry. I grip my keys between my knuckles as a makeshift weapon.

This must be how it feels to be Emily. Or Alex. Or, I suppose, most women walking alone late at night—even those who haven't had a personal brush with death. Exposed. Vulnerable. Scared. I remind myself that I'm not a woman. I don't look like a soft target. I'm a tall, fit man in his prime. The opposite of an easy mark. Of course, if I'm attacked it won't be a crime of opportunity. It'll be a deliberate, targeted strike. So my reassurances ring hollow in my mind.

I jog the last several feet to the lobby door, my ID badge already in hand, and hold it up to the reader without breaking my stride. Once inside, I wait to hear the door's lock reengage behind me before I exhale and roll my shoulders.

The reception desk is empty at this hour. The card reader recorded my entrance and will record my departure when I leave, but I stop at the open log book and sign in out of habit. Then I make my way down the dimly lit, empty corridor. My footsteps echo sharply in the silence.

Before I reach the lab room, I detour to my left and push open the metal door to the break room. The motion-activated light clicks on, illuminating my path to the old off-white refrigerator and the vending machine next to it. Reflexively, I check the coffee maker on the counter to my right. As expected, the carafe is empty at this hour. And I don't want to wait for a pot to brew.

So, I pull open the refrigerator and scan its meager contents hoping to find the remnants of a staff lunch. Sodas, stale sandwiches, sugary muffins. But the janitorial crew must've cleaned out the fridge recently because there's nothing inside except a bottle of mustard and an open carton of milk. The vending machine beckons. I feed my credit card into the slot and hit the buttons to select a bottled water and a granola bar. The items fall to the bottom with a thud, and I collect my sad midnight snack.

I devour the bar during my short walk down the hall to the lab, then twist the cap off the water and take a long gulp of the cold liquid. I let myself into the large, eerily silent room, turn on the lights, and boot up the computer on my work station. While the desktop comes to life, I roll my neck and do a handful of standing stretches to work the stiffness out of my back.

I flip through the stack of reports in my in-box. Nothing urgent. So I turn back to the computer and open my email. I scroll past administrative announcements, a message from HR, and a reminder that I need to meet with the assistant district attorney next week to do trial prep for a case coming up. Then I see it. The file I requested from the cold case unit in Maricopa County came in while I was driving Emily to the cabin, and, miracle of miracles, it's fully digitized. I'm pumping my fist in triumph when the door bangs open.

I whirl around on the stool and pop to my feet. Graham Stone meets my surprised expression with a look I can't quite interpret. Is it sadness? Regret? I study my boss's downturned lips and furrowed brow. Disappointment, I decide.

"What are you doing here so late?" I ask, trying to hide my nervousness.

"I could ask you the same."

"I wanted to make some headway on the stabbing."

He nods, distracted, as he crosses the room to peer over my shoulder at the file on the screen. "Arizona?" He points to the letterhead on the screen.

I clear my throat. "I remembered a stabbing that happened when I was living out there. Very similar MO to ours. I wondered if it was ever solved or if they developed any suspects, so I reached out."

Graham bobs his head like he's impressed by my initiative, but there's still something off about his demeanor.

He leans in for a closer look at the victim's photo. I

remember this shot from the media coverage at the time of her murder. It's a candid shot, taken at the equine summer camp where she'd worked between high school and college. Her head is tilted, resting against the side of the horse's head. Both the young woman and the animal grin broadly at the camera.

Graham takes in the image, focusing on the copper color of the woman's hair. "Another redhead."

He flicks his gaze to the photo pinned on the bulletin board behind my desk. Giselle Ward, the latest victim. Our victim. Giselle is the reddest of redheads. In the picture, Giselle is dressed in a ballet costume—a leotard and tutu, up on pointe with one leg extended behind her in a high, straight line. Even pinned into a neat bun, it's obvious that her hair is the color of a blazing fire.

The point of the picture is to remind the investigators that our victim was once a vibrant, lively woman and not the bloodied, battered husk shown in the crime scene photos. We don't need the reminder. At least I don't.

"Dana Rowland," I say now.

"College student?"

"A freshman. She was killed during Spring Break in her dorm room. She stayed on campus to work out with the rest of the equestrian team."

He groans the knowing groan of a bureaucrat. "That must've been a shit show. Panicked parents from around the country demanding answers; administrators in crisis management mode trying to control the messaging."

I shrug. "I'm sure it was. I was sixteen at the time, so none of that registered." Another glance at Dana's photo. "Just the murder."

"This happened in your town?"

"No, Tempe." I shake my head. "It's nearby, though. We lived in Scottsdale. The university in Tempe was less than thirty minutes away, and Dana was from Phoenix." I pause. "You know anything about the Phoenix metro area?"

"Not really."

"In addition to Phoenix proper, the metropolitan area encompasses the towns of Scottsdale, Tempe, Mesa, and Chandler, among others. They're all in Maricopa County."

"So, basically your hometown."

I resist the urge to shift my weight. "You could say that, I guess."

There's a long pause while he eyes me. "You think we have a serial killer? Two redheads in their early twenties stabbed fourteen years apart?"

There's zero chance I'm answering this question, so I gaze steadily back at him until he answers it himself.

"You know the saying. Two's a coincidence."

I finish the old saw, "Three's a pattern."

Of course, Graham doesn't know there *are* three stabbing attacks on college-aged redheads if you count the attempt on Lexi Lincoln. Four, if you count the murder of Cassie Baughman. While Cassie was a blonde, not a redhead, she was sleeping in Emily's bedroom the night she was butchered. Four events spaced at seven-year intervals in Maine, Arizona, Ohio, and Pennsylvania. It's a pattern all right. But I have no intention of connecting the dots for him. And what he says next makes me damn glad I didn't.

He frowns. "Worth looking into, though. Forward me the file."

I pull back in surprise. "You're going to follow up on it?" Graham hasn't done field work since—well, I don't know when. He was the supervisor in charge of the lab when I was hired. So, at least as long as I've been here.

He sighs heavily. It's almost a moan. "Not me. But not you either. Sit down, Tristan."

He gestures toward my stool, and I lower my butt to it reluctantly. Does he intend to loom over me while we have the unpleasant conversation that's clearly coming? But he rolls over the stool from the next workstation and sits so close to me our knees almost touch.

"What's going on?"

Whatever Graham has to say, I want to get it over with. Peel the bandage off and move on, that's my mantra. Dr. Wilde thinks I could do with slightly more introspection and sitting with my feelings. I think he's full of it.

Graham's sick expression makes me think he's not one for sitting with his feelings either. He confirms this hunch a second later when he says without preamble, "You're suspended."

I stare at him for a long moment while my tired brain

tries to make sense of the short sentence. Failing to do so, I end up repeating, "I'm suspended?"

He gives a brisk nod of confirmation, then tries to ease the blow. "With pay, of course. It's procedure whenever an analyst contaminates evidence. It's out of my hands, Tristan."

My head spins. "I contaminated evidence?"

He cocks his head and frowns. "Didn't you get a message from Human Resources? You should have."

"Oh. I guess I did. I saw the Rowland cold case file in my inbox and skipped down to that," I explain. Now I'm frowning. "I can't believe I contaminated evidence, Graham. You know how careful I am."

"I do, which is why it's so surprising that you'd screw up. Especially on such an important case." Another big sigh. "But DNA doesn't lie."

"An important case? Are you saying it's the Ward case?" My heart is pounding wildly. This can't be happening.

"Afraid so. Remember that brown hair they found on her body?"

I nod, swallowing hard. "Sure. There was no root attached, so I couldn't order nuclear DNA testing."

"I saw that in your report. I sent it out for mitochondrial testing."

"Why?" I give him a confused look. Mitochondrial DNA is used to identify bodies or missing persons, but it's of limited utility in a murder investigation. It's not unique to the individual the way nuclear DNA is.

His eyes narrow. He doesn't like being second-guessed. "The killer left us a jack-all to go on. I figured if nothing else, we could use mitochondrial DNA to rule out her siblings."

Right. Giselle Ward had two sisters and a brother. "So you used her DNA as the reference sample?"

"Correct. And there wasn't a match to that sample." He pauses. "But there was a match to *your* sample."

My heart picks up the pace from pounding to galloping. "My sample?" I ask, buying time to think.

Every crime scene analyst provides both a nuclear DNA and mitochondrial DNA sample when they join the lab. It's a sound practice. It avoids screwups like the Phantom of Heilbronn, the prolific female serial killer who German police were unable to catch because she turned out not to exist. A woman working in a cotton swab factory had accidentally contaminated the Q-tips used to collect DNA evidence with her own. There have also been cases of secondary transfer, where a person's DNA appears on an item it's been established they've never touched. Forensic science is science, but it isn't infallible. So, the analysts provide reference samples, just in case there's an anomaly.

Graham gives me a bracing clap on the shoulder. "Chin up. A two-week paid suspension while we investigate how the transfer happened isn't the worst thing in the world."

He's right. It's not. But being taken off *this* case, right now, is. Still, there's no point in arguing. He must see the defeat in my face because he stands, yawns, and stretches.

"By rights I should stick around and escort you out …"

That is the procedure. But it's almost one o'clock in the morning. And he's about to be down one investigator on the biggest case in the lab. The coming days are going to be hectic, and he knows it.

"Go home and get some sleep. I'll just respond to these emails then shut down my computer and leave. I'll be right behind you," I promise.

He pretends he's considering it. Then he says, "Okay. Appreciate it. I also appreciate your handling the news so professionally. Two weeks will go by before you know it."

I force a smile. "Right."

He pauses with his hand on the door and looks back. "Forward me that cold case from Arizona."

"Will do."

He pushes the door open and heads out into the hallway. I pull up the email from the Maricopa County Homicide Cold Case Unit and forward it twice: first to Graham Stone's email, and then, in violation of department protocol, to my own personal email address. I delete the second forward from my 'Sent' history for all the good it'll do me, which is probably none. I use my phone app to scan my notes on the Giselle Ward murder, then I shut down the computer, grab my bag, and turn out the lights.

As shaken as I am that my mitochondrial DNA came back on that hair, I'm relieved. A two-week suspension beats being named a person of interest in a murder. But my window of time is shrinking, and not having access to the lab and all its resources is going to make my plan harder to execute.

fourteen

Alex

I jolt awake, sweaty and gasping. I press my shoulder blades against the mattress and stare wide-eyed up at the ceiling I can't see in my dark bedroom. I listen for the sound that woke me, straining to hear over my ragged breath and thumping heart. Aside from my noises and the steady ticking of the old clock on my nightstand, the room is silent.

I sleep the sleep of the dead most nights. When Robert's home, he always remarks on how lucky I am to be such a sound sleeper. I tell him it's all the fresh air and sunshine. And it's true. I stay active all day, eat and drink well, and wear myself out so that by the time my head hits the pillow, my exhausted brain turns off. Then, I give myself over to sleep until the first gray light of morning starts to leak in through my curtains.

Not tonight, though.

After several long minutes of foggy-headed confusion, I accept that I'm not going to fall back to sleep. I could blame the coffee. Or the whiskey.

I'd planned to stay up late looking into Tristan and Emily Rose's past. But once I realized Tristan was Tom Weakes' son, I lost my appetite for the research project. After I puked my guts out, I was too keyed up to sit still, let alone sleep. So I pulled Robert's dusty bottle of bourbon out of the cabinet, poured two fingers of the liquid into a heavy glass, and then lay in bed reading my book—a biography of the bloodthirsty Harpe brothers, often called the country's first serial killers—until the booze did its job, and my eyes grew heavy.

I suppose I could also blame my choice of bedtime reading material. It's gruesome stuff, but typically, nothing interferes with my sleep. It's a point of pride. Sleeping soundly through the night without nightmares was one of my priorities after the attack. I thought if I could do that—sleep alone without fear—I'd be well on my way to reclaiming my life. I'm not sure how true that turned out to be, but I am generally well-rested.

Tonight, though, is a lost cause. I sit up, switch on the light, and take a long drink of water from the glass by my bedside. I'm wide awake. I glance at the clock. It's just after four o'clock. The sun won't rise for another three and a half hours, thanks to daylight saving time, which went into effect a few weeks back. A flash of irritation blazes in my chest as I sit on the edge of my bed to pull on my long, thick, wool socks. Blasted Emily Rose.

By the time I pad down the dark, quiet hallway to the bathroom, I'm already correcting myself. It's not her fault. Either she's the most gifted actor I've ever met or she had no idea that her questions about Windy Rock would upset me. How could she? But whether or not it's her fault, her presence here has interrupted my routines and now my sleep. Cranky, I brush my teeth and splash some water on my face. Although I sleep like a rock, when I'm up, I'm up. So, I might as well start my day.

In the kitchen, I prepare a bowl of oatmeal and get my coffee going by the dim nightlight built into the stove's hood. I'm not yet ready to face overhead lights. I flip on my laptop so I can attend to some emails and check my bookings. But my digital routine is interrupted as well, this time by the weather bulletins. The storm has definitely shifted and picked up speed—it's made landfall in Georgia and it's barreling up the coast at us.

I study the weather alerts, paying particular attention to the storm track models. By the time I'm done, my views on my early morning wake-up have switched from irritated to grateful. It's even possible that what woke me was the precipitous drop in barometric pressure ahead of the storm. Maybe my interrupted sleep is a blessing, not a curse. Regardless, I can make use of this time. I gulp my coffee and shovel the oatmeal into my mouth.

I toss the bowl and mug into the sink and fill them with soapy water to soak. I'll deal with them later. Then I pull on my coat, hat, and boots. I clip a headlamp to my wool cap before putting my gloves on. Finally, I slip a slim flashlight into my pocket, just in case. I activate the light on my hat as I step out onto the porch and its beam shines a few feet ahead of me as I stop to fill my lungs with the morning mountain air. The cold air burns.

I grab the axe that I leave propped against the wall near my door and walk down to the clearing to split two armloads of dried firewood. I've already gathered more than enough wood to last until the spring thaw. But with a storm coming, I want more. Plus, the activity gets my blood pumping and warms me.

I dump the half-logs in the bin by the door, return the axe to its spot, and do my rounds. I check the garden shed, tool shed, and barn, making sure everything is put away, battened down, and locked up. As I pass the empty chicken coop, I'm grateful, not for the first time, that I sold my chickens to the family down the valley.

For a while my brood provided me with eggs and companionship, but then a red fox slaughtered Henny Penny. My pain at finding the clump of bloody feathers left behind overwhelmed me. It was too much.

I prefer loneliness to loss. It's why I told Robert I didn't want to have children—I can't bear the thought of grieving another chicken, let alone a potential child. It's a dark worldview, and I know it. But it's mine.

I pause beside the fencing that does nothing to keep the rabbits out of my garden and let my gaze travel down the hill, falling on the dark cabin. Just then, the lamp in the bedroom comes on with a soft yellow glow. I jump back into the shadows even though there's no way the woman inside can see me and I have no reason to hide on my own property.

Emily Rose is either an early riser or a poor sleeper. Well, she does have a deadline looming. There's every reason to think she's up at this hour to tackle her manuscript. Still, it's awfully early. As I stand there in the gray half-light, watching the cabin, the skin on the back of my neck prickles as if I'm being watched, too.

I shift my gaze without turning my head and scan the area with my peripheral vision. I'm being ridiculous and know it—there's no one else up here. Still, I can't shake the feeling that there's someone in the dense woods across the clearing. I narrow my eyes, straining to make out a shape, movement, any hint of life. There's nothing.

I huff out a frustrated breath. Life on this remote mountaintop is many things. Sometimes I feel isolated, even lonely. But I've never felt afraid before. Not once. My seclusion has always been a source of comfort—knowing that I'm removed from all the violence and suffering that suffuses society makes me feel protected and secure. But not now. Now I feel vulnerable, exposed. I curse Tristan

Rose under my breath. His coming here has breached my defenses.

A sharp crack breaks the silence as if someone or something has stepped on a fallen twig. I freeze. I wish I hadn't left the axe on the porch. My throat goes dry. I can't swallow.

Finally, with shaking hands, I remove the flashlight from my pocket and switch it on, aiming the beam into the woods, low to the ground. I'm hoping to catch the glow of an animal's eyes—a fox, a squirrel, or one of the blasted bunnies. I see nothing.

I switch off the light, and as I do, I hear the rustle of dried leaves. I listen harder. No, it's just the wind gusting in advance of the storm. *Focus on the storm,* I order myself. Make the preparations to stave off a real threat instead of obsessing about imaginary ones.

Chastened by my own scolding, I finish my circuit, methodically securing items that might blow away, tightening ropes, testing locks. I consider going to the cabin to make sure it's storm-ready, too. I know Emily's awake. But it's far too early to pay a visit. I tell myself I'll drop by later, and turn to trudge back to the farmhouse. Raw from the wind and unsettled, I'm eager to get back inside and warm up with another mug of coffee. Daydreaming about my hot drink, I decide I've earned a dollop of fresh cream and a spoonful of sugar.

When I reach the porch, all thoughts of my treat vanish as I gape at what's not there. The axe is gone.

fifteen

Emily

The grief hour has followed me to this little cottage. At precisely 4:51 AM, I jolt awake, my heart pounding. As I reach over to switch on the lamp, my head throbs. I let out a soft moan as I flop against the pillow to assess my condition. In addition to the headache, I'm dizzy, and thirsty. My tongue is furry and my eyes burn. I had too much wine and too little food last night.

The hangover is no surprise, but I mentally kick myself anyway. I know better. The physical symptoms will dog me most of the day, but the worst will be the dreaded hangxiety. I know all about the post-drinking chemical changes—the decrease in GABA and corresponding uptick in glutamate in the brain and the spike in cortisol levels—that can make anyone feel anxious the morning after over-imbibing. But I'm not anyone. I have generalized anxiety and a panic disorder. And I'm taking SSRI medication. I shouldn't really be drinking at all, and I definitely shouldn't be polishing off a bottle of wine solo.

"Should've thought of that last night," I croak aloud. My voice is hoarse and thick.

Although, to be fair, accessing rational thought would have been a challenge last night, given that I was teetering on the edge of a full-blown panic attack. Beating myself up about it now isn't going to help. A cup of coffee and a painkiller might, though. So I throw off the heavy quilt and swing my legs over the edge until my feet connect with the bare floor. The cold seeps through my socks as I sway to standing. The room spins, and I grab the head-board to steady myself. Coffee and some dry toast or crackers to settle my stomach, I amend. And two painkillers.

I reach for my heavy cardigan and gingerly ease my arms into it without moving my neck or head. Then I take some slow breaths to stave off the nausea the motion causes and shuffle toward the door. As I pass the window, I pause to glance outside, but there's nothing to see. Only a wall of black. It's the deep darkness of night in the country with no illumination from streetlights, neighbors, or passing cars. I suppose the stars might provide some light, but I can't see them—or the moon. I can't even make out the faint outline of Alex's farmhouse or the shadows of the dense trees I know are out there.

I pull my sweater tighter around my torso and am about to walk on when I catch a flash of light out of the corner of my eye. I whip my head back toward the window and instantly regret the sudden movement. But my queasiness takes a back to seat to the fear surging through me as I press my forehead against the cold pane of glass. The bright ray of light is unmistakable. It can only be a flashlight's beam. As if to prove the point, the beam sweeps in a wide arc, lighting up the copse of trees to the left. Someone's out there, and, judging by their position, they're looking at the cabin, watching me. I stare through the window until my eyes burn, straining and failing to make out some detail—anything at all—about the watcher.

It's probably Alex, I tell myself with no conviction whatsoever. Why would she be awake and prowling around her farm in the dark at this hour?

The flashlight clicks off, and the clearing plunges back into darkness. My pulse pounds against my throat. I close my eyes and do a breathing exercise, the one that most reliably calms me down—breathe in for a four count, pause, then out for a seven count, pause, then repeat. After six or seven cycles, my heart rate is close to normal. As a bonus, all the oxygen helps my throbbing headache. My skull still feels like it's being squeezed in a vise, but the intensity has subsided some.

I'm steady enough to make my way into the tiny bathroom, where I shake two ibuprofen from the travel-size tube and dry swallow them along with my Lexapro. Then I grip the railing and head down the steep narrow stairs taking careful, mincing steps.

I grab my mason jar of cold brew from the small refrigerator and find a package of saltine crackers that Tristan sent along to go with his homemade carrot-ginger soup. I stand at the butcher block island while I nibble the crackers and sip the coffee slowly, not wanting to overtax my stomach. I can't allow the light I saw outside derail me. I already wasted last night by obsessing and worrying. I *need* to write.

I block out all thoughts of dangers lurking in the dark, memories of death and fear, and my anxiety about meeting my deadline. All I can control is whether I put my butt in a chair and my fingers on the keyboard. So I do.

I skip my morning writing rituals. No meditation, no candle, no free writing in my journal about the work. I just fire up my laptop, open the manuscript file, and write.

After a hundred halting words, I start to find my rhythm. The words flow as I lose myself in my story. My sour stomach, steady headache, and fatigue from a crappy night's sleep fall away. Time passes without my noticing as my fingers fly over the keys. The scene between Maleen and Ruth unfolds in my mind like a movie I'm watching and I type as quickly as I can, as if I'm taking dictation from my imagination. I suppose I am.

sixteen

Tristan

I try my damnedest to focus on the cold case file I smuggled out of the office. But my mind keeps going back to the Giselle Ward case. I still can't quite believe I've been suspended. In fact, I *didn't* believe it.

When I woke up, I started automatically getting ready to go into the office. Even though it's a Sunday, I'd planned to go in to work on the Ward case. I was halfway through brushing my teeth before I remembered I don't have a job to go to, at least not right now. I can't accept that I contaminated evidence. I'm always so careful. And of all the times to screw up, this is the worst. I need to work this case so I can make the connection between Giselle's murder and Dana Rowland's in Arizona.

My thoughts turn to Emily. I glance at the clock. It's still a bit early to call, and since I can't reach her directly, I'll have to go through Alex. I worry about Em being up on that mountain when the storm hits. The Weather Channel map has the Blue Ridge Mountains as the dead center of the storm. It could get wild up there. Then I remind myself that Alex is there. She's clearly self-sufficient. She'll be able to take care of Emily.

I'd like to get my hands on the police files from the attempt on Alex's life to see what evidence the authorities gathered back then. If I hadn't just been suspended, I could request them through my office, no problem. But I have been, so I can't. The other option would be to rely on personal connections with someone up in Windy Rock to get access to the records in an unofficial capacity. But we left Windy Rock when I was nine, and I haven't set foot in the town since, so that's not going to work either.

I chew on the inside of my cheek while I muse, then I open a browser window and search "Alexandra Lincoln stabbing Windy Rock." The hits come back quickly. I'm surprised at how many results there are given the age of the case. I scan the media reports.

I didn't know much about the stabbing when it happened. I was just a kid and our parents and teachers limited our access to information about what happened, which was surprisingly easy to do in the pre-internet, pre-smartphone days. I heard things here and there, snippets of conversation between adults who didn't realize we were listening, but not enough to piece together details. Lexi had been attacked. She was in the hospital in Bangor, and she couldn't remember who'd done it. This was the sum total of my knowledge.

Then my dad threw himself off the cliff into the ocean, my world tilted, and I forgot all about Lexi Lincoln. My throat tightens as I think of my father and the immediate aftermath of his death. My mom hurried us out of town so fast that the closeness in time between his suicide and the attempt on Lexi's life never clicked for me until years later.

Back then, when it happened and mom told me we were moving, I was devastated Tate wasn't coming with us. I'd expected her to fight him on staying behind to finish out his senior year, but she didn't. She was so focused on getting out of town that she just let him stay. I wonder now if that's all it was or if she knew more than she let on. We've never talked about it. We've talked *around* it, but we've never talked *about* it.

I close the browser, stand up and stretch, and go out to the kitchen for another cup of coffee. Is it finally time to have the conversation that my mother and I have been putting off for two decades? The thought alone makes my gut seize and my throat clench, so I decide the answer is no, this is not the time. I need to focus on the investigation. But it's no surprise that this case, the Rowland case, and, especially, crossing paths with Lexi/Alex is dredging up old emotions and fragments of memories, bringing all that detritus to the surface.

I shake my head to dislodge the thoughts, and promise myself I'll talk to Dr. Wilde about it during our next call in September. After that, maybe I'll be ready for a long-overdue heart-to-heart with my mom.

I drain the coffee in three long gulps and return to work. I have the files from Arizona spread out on my desk and the pictures I took of the Ward file up on my phone. I look at Dana Rowland's photo, then Giselle Ward's photo, Dana, then Giselle, back and forth. They were both willowy redheads and both extremely fit—an equestrian and a ballet dancer, stronger than they looked. Alex is a redhead, too. Shorter than the others but she's more substantial-looking, muscular and sturdy. The image of her hefting the armload of firewood one-handed pops into my mind.

Cassie doesn't fit the type at all. She was a curvy blonde. But then, there's no reason why Cassie would fit the type. She wasn't the intended victim the night she was killed.

Emily was.

I wonder, as I often do, if my wife knows. Sometimes I think all her fear and anxiety are the understandable result of finding her roommate butchered in her bedroom.

But sometimes, I think it's more than that—that she must know. Her reaction to the scent of sandalwood, her insistence that someone was watching her from the Simmons' garden, and her flat refusal to do any publicity for her books—these all suggest she believes she's still in danger.

If that's what she thinks, she's right.

seventeen

Emily

I reach for my mug and raise it to my lips, my eyes still on my laptop screen, immersed in my story world. I open my mouth to drink, and nothing happens. I shift my gaze to the mug. It's empty. I laugh at myself.

It's been a long time since I've been this caught up in my work. The buzz, the dopamine hit, has been driving me forward for hours. It's time for a quick break. I should stretch my legs, pee, and get something to drink. After overimbibing last night, I need to stay hydrated. I scan the last few paragraphs I wrote, then I hit save and stand up.

I mull over the story as I walk out into the kitchen in a

daze. Ruth's predicament resonates. Maleen's her closest friend, yes. But she's also her boss. They aren't social equals, and Ruth's boxed in long before she's walled up in a lightless tower. The trick is to make Maleen relatable in this scene. Why does she need Ruth to side with her against the king? He's Maleen's father. She should stand up to him by herself, shouldn't she?

I pour a glass of water and drink it absently while I ponder the question.

It comes to me all at once. This happens sometimes. These flashes of insight are rare for me, which makes me love them all the more.

Maleen's character arc is one from passive to active, patient to impatient, awaiting rescue to rescuing herself. At this point in the story when the king has forbidden her to marry the man she loves but hasn't yet threatened to imprison her, she believes someone will take care of this problem—take care of her. It can't be her lover, she knows the king will simply kill him. And it doesn't occur to her that it can be her. She hasn't had the life experience yet that will allow her to defy her father and walk away. So, she turns to her truest friend for support. Maleen's need for Ruth's help is myopic and she's thoughtless, but she doesn't realize the enormity of what she's asking. She can't understand what it would mean for Ruth to back her against her father.

I nod to myself, satisfied, drain the rest of the glass, and place it on the counter beside the sink. Maleen needs to grow as a character, and she will. But her desperate need for Ruth's support makes sense at this point in Maleen's journey. She doesn't know what's coming.

Just as I didn't know that I was condemning Cassie to die an unimaginably horrible death when I asked her to cover my shift for me that night.

March 2017

"I'll owe you," I wheedled, fixing Cassie with a wide-eyed look.

"Em, I'm tired." She pursed her lips and raised an eyebrow, unimpressed with my puppy dog eyes.

I gnawed at my lower lip, trying to work out how to convince my best friend to do this favor for me. I *really* want to hear Roland James read from his latest poetry chapbook. He's my favorite poet, hands down. And I completely lucked into this ticket. The bookstore hosting him is two hours away, the reading doesn't start until 8 PM, and Professor Lindell is not a night owl.

I was in the professor's office, dropping off some research she'd asked me to pull together, when I noticed the ticket on her desk.

I'll admit it, I squealed. "Ooh, you're going to hear Roland James read? He's amazing!"

She peered at me over the tops of her glasses, confused. I pointed to the ticket and her eyes traced my finger.

"Oh, that." She waved a hand. "Rolly sent it over. But Pages and Sages is all the way over in Greenwich Springs, and I have an early committee meeting in the morning." She paused. "If you want it, take it."

My eyes widened. "Are you serious?"

She nodded. "Of course. I'm not going to use it." Then she studied me closely "You like his work?"

"Roland James? Of course. His writing is so evocative and lush."

"Huh, go figure. I find it smarmy." She plucked the ticket from her desk with her thumb and index finger and extended it toward me as if it had cooties. "But I might be conflating the man and the work."

I snatched the ticket as if she might change her mind. "You know him? Mr. James?"

She lifted her silver eyebrows. "Yes, I know Rolly. Or I knew him, at least. I was the literary magazine advisor a million years ago when I was an adjunct and he was an undergrad."

"Wow." I pocketed the ticket. "Lucky you."

She lifted one eyebrow and gave me a wry smile. "Good night, Emily."

"Good night, professor. And thank you *so much*."

I felt like Charlie scoring the Golden Ticket. Now I needed to persuade Cassie to cover my shift at the restaurant, so I could use it.

I took a breath. "Cass, you know Roland James is my favorite poet."

"I do," she agreed.

"And seeing him read is one of my dreams."

"I know."

"But this isn't *just* a reading." I pulled out the ticket and read from it. "It's an opportunity to take part in an intimate conversation with the Midwest's premier voice of our generation."

She wrinkled her nose. "Isn't he, like, forty?"

"Late thirties at most," I corrected before conceding, "Okay, not *our* generation. But a generation. Cassie, please. I'll give you my tips from next weekend. And I'm working brunch. On a football weekend."

"All your tips?"

"All of them," I confirmed.

"You make poor financial decisions," she told me. Then she grinned. "I'll do it."

And that decision, which would turn out to have no financial consequences for me, had terrible life consequences for both of us—her more than me, to be sure. When Cassie dragged herself home from the sports bar a little before 3 AM, dog-tired and smelling of fry grease, I was two hours away in Roland James' hotel room nursing a scotch while he asked question after question about my writing. My enthusiasm and his attentiveness bubbled over into something more, something tangible, and we ended up in his bed—a slow, sensuous tangle of bodies and sheets that left me floating over my body.

By the time I charged into our apartment, dripping wet from the rain and bursting to tell my best friend about the most transcendent sex of my life, she was lying beside my bed in a puddle of her own blood, her sightless eyes staring up at my bedroom ceiling.

I drag myself back to the present, my chest heaving.

"I didn't know," I remind myself fiercely.

It's true that I couldn't have known what would happen to Cassie that night. And there's no guarantee that if I'd been there, the killer wouldn't have killed us both. But still, I can't shake the belief that I'm responsible.

I swipe angrily at the tears pooling in my eyes. "Channel this into a scene," I say aloud. "Make the reader feel Maleen's regret once Ruth's locked up in the tower with her."

I take a deep, shuddering breath and am halfway back to the small writing desk when a loud thump hits the door. I freeze. The pounding continues, and I peer through the window, catching a glimpse of Alex's profile. A flash of irritation blazes in my chest at being interrupted before I've even started again.

Part of me wants to ignore her and simply return to my work. But I don't have it in me to be so rude, so I sigh and cross the room.

I unlock the door and greet my host. "Yes?"

Alex stomps her feet and rubs her hands. Two bright red patches flame on her cheeks. The cold, biting air swirls around her. I shiver. I hadn't planned to ask her in, but the alternative is to let the whooshing frigid air fill the small cabin, so I step back and gesture for her to enter.

She reaches down and grabs something off the porch before she storms inside. I edge around her to close the door against the wind and then eye her cautiously.

"Is everything okay?"

Alex scans the room. I don't know what she's looking for, but she makes a slow, thorough inventory. This woman is creeping me out. And she's gripping an axe.

"Alex?" I repeat.

Finally, her eyes land on my face. "I don't know if you listened to the weather this morning, but we're in the track of the storm."

Listen to the weather? I couldn't if I wanted to. "No."

As if reading my mind, Alex says, "There's a battery-operated radio in the dining room. You won't get a lot of stations, but the station out of Boone usually comes in."

"Oh, I wasn't ... I'm not planning to go anywhere, so I don't really have a need to monitor the weather," I tell her.

"Right. You're here to write." Alex's tone suggests this isn't true.

I frown. "Right."

Alex walks past me to the small writing desk and peers at the words on my screen, making no effort to hide the fact that she's reading my manuscript.

What the hell?

I push past her and close the laptop lid. "Hey! I don't let people read my works in progress." I shake with anger at the violation. I take a few seconds to breathe and regain control before continuing. "Not to be rude, but aside from letting me know that a storm's coming, why are you here?"

"It's not just any storm. It's an enormous storm. They're saying it'll be at least as bad as the Storm of the Century."

I look at her blankly.

"The Storm of the Century? March of 1993?"

I laugh. "I wasn't even born yet."

"I was ten. We got a foot and a half of snow. No school for almost a week." At the memory, her mouth relaxes— not into a smile exactly, more like a less severe frown.

"It'll be rain here, though, right? This storm, I mean."

"Don't be so sure. That superstorm in 1993 dumped two-and-a-half feet of snow here in the mountains. And the temperature dipped down to negative twelve."

I stare at her. She mistakes my mounting anxiety for disbelief.

"I looked it up," she assures me.

"Do they plow up here?"

She barks out a laugh. "No."

"But the roads will clear by the time Tristan needs to come and get me next weekend. Right?"

Alex shrugs. "We have more immediate concerns than your departure."

"Like what?"

"You've never lived in the country, have you?"

I flush and shake my head, feeling foolish. "No."

"We could lose power. We likely *will* lose power. The unplowed roads will be impassable. There's a good chance the pipes will freeze."

I process this. "Does that mean we won't have refrigeration or running water?" My face and hands tingle. A sign of an impending panic attack.

"It's a possibility."

I have to get this woman out of here before I melt down in front of her. I slow my too-fast breathing and focus on the feeling of the cold, hard floor under my thick wool socks in an effort to ground myself.

She cocks her head to the side like a bird and watches me with concern.

I take another breath and croak, "How likely is it that this storm will hit us?"

"There's no question. It's bearing straight down on us. The wind's already picked up. The storm is moving faster than the models predicted. The front edge will be here by this evening and we're in for a wild ride overnight. Make sure all the windows are shuttered and the doors are locked. You have flashlights and candles and more than enough wood to make fires in case the electricity goes out. How are you on food?"

"I'm all set. Thanks for checking on me. But I really do need to get back to my manuscript, especially if I'm going to lose power and won't be able to charge my laptop." I flash a shaky smile and hope she gets the hint.

Alex's eyes flick to the pile of notebooks on the desk. "I guess you'll have to write longhand."

"I guess." My tone is dismissive. I'm not usually this rude but she pissed me off by looking at my work *and* I'm staving off a panic attack through sheer effort. I need her to leave.

She turns to go. Finally.

I'm crossing the room to open the door, when she wheels around, swinging the axe.

I jump back. "Watch it!"

"Did you take this from my porch?"

"What?"

"The axe disappeared from my porch this morning. And when I got here, I saw it leaning against the cabin wall."

"That's not possible."

"Yet, here it is."

What's her game? She's got to be gaslighting me. But why?

I draw my eyebrows together and crease my mouth into a frown. "Alex, I didn't take your axe. I haven't been outside since my walk yesterday evening. Why would I take it? You already brought me all the wood I need."

I stop short of noting that I've never split wood in my life. From the way she's eyeing my thin arms, I can tell she's thinking it. I hug my cardigan around my midsection in a self-protective gesture, as if I can ward off her judgment.

"It didn't walk here by itself," she persists.

"Maybe whoever was outside this morning put it there. Why, I have no idea."

Alex blinks. "Who was here? When?"

"I don't know. Before sunrise. I don't sleep well. I decided to come down here and write. On my way past the window, I saw the beam of a flashlight, like someone was standing in the clearing near your barn. But when I looked again, the light was out, and I couldn't see anything in the dark. I assumed it was you checking on your farm."

"What time was this?"

"Um, around five. Maybe a little later." But not much later, because I know exactly when I woke up.

Her face pales, and her jaw tightens. "That was me. But I didn't move the axe. You didn't see anyone else?"

"Like who?"

"Like anyone—a delivery person or maybe a hunter or hiker who wandered off the public lands."

"I don't know," I say after a long pause. I'm uncomfortable at being put on the spot. "I'll be honest, I drank a lot of wine last night. Too much. I was a little hungover this morning. I'm not sure what I saw, but I am sure I didn't take your axe. That's all I can tell you."

Alex holds my gaze wordlessly for several seconds that feel like hours, then she nods. "I'm taking this with me." She hefts the axe.

I lift my hand. "You should. It's yours, after all."

She finally leaves. I lock the door behind her and then slide down the wall to the floor, where I tuck my legs under me, rest my head against the cool wall, sweating and dizzy, and close my eyes.

eighteen

```
Alex
```

I'm still in a huff when I reach the farmhouse. I throw the axe against the woodpile with a *thwack* and stomp up the stairs to the front door. My agitation surprises, and worries, me. I'm usually placid. Sometimes my unbothered affect requires a lot of effort, but I rarely—no, never—lose my temper. I don't allow myself to because I'm afraid that losing my grip on my temper is the first step on a steep downward trajectory of losing control of all my emotions.

I shove the key in the front door and shoulder the door open. Once inside, I lock the door and press my back against it, breathing hard. I calm down enough to realize that leaving a sharp blade lying unsecured in a windstorm is stupid. It's a bad idea even *if* nobody takes it. I unlock the door and hurry outside to retrieve it.

A wind gust blows my hood up over my eyes as I'm running back to the house. As I push the hood back, I swear I see someone behind a screen of evergreen trees. A shape, nothing more. But when I stop and focus, all I see are swaying firs. Still, I take a step closer to the stand of trees, gripping the axe tightly.

"Hello?"

The wind tears my voice from my throat and swallows the sound.

"Get off my property," I call, louder this time, ignoring how ridiculous I feel shouting into the empty woods.

I stand there a moment longer before I turn back to the house. I force myself to walk at a casual, unbothered pace even though my heart is thumping wildly and I want nothing more than to sprint to the safety of my home.

Back inside, I lock the door and carry the axe with me to the closet, where I hang up my coat and remove my boots. My pulse still races from the glimpse of the person watching me—if someone was even there. But at least my anger toward Emily has cooled.

There's no good reason for my rage. Yes, she's married to Tom Weakes' son, and I hate that fact. But she's not a threat to me, and I believe her that she didn't take the axe.

She may be harmless, but, based on her reaction to the news of the storm, she's also likely to be useless if it turns out to be the monster the meteorologists are predicting. Right now, she's an irritant at worst.

No, I admit, my fury has little to do with Emily Rose. I'm in a tailspin because there *is* someone out there, watching me. I felt their presence this morning and again, just now. This enrages me. This mountaintop home is supposed to be my sanctuary, my quiet, safe space tucked away at the end of the world. Much like Emily did when I read a few lines of her book, I now feel violated and exposed. And I hate it.

And part of it, I know, is the impending storm. Bad weather has always been a trigger for me, although I've worked over the past twenty-one years to deal with the emotions raging inside of me.

It's as if an external storm activates a very similar internal one. Violent crashing images that I can't make sense of will flash like lightning in my mind. My thoughts will be thunderous and unstoppable. And my body will seize up with terror.

I rest my palms on the table and fill my lungs. I breathe. I'll get through this just like I've survived every other storm since the night of my attack.

My eyes fall on the axe where I've left it on the kitchen counter, and I realize it's more than the storm. It's more than Emily Rose having a connection to my past.

The axe being moved calls up memories from before the attack, a time whose memories were not wiped away.

In late January or early February, a month or a month and a half before I was attacked, I started to notice my things were out of place in my apartment. I'd come home from work and throw my keys in the bowl I kept on the table in the entryway, but the bowl wouldn't be there. It had been moved to the living room. My hairbrush wasn't where I left it. The light in my pantry was on when I was sure I turned it off. The door to my closet was open, but I knew I'd closed it.

It would've been easy to blame a roommate or a cleaning person, but I lived alone and couldn't afford a housekeeping service.

The disturbances kept happening. They were always little things, but after a few weeks, there were enough of them that I began to doubt my sanity. Then I wondered if I had a medical condition. Was I sleepwalking or blacking out? How early, exactly, could the onset of early-onset Alzheimer's happen?

I'd eventually been concerned enough to schedule an appointment with the general practitioner in town, but it was flu season, and the earliest appointment I could get was in March. When the appointment finally rolled around, I missed it. I was busy fighting for my life in the ICU.

The axe disappearing from my porch and showing up

at the cabin brings the memories of that disorienting, unsettling period rushing back.

Stop.

I have to stay focused and grounded in reality if I want to make it through the coming storm. I can't allow myself to slip into hysteria based on things that happened over two decades ago.

I pour a glass of water and make a peanut butter and jelly sandwich. I eat it while I check my email and respond to Robert's last message. I warn him I'll probably be without power for the next few days so he won't worry. I consider calling his brother and sister-in-law to check in. I desperately want to talk to someone who's not tied to Windy Rock or the events that happened there. But I don't do it. They'll know the storm's bearing down, and I'm not sure I'll be able to hide the worry in my voice.

I take my plate to the sink and brush the crumbs down the drain, wash and dry the plate, and return it to the cabinet. I head back to the computer to see whether Robert's responded to my email—unlikely so soon, but possible. He hasn't, but I see a notification from the Stay Your Way site, so I open the page and navigate to my inbox.

It's a message from Tristan Rose. He's concerned about the storm and wants to make sure Emily and I will be okay.

My finger hesitates over the reply button, and I realize I don't want to respond.

"If he's really worried, he can call the number I provided when I sent the directions," I say aloud.

Maybe I'll have phone service when he calls, and maybe I won't. I don't owe Tom Weakes' son a damned thing. I tell myself this, but it's not strictly true. I've taken his money, and he has the right to know whether his wife is safe. Still, I power off the computer without answering the message. My decision to ignore it sits heavy in my gut, like a rock.

I need to shake off this feeling—all these feelings. I lace up my running shoes, planning to head out for a jog before the storm hits, but as I'm opening the door, the wind rips a board from my abandoned chicken coop and sends it sailing across the yard. I back my way into the house and slam the door shut against the howling wind.

After unlacing my shoes and returning them to their spot in the closet, I can feel my anxiety and restlessness mounting. My mind goes to the whiskey in the liquor cabinet. I check the clock. It's only one in the afternoon, far too early for a drink.

So I pick up my book, not considering whether the gruesome tale of the serial-killing Harpe brothers is really the best distraction, and head into the living room. I turn on the lamp near the couch and read until my eyes grow heavy. I don't normally nap, but I was up early, and it's been a stressful day. I tell myself there's a good chance it'll be a dramatic evening and overnight, so I might as well sleep while I can. I switch off the light and pull the blanket down from the back of the couch, snuggling into the pillow. As I drift off, a slightly sweet and spicy scent wafts up from the soft blanket and fills my nostrils. My eyes flutter open as my brain tries to place the smell.

But I'm too tired to run down the memory. I close my eyes and turn onto my side. Within a minute, I'm asleep.

nineteen

Tristan

I check the time and am surprised to see it's mid-afternoon.

I missed lunch, working through the mealtime. My stomach growls as if it had been waiting for this realization to strike. So I gather my scribbled notes into a tidy stack, then go out into the kitchen.

I sent half the leftover lasagna with Emily to the cabin and kept the rest for myself. I remove the container from the refrigerator and pop it into the microwave. While it heats, I stand at the kitchen window and look out into our backyard. The storm's not going to come this far north, or if it does, it won't be anything major. But even so, it's windy. The trees are waving their limbs. It looks like they're dancing. And the few daffodils that have popped up in the garden have their heads bent as if they're ashamed.

I glance over at the Simmons' yard and my thoughts turn to Emily's scare the other day. Then I remember my promise to her to let our neighbors know she saw, or thought she saw, someone. I'd meant to text Tyrone and ask him to check the feed on his security camera, but it had slipped my mind in my hurry to take Emily down to the cabin and get back home. I pull my phone out now and am about to thumb out a text when I think better of it.

I call instead. After three rings, I get Tyrone's voicemail. I wait for the beep, then say, "Hey, Ty, it's Tristan. Everything's fine. Hope you and Lashina are having a blast. Would you mind checking your security footage for Friday, right around noon? Em thought she saw something in your garden. If there was an animal there, it didn't cause any damage, but it wouldn't hurt to take a peek at the video feed. Talk soon."

I end the call, wondering why I didn't say Emily thought she saw a person. Is it because I truly don't think she did? My wife may be skittish, but she's not divorced from reality. Before I can probe my motivation further, the microwave dings.

I remove the plate of lasagna, stirring it with a fork to ensure it's heated evenly, and pour a drink. Then I sit down at the kitchen island to eat my lunch. I'm a third of the way through the meal when my phone buzzes with a notification. I pick it up hoping Alex Liu has answered my message, but she hasn't. Instead, I have a text from Tyrone:

> Checked the feed. Emily saw something alright. But it's not an animal. Sending the file.

There's a link. I forward it to my email so I can view it from my computer and push the rest of my meal away, no longer hungry.

Back at my desk, I open Tyrone's video and watch the fuzzy security camera footage. The Simmons' camera is aimed not at his garden, but at the detached garage at the back of the yard where Ty keeps his vintage Indian Scout motorcycle. Still, the edge of the frame captures the part of their garden closest to our fence line, and I can see the clear shape of a man—not a bear, not a deer, but a human being positioned so he can see right into our house and watch Emily work.

My heart thumps as I magnify the video, but with the increase in size, the image loses all definition. It's nothing but a blurry mass. I swear under my breath. If I were at work, I could send it to the technology specialists to enlarge and sharpen. But I'm not, so I can't.

I slam my fist down on the desk. Being sidelined right now is worse than bad timing. My suspension is hamstringing me. I breathe through my nose slowly, trying to gain control of my frustration. I can hear my mother's calm, soothing voice guiding me: "Getting mad almost never improves a situation, Tristan."

My dad and Tate shared a vicious temper that Mom worked hard to train out of me. Tom Weakes punched his fist through the drywall and threw plates and bottles at the target of his rage. Tate stomped and stormed and swore and got into schoolyard brawls over the slightest perceived insult. But me? I had a pillow to scream into, a journal to write my thoughts in, and a glitter-filled calm down jar.

When I was very young, I thought my mother's efforts to help me process big feelings nonviolently were stupid and embarrassing. By the time she and I moved to Arizona, I understood that, far from being dumb, the endeavor was crucial. Then she married Jon Rose and gave me a male role model who could control his emotions. I realized his quiet strength was more masculine and mature than any of my father or brother's volatile explosions. I pride myself on being the man he raised me to be from the age of nine. I need to remember Jon's example now.

I text Tyrone back to thank him for the video and assure him I'll keep an eye out for the trespasser.

He responds immediately.

> Seems like he's more interested in your place than mine. Take care of that wife of yours.

I send a thumbs-up emoji and close the chat.

I run my fingers through my hair, leaving it standing up in little spikes. Emily always laughs when I do this. For a moment, I miss her so much I feel it in my body—a physical ache. I remind myself I need her to be gone now because I have to focus.

So I focus. I turn to the Giselle Ward evidence. I know damned well I didn't contaminate a sample. I couldn't have—I'm always so careful. But there's no other explanation for it. The county crime lab isn't a hotbed of careerist backstabbers or ambitious climbers. I doubt very much that anyone at work has set me up. I have good working relationships with the police, particularly the homicide detectives, and the DAs. My reputation is—was, at least—impeccable. No one in my professional life would want to sideline me during the Ward case.

Could I really have screwed up so monumentally?

I blow out a long breath, and the thought I had on the highway—the one I couldn't quite wrap my arms around and chalked up to a caffeine buzz—suddenly rushes to the forefront of my mind. Alex, Dana, and Cassie were attacked seven years apart, all during storms. To be fair, Dana Rowland's murder didn't occur during a rainstorm or snowstorm. She was murdered during a haboob, a fierce dust storm. Created when a thunderstorm with high winds collapses over dry terrain, a haboob is terrifying. Imagine enormous, rolling walls of dense dust that blanket the sky and block out the sun.

The one that hit the day Dana died was massive, reaching over four thousand feet high and stretching more than one hundred miles wide. It picked up and hurled rocks, boulders, and debris, downed power lines and trees, and turned over cars. It was every bit as dramatic as a nor'easter, a blizzard, or a hurricane.

I suddenly shoot out of my chair. "Cassie isn't the victim who breaks the pattern. Giselle is." My words are loud and sharp, breaking the stillness of my quiet, empty house.

I don't have to check the weather report to confirm. I have vivid memory of the day Giselle Ward's roommate found her bleeding out in a sticky puddle in the hallway between her bedroom and the bathroom. It was the kind of day that makes March in Pennsylvania bearable. Warm sunshine, a light breeze, bright blue skies, and a temperature in the high 60s—it was a promise of the spring to come. There was no storm. Not even a drizzle of rain.

Just as quickly as I bolted from my chair, I slam back down into it with a thud and a sudden, sick realization: I've been set up. Giselle Ward, a redhead, stabbed to death seven years after the attack on Cassie, is a placeholder. Her murder is a red herring, a distraction to keep me busy while her killer puts plans in motion. This is payback.

2010

I was at track practice when, from out of nowhere, the haboob hit. Usually, there's some warning before a dust storm forms, but not this one. We were doing laps around the oval when Coach Teal blew his whistle and shouted for us to get our asses into the gymnasium to shelter in place.

We sprinted flat-out, running faster than we had at any point in practice, as the wall of dirt rose up and blotted out the sun, turning the sky black.

By this point, my mom and I had been in Arizona for seven years, and I'd lived through my fair share of these storms. But this one was next level.

We sat in the locker room, eight teenaged boys marinating in the scent of sweat, musty towels, and Axe body spray until Coach gave us the all-clear to leave.

Navigating the short distance to my car in the student parking lot was like walking through a war zone. Bushes had been ripped up by their roots. Dirt was churned. Trash cans were on their sides, litter strewn everywhere. I drove home hunched over the wheel, white-knuckling it. Every traffic light between school and home was out. Car alarms wailed, and emergency vehicles flew by at every intersection, sirens blaring.

When I finally walked into the kitchen through the back door, I tossed my keys on the kitchen table and slumped into the closest chair. "That was brutal," I moaned.

There was no response. I knew my father—stepfather

—was out of town, traveling on business, but Mom should have been home. And ordinarily, her reaction to an announcement about a bad day was to flutter into the kitchen and offer me a snack and an ear to pour out my tale of girl trouble, a slow heat time, or too-heavy home-work load. But today, nothing.

I combed the house room by room, calling her name. She wasn't in the laundry room. She wasn't upstairs reading or napping. The house was empty. No Mom, no note affixed to the refrigerator with a magnet, no clue as to where she might be. I'd parked on the street in the drive-way, so I went out to the garage to check if her car, a silver Honda Civic, was there. It was. But she was gone.

My chest was tight with worry by the time I grabbed the cordless phone from its base and punched in Jessica Chavez's number. The Chavezes lived across the street, and Mrs. Chavez was my mom's closest friend. Mom had probably gone over to have coffee and gossip and lost track of time.

Mrs. Chavez answered on the third ring. "Hello?"

"Hi, Mrs. Chavez, it's Tristan. Is my mom there?"

"No, honey, she's not here. She's not back?"

"Not back from where? Her car's in the garage."

There was a pause, brief but noticeable. Then she said, "I saw her leave your house. It was after the worst of the storm had passed and I was checking my trees for damage. One of those Hummers pulled up in front of your house. It idled for a while until she came outside and got in the passenger seat. I waved to her, but I guess she didn't see me."

My stomach twisted and I gripped the phone. "Are you sure it was a Hummer?"

"I'm pretty sure. It was one of those big boxy trucks that looks like a Jeep on steroids. Isn't that a Hummer?"

"Yeah."

"Then that's what it was. A black one."

I started to sweat. I only knew one person who drove a black Hummer, and he pitched himself into the Atlantic Ocean seven years ago. Mom had sold that thing before we left. Unless ... I squeezed my eyes closed, trying to block out Tate, red-faced and screaming at her that he wanted Dad's car. Could he have bought it back from the lot?

"Did you happen to notice if it had out-of-state plates?"

"Hmm, I can't say that I did. Tristan, is everything okay?"

"Yeah, yeah. I'm just worried that she's not home yet," I choked out the lie. "The roads were a mess when I left track practice."

She cooed, "Such a good son. I'm sure your mother is doing fine, just fine. Do you want to come over here and have dinner with us?"

"No, thank you, Mrs. Chavez. I'm sure you're right, and she'll be home any minute."

She sounded hesitant about leaving me there alone,

even though I was sixteen. "Well, okay. If you need anything, you let me know."

"I will."

As I ended the call, the loud rumble of an engine sounded out front. I ran to the living room window. Sure enough, there was a big black Hummer hulking in front of the house. Dad's Hummer, I was almost sure of it.

When Mom got out of the truck and ran toward the front door, her face was streaked with tears, and I was positive. I wrenched the door open.

"Mom, what's wrong?"

She ran straight into my arms, sobbing. I patted her back awkwardly and looked over her shoulder in time to watch a tall, burly man exit the driver's side of the vehicle. He slammed the door shut and stalked slowly up the walk toward us. Tate.

The seven years since I'd seen my brother hadn't been kind to him. His hair was greasy and lank. His eyes were bloodshot and his skin was sallow. Dirt clung to his nails. In contrast to his broad chest and shoulders, his cheeks were sunken, almost hollow.

"Mom, go inside," I said, my voice shaking.

She craned to look over her shoulder at Tate's thunderous face. "Honey, no."

"Go inside," I said more forcefully. I gave her a small push toward the open door. Reluctantly, she went inside and shut the door behind her.

"Hey, little man," Tate said.

I ignored it. I knew he was trying to get a rise out of me, and even at sixteen, I had the self-control to ignore it.

"What are you doing here, Tate?"

"Jesus, visiting my mother and brother. Bring it in." He stretched out his arms.

I curled my lip. "I don't think so. You need to leave."

"You need to watch how you talk to me. I'm your older brother."

"You're nobody," I told him.

He laughed a bitter laugh and spat a stream of chewing tobacco on the patio.

"Don't," I warned. "Don't do that."

He spat again, and I balled my fists.

His eyes tracked my movement, and he smirked. "Try it, little man."

In my peripheral vision, I could see our mother peering through the curtain in the living room, watching us.

"Tate," I said as calmly as I could. "Mom doesn't want anything to do with you. I don't want anything to do with you. I don't know why you're here, but it's time for you to go."

"You two think you can turn your back on me—on Dad?"

"Dad's dead," I told him flatly.

"He was your father."

"I have a father. A decent one."

He whipped out his hand and slapped me, fast and hard. "Watch your mouth. Next time it'll be a closed fist."

"Like father, like son," I shot back, my cheek stinging.

His eyes narrowed. "You're soft."

Adrenaline poured through my body. I was somehow both hot and cold and vibrating with nervous energy, but I kept my voice level.

"And you're trespassing. Get off our property."

His face darkened, and his eyes shifted to the window. He flipped our mother the bird and turned as if he were leaving. Classic Tate. Barrel in, cause a scene, and leave. I sighed with shaky relief as he stepped away from the patio.

Then he wheeled back around so fast I didn't even notice that he had our garden flag in his hand until it connected with my shoulder. As I wondered if the haboob had uprooted it, he swung it at me again. Another heavy blow landed—this one to the side of my neck.

That red mist people describe when they're enraged? I saw it. I lunged at him, wrenching the iron stake from his hands. I threw it aside and punched him, splitting his lip. Then we were on the ground. He was bigger, stronger, faster, and—it has to be said—meaner than me. I got a few good punches in, but he pummeled me into stillness and then kicked me, his work boots connecting with my ribs in a series of breath-stealing staccato strikes.

Then, as I was dragging myself to my knees, our mother rushed out of the house, phone in hand, and screamed at him to leave before she called the police. He left. But first he ripped every plant out of our succulent garden, scattering them across the lawn, then sauntered down the front walk, pausing to spit tobacco juice on the sidewalk before getting into his truck and speeding away, tires squealing.

Mom helped me inside, cleaned me up, fixed me a bowl of soup, and made me promise to never tell my stepfather that Tate had come to the house. The next day, we went to the nursery for new succulents and replanted the garden. When he returned from his work trip, he asked what happened to the old plants. We told him the haboob had torn them up, which was more or less true.

I only asked my mother once where Tate had taken her that day. After I'd had some soup and the painkillers had kicked in.

She took so long to answer that I thought she wouldn't. But then she said in a dull voice, "He told me he'd been working at Arizona State. Landscaping. He said he thought I'd like to see the orchard."

That didn't sound like the Tate I knew.

"What happened, Mom?"

She turned away, her shoulders shaking. "The orchard was blocked off."

"Downed trees from the storm?" I asked, confused.

She started to cry. "No, police tape. It was a crime scene. One of the dorms behind to the left of it ... someone was hurt there." She let out an inhuman wail, like a wounded animal. Then she ran, sobbing, up the stairs and into her bedroom.

I could hear her crying up there, but I wasn't sure how to comfort her. So I stayed where I was. Eventually, I turned on the TV hoping for a distraction. Instead, I got a breathless local news report that Dana Rowland, a student at ASU, had been brutally murdered, stabbed to death in her dorm room during the storm. I jabbed the remote to shut off the TV and sank to my knees on the carpet.

Later that night, I knocked on my mother's bedroom door.

"Come in," she called in a faint voice.

She was sitting in the big chair in the corner where she liked to read. She called it her book nook. Her expression was vacant and tired.

I crouched near her chair. "I saw the report about that college girl."

She hugged her arms around herself and rocked back and forth.

"Mom, we have to tell the police."

She turned her head and gave me a bleak look. "Tell them what, honey?"

I swallowed hard. "Tell them what we know. That Tate—"

She shook her head. "We don't *know* anything. Dark suspicions aren't facts."

"But they can investigate. That's what they do," I argued.

"Is it? That's not what the police in Windy Rock did when Lexi was stabbed."

It was the first time since we'd moved away that she'd brought up the attack in Windy Rock. My frustration outweighed my surprise, and I frowned, wondering how to make her see we couldn't stay silent.

Finally, she gripped my hands in hers. Her skin was cold as ice.

"Tristan, if the police interview Tate, he'll know who pointed them in his direction. Think hard about what he might do." Her eyes pleaded with me, full of fear and help-lessness.

I hung my head and dropped my gaze to the carpet.

She kissed the crown of my head. "You're a good boy. You'll be a good man."

When my feet cramped, I stood up, brushed my hand against her cheek, and left her sitting in her book nook. Then I crept downstairs.

My heard pounded and my fingers shook as I called 911 and anonymously suggested the authorities take a close look at the gardening staff at ASU—in particular, a man named Tate Weakes.

part ii. the darkness

[T]he King flew into a passion, and ordered a dark tower to be built, into which no ray of sunlight or moonlight should enter. When it was finished, he said, "Therein shalt thou be imprisoned for seven years, and then I will come and see if thy perverse spirit is broken." Meat and drink for the seven years were carried into the tower, and then she and her waiting-woman were led into it and walled up, and thus cut off from the sky and from the earth. There they sat in the darkness, and knew not when day or night began.

—*Maid Maleen,* as retold by the Brothers Grimm

Ruth seemed to grow stronger in the dark. Like the nocturnal moonflower, with its glowing white trumpet face opening to the night sky, Maleen's friend found solace and sustenance even without sunlight. She stood straight and solid, unbowed by their confinement.

But she watched her friend surreptitiously. Worry thrummed in her chest as she peeked through her thick eyelashes at Maleen. The princess seemed to grow paler, softer, and wispier with each day and night that passed. Ruth feared eventually Maleen would disappear, dissolve into the darkness like spun sugar under water. And then, she would be alone—truly alone—in this living tomb.

—*The Tower,* by Emily Rose

twenty

Emily

It starts to snow not long after Alex stomps out of the cabin. I can see the first flurries from my spot on the floor near the door. By the time my heart rate returns to normal and I pull myself to my feet, fat white flakes are falling. I press my head against the cool pane of glass and watch from the window for a while before returning to my manuscript. I have a half-formed thought that I might go outside for a break at some point, but while I'm typing away, the snowfall intensifies into the promised storm. I'm so caught up in the story I don't even notice.

Despite everything, including the strangeness of my

host and the now-raging storm, I'm glad Tristan suggested coming here. I feel more in tune with my book than I have in a long time.

I write for hours until I reach what I think will be the midpoint, the spot where Maleen finally realizes nobody's coming to save them. She and Ruth have been forgotten. In the original fairy tale, the king says he's locking up the princess and her lady-in-waiting for seven years, and they resign themselves to their fate, believing it's temporary. Outside the windowless tower, though, the kingdom falls into war and ruin, and the king is dead. So when the seven years are up, they're not released. It's the point of no return for the character. It'll be the impetus that makes Maleen find the strength to save herself.

I'm excited to reach the scene, and my fingers fly over the keys. I can barely keep pace with the story as it unwinds in my mind with startling clarity. I'm riding a huge wave of dopamine, prepared to keep drafting until I crash.

This is flow. The writer's high I crave. When the story takes over, time loses all meaning, and I'm immersed in my work. Completely focused.

Until, at some point, the lights go out. I glance up, startled. Outside the wind howls, and the storm rages. I block it out and return to my book.

I keep writing, hoping the lights will come back on, but when I finish the scene and stretch my cramped fingers, the cottage is still dark. Alex warned me this would happen, I remind myself. I have flashlights and candles, and I'm tempted to press on, stay with the story, but if the lights are out, the heat is off. I need to start a fire before the cabin gets any colder.

I stand and eye the pile of logs in the small fireplace with suspicion. Then I walk over for a closer look. I realize that, while I've watched Tristan start a fire at least a dozen times, I've never actually done it myself. But how hard can it be?

I find the flashlight in the kitchen drawer and aim it at the hearth while I flick the wheel on the long lighter. The kindling catches fire, and for a moment, I think it's going to do its job and light the logs, but then the flame sputters and dies. I stare in disbelief. I swear the air is colder. I shiver. I don't know if the chill has already overtaken the cabin or if I'm imagining it. I try a second time, then a third without success.

The last thing I want to do is call Alex. The woman was so weird and overbearing when she stormed in here earlier. But what choice do I have? I'm shaking and on the verge of tears. I wrap a blanket around my shoulders and head upstairs to make the phone call.

I navigate the dark cottage cabin by flashlight, taking the stairs slowly so I don't lose my footing. It's so dark inside. I glance out the window on my way to the phone by the bedside. It's even darker out there. I see nothing but a wall of swirling, howling snow. The heavy snow blots out the late afternoon sunlight, and dark gray clouds fill the sky.

I shiver involuntarily, then turn away from the window and train the light on the pad beside the phone. The telephone number is written in precise straight digits. Not only is the phone a landline, but it's an old-school rotary phone. I trap the receiver between my neck and my ear and am reminded how I first encountered a rotary dial phone the summer I was twelve. I was at sleepaway camp, and we could call home on Sundays from the phone mounted on the wall outside the mess hall. The counselors laughed at all of us for our lack of familiarity and eventually told me the reason I couldn't hear my dad clear was because I was holding the receiver upside down. I smile at the memory as I dial Alex's number. I listen as the phone rings once, twice, three times.

"Come on," I hiss. "Answer." I picture myself dying of hypothermia in this stupid cabin.

Finally, after I lose count of the rings, Alex's voice comes on the line. "Hello?" It's groggy and hoarse as if she'd been woken from a deep sleep.

"Um, Alex, it's Emily. Did I wake you?"

She doesn't answer the question. "What's wrong?"

"The power went out."

"I told you that would happen."

"I know, but I can't get the fire to light."

Alex goes silent on the other end for a beat. Then, "What do you mean, you can't get the fire to light?"

"I don't know. I don't know if the starter's wet or I'm doing something wrong. I can't light it. It's getting really cold in here."

I cringe at Alex's exasperated huff. I feel stupid enough. This woman doesn't need to make me feel worse, but she does, of course.

"I'm sure you're doing something wrong. Do you need me to walk you through it?"

I crane my neck to glance out the window. Through the screen of white, I can see a diffuse yellow glow coming from the farmhouse. "Why isn't your power out?"

"What?"

"A light is on in your house."

"Oh, the backup generator must have kicked on."

"Will that happen here?"

"No, the cabin's not on the generator. And honestly, Emily, I'm not going to have power for long because my propane delivery was delayed last week."

I don't really understand how generators work or what propane has to do with anything. But I do know that Alex has power now.

"Can I come up? Just for a little while," I hurry to assure her. I hate how plaintive I sound.

"I'll come down there and show you how to make a fire," she suggests. "Better to teach a man to fish and all that."

"No. Forget it." I hang up the phone, frustrated and about to cry.

I pull an extra sweater, the heaviest one I'd packed, from my bag and yank it over my head. I tell myself that with enough layers and blankets, I'll be fine and thump back down the stairs less carefully this time, propelled by adrenaline.

I pull out the chair, sit down in front of my laptop, and place my fingers on the keys. Then I stop. I don't know how long the cabin will be without electricity. And even if, by some miracle, I manage to light a fire at some point, that won't power my laptop. It's better to save my work now and switch to a notebook, even though I don't want to. My muse is geared up and ready to write, but losing all my work would be stupid. Tragic even. I have to be smart even if it means losing my flow state. So I sigh, hit save, and close my file.

I go from room to room, gathering as many candles as I can find because I don't want to waste the flashlight battery either. I'll write by candlelight like some sort of romantic poet. I wonder if Emily Dickinson wrote by candlelight or maybe Charlotte Bronte. I'll bet Mary Shelley did.

I light the candles and pretend the ambiance is inspiring. Then I scratch my pen across my notebook until my fingers cramp. As I stop and shake out my hand, my gaze is drawn to the unlit fireplace. I could give it another try, but failing again will send me into a tailspin. Maybe Alex will take pity on me and come over to start the fire even though I told her not to and hung up on her.

I walk out to the kitchen to make myself a cup of tea and realize that I can't use the electric kettle or the microwave to heat the water. I give a small scream of frustration that morphs into dark laughter. Alex is no more coming to save me than the king is coming to release his daughter and her friend from the tower. Like Maleen, I'm going to have to save myself.

I sigh deeply. That means tackling the fireplace. My gaze falls on the bottles of wine lined up beside the sink. One is a Chianti, which Tristan packed to go along with the lasagna. I smile as a thought forms. There's more than one way for a princess to save herself.

I grab a cloth bag and pack up the container of food and the bottle of wine. Then I tuck in the half-loaf of Tristan's homemade bread. I blow out the multitude of candles and bundle up as warmly as I can before slipping the flashlight into my pocket and shouldering the bag. I straighten my shoulders, open the door, and step outside into the tempest.

It takes longer than I could have imagined to traverse the distance between the cabin and the farmhouse. It feels as if the fierce wind drives me back a step for every step forward. I begin to wonder if I'm actually making progress or just walking in place. Not only is the wind strong, it's piercingly cold, and the snow is wet and thick. Heavy flakes coat my eyelashes. I blink them away, and they land on my cheeks, stinging my skin as they melt. The snow is already piled ankle-deep as I trudge toward the house.

Finally, my slow progress pays off, and I find myself on Alex's porch. I stare at the door with my hand raised and lose all confidence in my plan. I twist and look over my shoulder. I'm not trekking back to the cabin.

"The only way out is through," I tell myself. Then before I can second guess myself, I rap hard on the door. I hear Alex walking around inside and vow that if she doesn't open this door, I'll break a window to get in.

Alex yanks the door open and stares at me. "What?"

My teeth chatter as I force out the words from between my numb lips. "It's too cold in there. I can't light the fire. Please let me come in just for a little while."

She crosses her arms. "That's not how this works. You rented the cabin."

"I know how it works, and I know I rented the cabin, but it's really cold." And I muster a smile and hold up the bag. "I have food and wine. Really good food—lasagna and homemade bread. And a bottle of Chianti to wash it down. Please let me in. We'll eat, you can tell me how to start a fire, and I'll go back to the cabin. I promise."

She stares at me, impassive.

I stare back, hopeful.

"Listen, I'm not trying to be rude—"

I cut her off. "Alex, I can't be by myself during this storm. I have really bad anxiety. I have ever since ...." I trail off.

She narrows her eyes as if I've piqued her curiosity. "Ever since what?"

I don't talk about this with strangers—or anyone really, aside from Dr. Wilde. But if it gets me inside her warm house, I'll tell her.

I let out a long breath. "Ever since my roommate was murdered. She was stabbed to death during a bad storm, and I found her body. I'm going to have a panic attack if you don't let me in." My voice breaks on a sob.

Alex's face pales, and her eyes go wide. "Your roommate was stabbed to death."

I nod, swallow, unable to speak and I see her face shift. Her expression is more than pity, but I can't place it.

She shakes her head as if she can't believe what she's about to say and steps back, gesturing for me to enter. "Come on in."

She closes the door against the storm and my shoulders sag with relief.

twenty-one

<pre>Alex</pre>

Emily sheds her layers. Off comes the scarf, hat, gloves, heavy coat, and not one but two sweaters. She sits on the bench along the wall to unlace her shoes and looks up at me.

"Thank you." Her voice is soft.

I don't respond. I let her in, not out of sympathy, but out of surprise and curiosity. It can't be a coincidence that Tristan's wife's roommate was stabbed to death. I want to know the details. And Emily isn't lying about her mental state. I can see she's teetering on the very edge of a full-blown panic attack, which won't do either of us any good.

So I make myself smile. "Well, I can't resist homemade lasagna."

She manages a giggle. It sounds forced, but I'll take what I can get.

"Don't forget the wine."

I'm about to say I don't think it's a good idea to drink alcohol in her condition, but I stop myself. One, I'm not this woman's mother, and two, the wine might loosen her tongue and lower her inhibitions. And what I need from Emily is information, as much information as I can glean.

"Why don't we have a glass before we eat?" I suggest instead. "I'll uncork it while you warm up by the fire."

I hold out my hand. She grabs the bottle by its neck and passes it to me, then pads in her socks to the couch near the fire.

As I head into the kitchen to look for the corkscrew, I glance back to see Emily beginning to wrap herself in the blanket I used for my nap. Then she sniffs it and frowns.

"Everything okay?" I ask.

"Oh, um, yeah," she answers, but she neatly folds the blanket and places it on the far end of the couch.

"You're welcome to use that."

"No, that's okay. I have an aversion to the scent of sandalwood. It's a long story."

I shrug then continue into the kitchen. I uncork the wine and grab two glasses from the shelf. "There are more blankets in the chest by the window. Help yourself," I call over my shoulder as I pour two generous servings of the red wine.

When I join her in the living room, She's wrapped up in a quilt I bought at a farmer's market down in the valley. I pass her a glass.

"Thanks." She takes it with a small smile.

"To homemade lasagna?" I propose with false cheer.

We clink our glasses together and I sit in the rocking chair across from her. For a while, we sip in silence. The storm howls. She watches the flames flicker and dance in the fireplace. I watch her face.

I want to make sure she's calmed down before I bring up the stabbing. She has, so I take a drink and say, "I'm sorry about your roommate."

She snaps her eyes toward me in surprise, almost as if she forgot she told me.

"Oh," Emily begins, her voice shaking. "Thanks. It happened a long time ago."

"How long?" I ask.

"I was in college. It was seven years ago this month."

"And you found her."

She bites her lip. "Yeah."

This is like pulling teeth. But I persist, keeping my tone friendly and concerned. "It was storming?"

She lets out a ragged sigh. "Right. Our apartment leaked—in Cassie's bedroom. So when it rained hard, she just slept in my room. Our landlord kept promising to fix it, and there were only a few months left in the semester.

So we just dealt with it. The night she died, I had been at a poetry reading a few towns over from ours. The storm came out of nowhere. It was a downpour. Visibility was so bad, and it took me a long time to get home. It was intense."

"Mm-hmm," I say to encourage her to keep talking. "I've lived through storms like that."

We both glance at the window, probably thinking the same thing. We're living through one right now. As if to prove the point, the wind picks up, knocking a chunk of snow from the roof. It lands on the porch with a thud. We both jump.

I tell myself to keep it together. This woman and her story must be getting to me. Despite my history, I rarely have a strong startle response.

"Anyway," Emily continues, clearly invested in finishing this story now that she started it. "It was almost five in the morning by the time I finally got home. I was drenched just from running from my car to the building. And I remember, standing on the floor mat inside the door dripping and I swore I heard it raining inside."

"The leaky roof," I guess.

"No, it was more than a leak. I could hear the whole storm, the wind, the lightning, all of it. It sounded too close. When I went into my bedroom, that's what I saw first, that the window by my bed was broken. It was storming in the bedroom. The rain was coming in through the shattered pane and it was nearly as windy in there as it had been outside.”

“That's how the killer got in? Through your bedroom window?”

“Yes. I was so focused on the rain coming in the window that I almost tripped on Cassie before I saw her on the floor by my bed. She must have been asleep because the blanket was hanging off the edge of the bed, soaked in her blood. There was so much blood.” Her voice quakes. “She was covered in blood, and her throat was hanging open. She looked like she was staring up at the ceiling, but I knew she was dead.”

She closes her eyes as if that might block out the images in her head and drains her glass. I ease it from her hand to refill it, then top off my own because I'm nearly as shaken as she is.

When I return to the living room, her eyes are open and she's just staring off into middle distance. I don't like to touch people or be touched unless it's by Robert, but something about the abject misery on Emily's face makes me reach out and squeeze her hand.

“I know what you've been through,” I tell her.

Emily laughs shortly. “You can't.”

“You'd be surprised.” I hand her the glass and sit down next to her.

Emily wipes her tears and flicks her gaze toward me. “What, you found your roommate stabbed to death, too?”

"Not exactly. I'll tell you the story, but first can I ask you a question?"

She nods wordlessly.

"Was Tristan with you at the poetry reading? Did he come home with you that night?"

She gives me a confused look. "What?"

"Tristan. Your husband," I prompt.

"Oh, no, we didn't start dating until after. I met Tristan almost a year after Cassie died."

This isn't the response I expected. I press my lips together and try not to frown. "How did you meet him?"

Emily smiles despite the pain on her face. "I ran into him, literally, in the lobby of my psychotherapist's office."

"And the rest is history."

"Something like that."

"What do you know about his family?" I probe.

It's her turn to frown. She draws her pretty eyebrows together and shakes her head. "Not much. His stepfather died before we got married. I only met him a few times, but he was a nice man, a good man. He always treated Tristan like his son. Jon adopted him. It was what Tristan wanted for his twelfth birthday."

"And his mom?"

"Tara's quiet. Kind of like me, I guess. She always seems a bit sad, subdued. But she's been lovely to me. I don't know much about what happened between her and Tristan's dad. He doesn't talk about it. He doesn't talk about Windy Rock at all, really."

I hesitate, take a breath, then steel myself. "How close is he with his brother?"

She blinks. "Tristan doesn't have a brother."

I feel my eyes widen. "Yes, he does. Tate. Tate Weakes."

She's shaking her head. "No, I don't think so. Tristan's never mentioned a brother. Neither has his mom. There's no pictures of a brother. Maybe you have him mixed up with someone else."

"No," I insist, surprised by the force in my voice. "Your husband has a brother."

twenty-two

Emily

My head buzzes, and it's not from the wine. I can't believe Tristan has a brother he never told me about.

I sense Alex's eyes on me as I stare into the fire, playing back every conversation I've ever had with Tristan or his mom. Could one of them have mentioned this brother and I somehow missed it or forgot? This feels impossible, but I'm desperate for an explanation other than the obvious one, which is that Tristan hid the fact that he has a sibling from me. I can't wrap my mind around it.

"Tristan has a brother," I say softly. "And his dad's last name was Weakes?" I look at her for confirmation.

She barks out a laugh. "Are you kidding me? You didn't even know his *name*? Do you know anything about your husband?"

I bristle, defensive. Probably because what she's saying has a kernel of truth to it. "It's not like that. I know all the things that matter. His legal last name is Rose. It was Rose when I met him. Why would I ask?"

"Why would you have to ask?" she shoots back. "Why wouldn't he just tell you?"

I consider this for a moment. Why wouldn't he?

Finally, I shrug. "He doesn't like to talk about Maine. When he does mention it, it's only in passing. He told me his dad died there when he was young, and he and his mom moved away soon after. She remarried pretty quickly, and his stepdad adopted him. He's told me plenty of stories about Arizona."

"But not Windy Rock."

"Right, not Windy Rock. I always assumed it's a difficult subject for him to talk about."

"Oh, I'm sure it is," she agrees, "but you're his wife. You must talk about difficult things." A pause. "Don't you?"

I bristle. "That's not fair. We started dating when I was grieving my best friend's murder. I mean, I'm still grieving, I probably always will be. But it was fresh then. It had only been a year."

She gives me a thoughtful look. "I'll bet Tristan was so

supportive, helping you through that dark period, wasn't he?"

My stomach twists. I really, *really* do not want to tell this prickly, judgmental woman the truth. But some part of me knows I need to.

"He doesn't know about Cassie."

She blinks, and it takes a moment for what I'm telling her to register.

"Tristan doesn't know your roommate was murdered?" she asks slowly.

I nod.

Her jaw drops. "How is that possible? You went to college in a town with a population of twenty thousand people, give or take. How did he miss a murder?"

Before answering, I raise an eyebrow at the fact that she researched us. She has the self-awareness to flush. "He wasn't living there yet. He started graduate school five months after it happened, and I guess …," I pause to search for a way to explain. "When I met him and realized he didn't know that I was the murdered girl's roommate, it was such a relief, refreshing. You can't imagine what it's like. Once you've been connected to a horrific crime, you never get your life back. To everyone who knows about it, I'll always be that girl who found her dead roommate's body. But with Tristan, I was just Emily."

Her face softens. "I don't have to imagine it. I know."

Now I'm the one who's confused. What does she mean? How could she possibly know?

I'm about to ask her, when she bolts to her feet. "Let's eat."

twenty-three

Tristan

By 5 PM, my brain is mush. I can't work anymore, and I know I'm missing something. I need to speak with my mother. I'm reaching for the phone when it rings. I pick it up to answer it, and my jaw hinges open when I read 'Mom' on the screen.

I fumble with the button to pick up the call and walk out into the kitchen. "Mom, I was just picking up the phone to call you."

"Oh?" Her voice is strange, shaky, and full of emotion that I can't place. "You must have sensed I need to talk."

"Is something wrong?"

She doesn't answer directly. "I have … news, Tristan."

"Are you sick?"

"No, no, it's nothing like that," she hurries to assure me. I lean against the kitchen counter and wait. "I guess I just need to come out and say it. Your brother is dead."

My mind goes completely blank. I say nothing.

"Honey, are you there?"

I struggle to remember how to speak and finally manage to string sounds into words and the words into a sentence. "What do you mean, Tate's dead?"

"Believe me, I'm as shocked as you are."

"I didn't know you were in contact with Tate."

"I'm not. I wasn't," she stammers. "I haven't spoken to Tate since that bad haboob. When was that? Maybe twelve —?"

"Fourteen years ago," I tell her with the certainty of a person who's just relived that day.

She considers my answer for a moment, then says, "That's right. It's been fourteen years. I haven't talked to him since … all of that."

"Then how do you know he's dead?"

"I got a phone call. Apparently, your brother was living in Ohio. His psychiatrist called because Tate had listed me as his next of kin."

My stomach drops. "Tate was seeing a psychiatrist?"

"I couldn't believe it either," my mother says, misunderstanding the tone in my voice. "But Dr. Wilde said he's been treating Tate for six years now."

Dr. Wilde? My heart thumps so loudly I wonder if my mother can hear it through the phone.

I guess not, because she doesn't miss a beat.

"The police called his office because his number was the only one saved in Tate's phone."

My mind spins, racing to make sense of what she's saying. As far as Dr. Wilde knows, *I'm* Tate Weakes. And I am very much not dead.

How do I explain her estranged son isn't dead but instead has engineered some sick, messed-up hoax?

"Who found him?"

"The doctor didn't have any details. He didn't even know who called. Just that it was the police. The person left a message with his service, but no name."

"That's odd," I manage.

"Another odd thing is that Tate didn't tell his psychotherapist we were estranged. The doctor seems to think we had a relationship."

This is exactly what Dr. Wilde would think because he and I have talked at length about how my mother and I have never dealt with our shared ordeal and the impact that silence has had on our relationship.

I let her keep talking because I know she needs to, but I'm lost in my thoughts, only half-listening, until I hear the words, 'crime lab.'

"I'm sorry, Mom. I missed that."

"I said I wonder, since you work for the crime lab, if you could reach out to the authorities in Ohio to find out what happened. Maybe ask how he died and how we can get his body back? I don't know what else to do. I wouldn't even know where to start." Her voice breaks.

"You start by going over to Mrs. Chavez's house. Stay with her. Let her comfort you. I'll make all the arrangements. I'll take care of this."

All these years later, Jessica Chavez is still my mother's neighbor and best friend. She won't hesitate. She'll take one look at my mom and envelope her in a badly needed hug.

"That's a good idea. Maybe I'll do that," she says, too vaguely for my liking.

"Let's do it this way. Stay on the phone and walk across the street to Jessica's now. I'm not going to hang up until I know that you're with her."

"Honey, I'm going to be okay."

"Humor me anyway."

"Tristan," she begins in a tentative voice.

I immediately know what she's about to ask and my chest tightens. "Yeah, Mom?"

"You don't think ... what if Tate killed himself? Like your father did. What if he did something and couldn't live with himself anymore?"

It's an understandable question. Unless, of course, you know damn well, like I do, that Tate's not dead. But I certainly can't tell her that.

I exhale slowly. "Look, we don't know anything about Tate's life. Let's not jump to conclusions. Maybe he got hit by a train. Maybe he had cancer. Maybe he died rescuing a bunch of stray animals from a fire. Don't let your mind immediately go to suicide—or any of the rest of it."

"You're right." I hear rustling as she puts on her shoes, the jingle of her keys. Eventually, the door opens and closes, and the faint sound of street traffic filters through the phone as she crosses the street. "Okay, honey. I'm at Jessica's." The doorbell rings.

"I'll take care of this," I promise.

"I know you will."

"Oh, Tara. This is a nice surprise." Jessica's voice, distant, comes through the phone. She must see something on my mother's face because her voice falls. "Oh, sweetie, what's wrong?"

"My son is dead," Mom blurts.

"Tristan's dead? Oh my God, what happened?"

"No, not Tristan."

"I don't ... what?"

I realize my mother has never mentioned another son to Jessica. The apple doesn't fall far, does it?

"Mom, hand the phone to Jessica, please," I say.

A moment later, my mother's friend's voice is in my ear. "Tristan, what's going on? Your mother said her son is dead. You have a brother?"

"It's a really long story, and I'm sure my mom will share it when she's ready," I hedge. "Please tell me you'll take care of her because I can't get out there for a while."

Confusion still clouds Jessica's voice, but she reacts as I know she will.

"Of course. She'll stay with me. I wouldn't hear of anything else. I'll take good care of her."

"Thank you."

"Tristan you know you don't need to thank me. You and Tara are like family. I'm so sorry for your loss."

Right. My loss. I roll my eyes but murmur something appreciative.

She passes the phone back to my mother.

"It's going to be okay," I tell her.

"What do I tell Jessica about Tate?" she whispers, although I'm sure the woman is standing right there and can hear her.

"You should tell her as much as you're comfortable sharing."

"Oh, that's not—"

"Mom, it's time," I say as gently as I can. "She's your friend. She'll understand and support you."

"I don't know," she hedges.

I'm sure the idea terrifies her. I know it terrifies me. My mother and I have been keeping secrets for as long as I can remember. I equate secrets with safety. No doubt she does, too.

"You don't have to decide right now, but promise you'll think about it. I'll talk to you soon."

"Okay, baby. Thank you."

"Of course, Mom. Love you."

"Love you more," she says, as she always does, and we end the call.

I drop my head into my hands and stare down at the table trying to work out my next move. And Tate's.

twenty-four

Alex

After our second glasses of wine, I suggest we eat. Emily's looking glassy-eyed, and I don't know her well enough to know whether it's the effect of the wine or the aftermath of telling her story. Either way, food can't hurt. And if I'm being honest, her comment about always being identified with her past—being defined by it—hit me hard. I know I need to tell her my story, but I want to put it off a while longer.

So we move into the kitchen and I slide the lasagna out of the container and into a casserole dish then place it on the counter while the oven preheats. She aims a pointed look at my microwave, and I shrug.

"Things taste better this way," I say. "Besides, it won't take long to heat this."

She removes the bread from its brown paper bag and scans the counters. "Cutting board?"

I hand her one from the stack in the top middle drawer and nod toward the toaster oven. "Why don't you reheat that, too?"

She's arranging the bread on the tray, her back to me, when she says, "I can't believe he didn't tell me he has a brother." The betrayal in her voice is palpable.

And even though I don't owe Tristan Rose a damned thing, I feel compelled to defend him.

"In fairness, Emily, if Tate were my brother, I don't think I'd tell anyone either."

She twists around to look at me. "Why?"

I exhale heavily. "It isn't my story to tell," I begin.

"I think we're past that, don't you?"

She's right, but, nonetheless, I feel dirty as I explain the little I know about the Weakes' home life.

"The Weakes family was troubled. I think today, people would probably intervene. I hope they would. But in the eighties and nineties, that's just not something people did, especially not in a town like Windy Rock."

She's already frowning. *Just wait,* I think.

"Troubled how?"

"Tom had a temper. And as a result, he had a hard time keeping a job. But Tara wasn't allowed to work outside the house because her job was to be a mom. So they were pretty much broke."

"Wasn't *allowed*?"

I nod. "That's the way I heard it, at least." I indulge my curiosity. "Does she have a job now?"

"She's a realtor. A successful one."

"Good for her," I say, and I mean it.

"I can't imagine the Tara I know letting someone push her around." She's shaking her head.

"People change." I should know this better than anyone.

"I guess. And they had two kids?" She asks like I might not be sure. She's really fixated on this brother thing.

"Yes, Emily. Two sons with a pretty big age gap between them. I think Tate is eight years older than Tristan. Maybe nine. Something like that."

"That *is* a big gap. Any idea why?"

"Not really. A few times, right after Tristan was born, I heard my mom and her friends speculating that Mrs. Weakes might have had fertility problems or miscarried or ..."

"Or what?" she demands as I trail off.

I let out a sigh. In for a dime in for a dollar. "They wondered if she might not have terminated some pregnancies along the way because the family couldn't afford another mouth to feed. But by the time Tristan came along, Mr. Weakes had been holding down a job for the longest stretch anyone could remember."

"Doing what?"

"He was a landscaper for a company that had a contract for both of the town's apartment buildings and the school."

The lasagna should be warmed through by now. So when the timer dings on the toaster oven, we plate the food and carry it to the dining room table. I bring the rest of the wine, too. I figure we're going to need it. I sprinkle some shredded Parmesan on my pasta and savor a bite. It's good, not too cheesy or spicy, and really flavorful.

Emily's toying with her fork, not eating. "When you say everyone knew Tristan's father had a temper, do you mean he was violent?"

"I don't know for sure, but it wouldn't surprise me to learn he was. It's not like Tara ever showed up with a black eye and said she ran into a door, but there was always a lot of yelling coming from their place. He was a big guy, a physical guy, and he didn't have a good handle on his emotions."

"It sounds like an awful situation."

"I'm sure it was," I agree. "And after Tristan came along, it got worse. Tate didn't react well to going from only child to the older brother with a baby getting all the attention."

"He was nine years old," Emily says, with a note of disbelief in her voice. "Surely he wasn't jealous of an infant."

"All I know is what I heard. And I remember one Saturday in particular when Mrs. Weakes was getting her hair cut at the same time as my mom. My mom told me to come by the salon to pick up some groceries that needed to be refrigerated. When I walked in, Tara was telling the hairdresser that her sister had sent her the money to get her hair done as a treat months earlier for her birthday, but she was afraid to make the appointment and leave the baby home with Tate and Tom. She literally said she wasn't sure what Tate would do, and she didn't know if Tom would stop him if he hurt the baby. I remember because Tristan was sleeping in a little bassinet at her feet."

She looks stricken. She puts down her fork and picks up her wine glass.

She takes a sip then shakes her head. "Sibling rivalry's not exactly a valid reason to disown your child, though."

I'm not sure the fear of bodily harm can be chalked up to sibling rivalry but I let the comment pass and continue, "When Tom died and Tara decided to move away, Tate was finishing up his senior year. He didn't want to go. He was eighteen, so she agreed to let him finish out the school year and graduate from Windy Rock."

"She left him behind?"

It's hard to explain this to a Millennial, but I try. "It wasn't so unusual back then. Tate stayed with a friend's family. He was supposed to, at least. He moved out of the friend's place—or got kicked out, more likely—and dropped out of school."

Emily processes this then asks the question I've been dreading. "Do you know how Tristan's father died?"

I drain my wine glass. "He killed himself."

twenty-five

We sit at the table. The food is gone. Our plates are empty, and the wine bottle is too. Alex stares at her hands while I stare at her.

I asked her to tell me about Tristan's dad committing suicide at least five minutes ago and she hasn't said a word in response. I shift in my seat, feeling awkward and ill at ease, and finally I leave her there, inspecting her palms, while I carry the dirty dishes out to the kitchen. As I place them in the basin and fill it with hot water and a squirt of dish soap, I look out the window over the sink. The farmhouse's exterior lights illuminate the ground. The snow is piled at least up knee-high now and shows no sign of slowing down. I'm grateful to be in this house with heat and electricity, and even I have to admit, Alex.

The conversation hasn't been fun—far from it—and she's not the warmest person I've ever met. But I wouldn't want to be alone in the cabin right now. Not even if it had power. So I need to draw her out. I need to pull this story out of her, in part to delay my departure, but also because I have to know what happened to Tristan's father. And I can tell that somehow his death relates to whatever it is that drove her out of Windy Rock.

I spy a dusty bottle of table red in a wine rack near her spice cabinet and grab it. It has a screw top, so I twist off the cap and carry the bottle into the dining room.

"Why don't we go back and sit by the fire, and you can tell me your story now?" I suggest.

Still fixated on her hands, she doesn't answer. So I pick up her glass and mine and carry them into the living room. It's a trick I learned from Tristan. Sometimes, when I'm lost in my thoughts and I can't seem to break free, he'll take a sudden action that pulls me along. Activation energy he calls it. All I know is it works. It gets me out of my head and back into my body.

Apparently, it works for Alex too, because after a minute, she pushes in her chair and joins me in the living room. I fill her glass and hand it to her. She takes a sip, then a deep breath. I steel myself, preparing to hear the circumstance of Tom Weakes' suicide.

But instead she says, "Twenty-one years ago, during a nor'easter, I woke up in my apartment—lightning crashing, thunder crashing, rain and wind just pounding the windows. I think so, at least."

"I'm sorry, what?"

"I don't actually have a memory of waking up that night. The doctors say it's a protective mechanism, selective amnesia."

I know what selective amnesia is. I've prayed for it, to no avail. My throat is dry. I drink some wine. We probably should have switched to water, but it's too late now.

"What's your mind protecting you from?" I ask quietly.

"There was a man in my apartment. He attacked me—stabbed me."

I gape at her until I find my voice. "If this is a joke, it's fucked up."

She gives me a sad smile. "I wouldn't normally do this, believe me. But you and I need to put all our cards on the table, Emily."

She unbuttons the top three buttons of her flannel shirt and pulls aside the base layer t-shirt underneath to reveal the top of a jagged, diagonal scar that starts at her collarbone.

I gasp.

"He cut me from here." She points to her collarbone

and traces a diagonal line all the way down the fabric of her shirt to her abdomen. "To here."

"Oh my God." I try to breathe.

"I don't remember any of it. I apparently fought him off because my neighbor called the police with a noise complaint. She told them a domestic violence incident in my apartment was making it impossible for her to hear her television program. That cranky bitch saved my life."

"What happened?" I say it mainly to encourage her to keep talking, but now that she's started telling her story, she needs no prompting.

"It took the police a long time to get there because of the storm. When they did, my bedroom window was open. The rain was pouring in and I was bleeding to death on my bedroom floor. They life-flighted me to the hospital in Bangor, and I—" She stops abruptly and takes a shuddering breath before biting out the words, "I shouldn't have survived."

"But you did."

"But I did. Everyone called it a miracle. It didn't feel like a miracle." She laughs bitterly. "It felt like I'd have been better off if I hadn't. I was in so much pain. I couldn't remember anything. I was terrified. I didn't know who'd done this to me or why or if they'd be back."

I reach over and gently squeeze her free hand as it dawns on me. "That's why you were so freaked out when I told you Tristan was from Windy Rock. Did you recognize him?"

"No. But I did some research last night and connected the dots."

I'm casting around for something comforting to say, but she's committed to pushing through to the end of her story. She swallows audibly, clears her throat, and says, "When I got out of the hospital, I did a stint in a rehabilitation center to re-learn how to walk and talk and use my hands again. But I never regained my memory of that night. In fact, I don't remember anything in the days leading up to the attack. But as soon as I could, I got the hell out of Windy Rock and never looked back. I met my husband in Boston, and when he was transferred out to the West Coast, I tagged along even though we'd only been dating for a few weeks."

Then I wonder—did Tristan recognize her? Or, worse, did he know ahead of time who she was? The thought makes me dizzy. "You weren't Alex Liu in Maine, right? Could Tristan have known who you were when he rented the cabin?"

She shakes her head. "I've gone over it a dozen times. I don't know how he could have found out. I've been extremely careful. He knew me as Lexi Lincoln." She pauses here to give me a knowing look. "In Windy Rock, I'm forever Lexi Lincoln, the girl who was stabbed."

My heart twists. This story is horrific—so much worse than mine. But I don't know why she's telling it. I'm here to hear it, to bear witness. But it's not related to Tom Weakes' suicide. Then I falter. It's not, right?

She searches my face as though she can read my mind and then says, "Three days after I was stabbed, while I was still in a medically induced coma, Tom Weakes jumped off the cliffs outside town into the ocean."

Bile rises in my throat. "A coincidence?" I croak.

She doesn't answer directly. Instead she says, "By the time I was discharged from the hospital to rehab, Tara and Tristan were long gone. They left Windy Rock for good the day after Tom's funeral, or so I heard. Tristan didn't tell you *any* of this?"

I shake my head. "Like I said, he never talks about his father. Mr. Weakes, I mean. When he mentions his father, he means Jon Rose. And he never talks about Windy Rock."

Alex watches me closely. I drink my wine and look back at her. She's waiting for something, but what? Then understanding hits me like a punch to the gut.

"You think it was Tom. You think Tristan's dad attacked you, tried to kill you?"

She responds in a measured tone. "I told you, I don't have any memory of the attack. But people talked. The timing was curious, if nothing else."

"Surely the police investigated him," I say, grasping at straws.

"After a fashion. There wasn't a lot to go on. Tara and Tristan had left town. I had no memory of the attack. And Tom was dead."

"But Tate wasn't."

She gives me a grave look. "That's right. Tate wasn't dead, and he didn't leave with his mother and brother."

I'm confused. No, I'm reeling. "Wait, do you think Tate did it, and his father found out and couldn't live with it? Or they did it together? Or what, exactly?"

"I don't know what to think. I've *never* known what to think. But now, I look at the facts. I look at you showing up here. Tristan Weakes' wife—"

"Tristan Rose's wife," I interrupt fiercely.

She raises an eyebrow and continues. "You just happen to be married to this person who's enmeshed with my past. And your roommate just happened to be stabbed and left for dead during a storm. That's ... well, it's something."

I'm not following her, so I come out and tell her, "I don't know what you're driving at, Alex. You're going to have to spell it out."

"Maybe Tristan and his brother aren't estranged," she says.

I stare at her in horror. "You think Tate and *Tristan* tried to kill you? And, what, teamed up to kill Cassie fourteen years later? That's absurd. Tristan was nine when you were stabbed."

"I know that, and I *don't* think Tristan was involved in my stabbing."

"But?" I demand, my voice shaking with anger.

"But," she says, "generational trauma is real. It has an impact. Isn't it possible—just possible—that if Tate and his dad stabbed me, years later, Tate stepped into Tom's role, brought Tristan in, and they stabbed your roommate? The echoes of the past and all."

I can't breathe. She's kidding, right? "You're not serious. Do you hear how ludicrous that sounds?"

She places her glass on the coffee table and spreads her hands wide in a gesture of appeasement. "It's a theory. Or it was. But you say Tristan isn't in contact with Tate, and Tristan wasn't even living in Ohio when your roommate was murdered. So I guess the theory falls apart."

My skin heats and my heart hammers. I narrow my eyes at her sudden change of tune. "You don't believe that. You don't think this is a coincidence."

To be honest, neither do I. Two stabbings and Tristan's on the periphery of both of them.

She gives a self-deprecating laugh. "Honestly, Emily? What I think is I must listen to too much true crime."

I look at her. "Do you?"

"Do I what?"

"Do you listen to true crime podcasts? Do you watch documentaries about murders?"

Her eyes flick involuntarily toward the book at the arm of the couch and I follow her gaze to read the title: *The Bloody Harpe Brothers: The True Terrifying Tale of America's First Serial Killers.*

"I guess I have my answer."

"Why do you ask?" she says, leveling me with a look.

"Because Tristan does. Incessantly."

"I've heard it's common for crime victims, survivors, and family members to be drawn to true crime in an effort to make sense of the unfathomable," she says.

I hold her gaze, unblinking.

She tilts her head, appraising me. "But not you."

"Not me," I agree.

"That's interesting."

I eye her, weighing whether to tell her.

"What?" She asks.

"What, what?"

"You've got something on your mind. What is it?"

There's no reason to hold back at this point, so I say it. "I don't need to make sense of it. I know why it happened. Cassie wasn't supposed to die that night. I was."

To her credit, she doesn't spout off the standard, 'It's common for survivors to blame themselves,' line. Instead, Alex Liu, survivor of a murder attempt, takes my statement at face value and asks, "How do you know?"

I tell her what I've never told anyone. "I know because he told me."

"He told you," she repeats.

As I'm explaining the note I found after Cassie's murder, an even worse thought hits me and bile rises in my throat. I clasp my hand over my mouth and jump to my feet.

"Bathroom's that way." She points.

I race down the hall and throw up into her toilet bowl. After my stomach is empty, I cup my hands under the stream of water in the sink and splash my face, rinse out my mouth. I spare a glance in the mirror. I look every bit as shitty as I feel.

When I walk back into the living room, she gives me a concerned look. "Feeling better?"

"No," I tell her. "I realized something. There aren't two stabbings where Tristan's the common denominator. There are three."

"Three?" she echoes.

I nod. "There was a murder in Little Sweetwater last week, where we live. A twenty-year-old woman was murdered last week. Her roommate found her."

"Stabbed to death?" Her voice shakes.

"Yes. And Tristan's working on the case."

My stomach heaves, but I know there's nothing left to vomit. So I force down my nausea and say, "And just like you and me, Giselle Ward was a redhead."

We stare at each other for a long wordless moment. I don't know what she's thinking, but I'm thinking it's possible my husband's a killer.

twenty-six

Tristan

For months after Tate showed up and beat the shit out of me, I waited to hear that he'd been arrested. I was sure my anonymous tip would help the police connect him to Dana Rowland's murder. But the news never came.

Now, I put aside the conversation with my mother and what I'm sure is Tate's latest gambit—faking his death—and take a long overdue, clear-eyed look at what happened in Arizona. Mom isn't the only one who hasn't been completely forthcoming.

Less than two weeks before the dust storm, before Dana Rowland's brutal stabbing, I got a card in the mail.

There was no return address, but it had a Tempe postmark. I didn't recognize the spiky printing on the envelope. I took it to my bedroom to open it.

It was a sixteenth birthday card, which was weird because I'd had my birthday in January, more than a month earlier. Weirder still, the image on the front was two cartoonish males sitting in a convertible. A speech bubble over the passenger's head read "Happy Birthday, little brother! Time for you to take the wheel!"

My throat was tight and dry as I flipped the card open. Inside, in that same jagged handwriting, there was a more personalized message:

> *I wasn't much older than you are now when Dad showed me what it meant to be a man. That pussy Mom married can't demonstrate, so it's up to me to be a role model. Meet me at the ASU bookstore on Saturday at 3:00.*

My stomach heaved, and I gagged but managed not to puke. "Not on your life," I muttered as I ripped the card in half, then fourths, and continued to rip the thin card and the envelope into smaller and smaller pieces until they were nothing more than two large handfuls of confetti. I crept to the hall bathroom, tossed the scraps into the toilet, and flushed it.

On Saturday, I went for a long trail run up through the

mountains. I ran for miles, to the point of exhaustion. I ran until my spent body and tired mind were too worn out to worry about Tate's overture and what it meant. I thought I could forget about it, and him. Then he showed up at the house days later.

I never told my mother about the card. Initially, I kept it from her because I knew the fact that Tate had tracked us down would upset her. And later, after the haboob, I kept it to myself because I suspected the card, my failure to meet him, or perhaps the combination of the two played a role in Dana Rowland's death.

One line from the note ran through my head in a nonstop loop for months, afterward: *"I wasn't much older than you are now when Dad showed me what it meant to be a man."* I could only guess what that initiation into manhood had entailed, but I knew for sure that I didn't want to be the kind of man my father had been and my brother had become.

What I didn't know—and still don't know now—is exactly how much responsibility I bear for Dana Rowland's murder. Was his plan always to kill her or did he do it to send me a message?

I click through the cold case files until I find what I'm looking for. Transcripts of the call providing tips and information about the Rowland case. I search through until I spot Tate's name and then read the follow-up: When the homicide detectives gathered university personnel for interviews, they did ask to speak to him, but he hadn't shown up for work since the day of the dust storm, not even to pick up his final check. Tate Weakes simply vanished.

I continue to read through the chronology. To their credit, the detectives did attempt to track Tate down. But a seasonal laborer moving on without leaving a forwarding address isn't, in itself, a red flag. They were understandably focused on suspects they could find—Dana's boyfriend, an old coworker who had a crush on her, a fraternity brother who'd harassed her at the university fitness center. Although none of these leads panned out, it's not surprising Tate fell off the detectives' radar.

What is surprising is that I didn't fall off Tate's.

January 2017
Wichita, Kansas

My twenty-third birthday fell right after the start of the spring semester. I'd taken a gap year between high school and college, bummed around Europe, then worked for a while at a ski resort in South America. The year had been good for me. It helped me figure out who I was as a person.

And by 2017, during the second semester of my senior

year, the person I was had no interest in partying. So, I waved off my housemates' cajoling requests to join them at The Coop and settled in for the night with the research materials for my genetics and genomics capstone project. I was reviewing a dense longitudinal study when the doorbell rang.

I ignored it. I was busy, and I wasn't expecting anyone. But whoever was on the porch hit the bell again and leaned steadily on it for several seconds before pulling back and jabbing at it repeatedly.

I swore and slammed my book shut. As I yanked the door open, I prepared to give whichever of my housemates had left without their key all kinds of crap.

But the man standing on my porch was not a housemate. Not a friend. Not even a missionary in a short-sleeved dress shirt looking to save my soul. Any of these would have been preferable.

"Hey, little man," he said.

I squared up, planting my feet in a defensive stance in case he took a swing and stared at my brother.

"Aren't you gonna invite me in?"

"No."

I moved to swing the door shut.

He reached out his hand and caught it. "Don't be a dick."

"What do you want?"

I kept my hand on the door. If I had to, I could force it

closed. I'd crush his fingers in the process, but I was okay with that outcome.

"I want to talk to you."

"Say what you need to say, then get off my porch."

He eyed me, and I could see what he was thinking. I wasn't sixteen anymore, and I'd put a lot of muscle on my lean runner's body in the seven years since he'd kicked my ass. If things got physical tonight, I'd hold my own a hell of a lot better than I had as a high school sophomore.

"Just wanted to wish you a happy birthday."

"Message received. Thanks. Bye." I started to close the door again.

"Come on, let me in. It's cold as balls out here." He looked around the deserted street.

I tracked his gaze. The house sat at one end of a residential side street—an alley, really. All the houses on the block were rental properties. Most were rented to undergrads. Many were in various states of benign neglect, and a few were in outright disrepair.

I wasn't worried about what the neighbors might think, but it was January in Kansas and I was letting the wintery air in. So, even though every fiber in my being was screaming at me to make him leave, I gritted my teeth and pulled the door open.

"The foyer, no further," I told him and slammed the door against the cold.

He looked around the unremarkable house. And as I watched him take in the place, I wondered, for the first time, what his living situation was. And then I wondered what it said about me that through the years I'd had zero curiosity about his circumstances and not a shred of empathy for him.

I'd spent the previous summer on a team doing inmate interviews at the state penitentiary for my sociology professor, and I knew that the worst thing I could do was hurry to fill the silence. People don't like silence, at least not normal people in social situations. Letting it drag on was an effective way to get someone to talk.

So I crossed my arms and stared at him. He looked less haggard than he had when I'd seen him in Arizona. His cheeks were filled out. He was cleaner.

He clocked me clocking him. "I don't do seasonal work anymore. I have a steady job. In Ohio."

"Don't care."

He kept talking as if I hadn't interrupted. "It's a nice little town. Reminds me a bit of home. Not that small, but smaller than the places where you've been living."

The casual way he said it made me wonder how closely he'd kept track of me.

He must have read the question in my face because he laughed. "Oh, I didn't have the kind of money to follow you around during your year of playtime, but I've kept tabs from a distance. Anyway, since you're graduating, you should think about coming to Ohio."

"I don't need career counseling from you. The university has a whole department for that. But that's not why you're here." I smiled tightly. "What do you really want? Money?"

His face darkened, and his hands fisted at his sides. "No, I don't want money." He took a deep breath as if he was controlling himself through extreme effort. "I'm here to renew my invitation."

"Your invitation?"

He stared at me, and I stared at him.

Finally, I remembered the birthday card and his offer to initiate me into whatever sick version of manhood he had in mind.

"No, thanks."

He shook his head, irritated by my flippant tone. "You're taking all these classes in the psychology of criminals. Meanwhile you have the opportunity to do some firsthand research."

"So you admit you're a criminal?"

He clenched his jaw but didn't answer.

I scoffed. "It doesn't matter. I already have my thesis project, thanks. Just like we have career counseling, we have academic advisors here."

I reached for the door, and he grabbed my sleeve. My eyes followed the motion.

"Don't touch me," I spat through clenched teeth. He pulled his hand back like my arm was on fire.

"Take it easy. I'm not here to hurt you."

I locked eyes with him. "Newsflash: you can't hurt me."

He laughed bitterly. "Oh, believe me, you spoiled little mama's boy, I absolutely can hurt you."

"Try it."

He ignored the challenge and went on in an unnatural, stilted tone like he was narrating a documentary. "Experts aren't sure how many killers work with a partner. The most famous team, of course, was Leopold and Loeb."

"The Harpe brothers are more notorious within the field of criminology," I told him in a flat voice.

He gave me a scornful look. "The Harpes were butchers. Leopold and Loeb were artists. They took the time to plan the perfect crime."

The admiration in his tone made my pulse thrum. Could I get him to confess to what he'd done? Aside from bringing closure to Dana Rowland's family, maybe I could actually find out what happened that night in Windy Rock.

"Did you really track me down to talk about what happened in Maine?"

"No. I told you. I'm here with an invitation."

"Right, the same invitation Dad gave you."

His face twisted into an angry sneer. "Dad didn't *invite* me to do anything. In my case, it was a demand."

"Tate, what happened?" I asked, my voice low.

"Dad had appetites, and he wanted to share them with me."

I asked the question that, as far as I knew, no one in

Windy Rock had ever asked him directly, "Did Dad attack Lexi Lincoln?"

His expression shifted. "Dad had different appetites."

I had no idea what this was supposed to mean. I kept my eyes locked on his as I struggled to make sense of his words. My brain sputtered like it was overheating.

He scoffed at my confusion and clarified, "Dad liked to watch."

"He liked to watch you hurt people?"

Another short, humorless laugh. "No, our father was a classic pervert, a peeping Tom. Guess his name fit. He liked to watch young women undress."

"He was spying on Lexi?"

A chilling smile stretched across his face. "Yeah, and that one night, he got a real show."

My brain finally came back online. As I realized what he was saying, the pizza I'd wolfed down earlier threatened to come back up, and I swallowed hard.

"You attacked her, and he saw it."

"How sick do you think he had to be to go out in that storm just to stand and watch a girl come home from work, make something to eat, and get ready for bed? I mean, that's not normal behavior for anyone, let alone a middle-aged man with a wife and two kids. But to do that in the middle of a freaking nor'easter? It was a compulsion, Tristan."

He was talking to me, but then again, he wasn't. He had a far-away look in his eye and he spoke in a soft, flat monotone. Still, I leaned in and listened, hoping to glean some understanding of what happened that night.

"He just stood outside her window in the driving rain being battered by the wind. It was pathetic. But all he wanted to do was watch, never act."

He'd never flatly admit that he broke into Lexi's apartment and tried to gut her. He was too smart to confess to attempted murder. But I was piecing together my own narrative of the events of that night.

"So it was Dad's fault you tried to kill Lexi?" I filled my voice with disdain, hoping to provoke him into responding.

He narrowed his eyes but kept his mouth shut.

I continued to goad him. "What's your excuse for what you did to Dana Rowland? Was Dad's ghost creeping on her? Did a dead man make you do it?"

His cheek twitched. And from that small reaction, I realized he didn't give a shit about Lexi or Dana, but on some level, he felt responsible for our father's suicide. From a clinical standpoint, this was an interesting development. Here was a killer who felt remorse not for his victims, but for our father—a man who was a cruel, unyielding abuser and, apparently, a voyeur.

"You need help, Tate."

"I do," he agreed readily. "I need a partner. That's why I'm here."

"You want me to help you kill women," I blurted.

He retreated from the statement in a hurry, "I didn't say that. What's wrong with you?"

I realized my error right away. Pushing him was a rookie mistake. My professor would be disappointed in me. I switched tacks. "You need treatment."

He shook his head. "I'm good, bro. You're the one who needs to decide what to do with his life. I know you're interviewing for jobs and applying to graduate schools. You need to pick a path and commit to it."

How did he know all this information about me? My chest tightened. He'd clearly been watching me, spying on me, and I'd been oblivious. It was a wildly unsettling realization, and I didn't know how to respond to it.

Meanwhile, he was getting antsy. He shuffled his feet. "That town in Ohio, there's a university there with a graduate program in forensic DNA. You could learn a lot there."

He brushed past me, opened the door, and walked out into the night. I stood in the hallway, slack-jawed and dazed, for several long minutes before I returned to the table where I'd been studying.

I spent the rest of the night sucking down energy drinks and trying to make sense of the encounter. I was sufficiently self-aware to know why I was drawn to forensic genetics. I wanted to help victims like Lexi and Dana and stop people like Tate.

But if I went to this town in Ohio where he lived and worked, I could stop Tate himself. I could find his next victim and save her before he acted. I knew he must have already selected her. He wouldn't have risked coming to see me over a hypothetical situation. He was going to kill again, and soon.

I should have called the police. But I knew Tate wouldn't have said as much as he had unless he knew no evidence tied him to Lexi or Dana. Tate was cruel and damaged, but he wasn't stupid. Far from it. And he was careful. I realized he never came out and told me the name of the town where he lived.

Calling the police in every small college town in Ohio to report that I had a feeling a young woman would be stabbed soon sounded like a great way to be dismissed as a crackpot or, worse, flagged as a potential offender. Instead, I hopped online and researched all the forensics graduate programs at universities in Ohio. In the end, I had a list of three.

I applied to and was accepted to all three programs. I scheduled trips out to Ohio to visit the campuses during my spring break. I didn't see Tate in any of the towns. But he must have known I was there. On the second night of my visit to Hope Falls, during a torrential downpour, a co-ed was viciously stabbed and left to die in her roommate's bed.

twenty-seven

Alex

Somehow, we polished off the second bottle of wine while I told my story.

I'm not drunk, I'm drained. I feel flat and empty. I don't talk about what happened to me. But on the rare occasions when I do, I feel this way—like I've been hollowed out.

I glance at Emily. She, I think, is buzzing.

She gives me a woozy half-smile and says, "It's getting late, and I need to wake up early to write while it's daylight. Unless you think the power will be back on in the cabin tomorrow?"

There's virtually no chance of that happening. But I tell her, "Maybe."

"So, are you still up for showing me how to make a fire?"

I look at the clock. It's late. It's dark. It's going to be freezing cold in that cabin.

"Why don't you stay here? I'll make up the guest room."

"Oh, no. I don't want to put you out."

"You're not. I'm offering. It'll only take me a few minutes to make the bed, and you'll be more comfortable here," I say firmly. "I'd be a bad host if I sent you back to that cold cabin."

She hedges. "Well, if you're sure?"

"I am."

We carry the empty bottle and the glasses out to the kitchen. It's true. She'll be more comfortable here, and I don't need a bad review on Stay Your Way. But it's more than that. I don't want her to be alone after the conversation we had. And I don't want to be alone. This truth surprises me because I'm accustomed to wrestling with my ghosts and demons by myself. I mean, Robert's always there for me emotionally. But he's not usually actually physically *here* for me. I find Emily's company comforting.

"Come on, I'll show you the guest room," I tell her.

As I lead her down the short hallway to the spare bedroom, she asks, "Does your husband know?"

I don't have to ask does he know about what. I stop walking and turn to her.

"Yes. Robert knows."

She gnaws on her bottom lip. "I think about it all the time—telling Tristan. But I just can't make myself talk to him about it."

"That's understandable," I tell her. "Like you said, He doesn't see you as The Girl Who Found Her Dead Roommate. You don't want to lose that."

"Still." She wrinkles her nose, unconvinced.

"There's something to be said for a fresh start."

"You didn't take one. You told Robert."

I give her a sad smile. "Your scars are psychic. Mine are physical. The first time I got undressed in front of Robert, I knew I'd have to tell him or lie. And you can't build a marriage on lies."

She pales, and I don't know if it's because she's thinking of my torn-up body or my pronouncement.

"I'm not judging your marriage," I hurry to assure her.

"But you're right—it's built on lies. Well, omissions. Things I haven't said."

"And things he hasn't said," I remind her. "That cuts both ways." It's intended to make her feel better, but I think it makes her feel worse.

"My marriage is a lie," she says more to herself than to me.

I open the door to the guest bedroom and usher her inside. I turn on the light and pull a set of fresh sheets and a stack of blankets from the closet. Her hands tremble as she helps me put the sheets on the bed.

I sigh. I'm bad at this—rusty and out of practice—but

she's teetering. "Listen, you'll probably feel better after a night's sleep. But if you don't and you decide you need to have a heart-to-heart with your husband, you can do that when you see him. There's no expiration date on honesty."

"You're right." She nods, but her grimace lets me know I'm even worse at providing emotional support than I thought I was.

I spread two warm blankets over the sheets and smooth the covers while she slides a pillowcase onto the pillow and plumps it up. I hand her an unopened tooth-brush package and a travel-sized toothpaste tube from the bedside table.

"Get some rest."

"Good night, Alex." Her voice is soft.

I walk through the first floor and turn out the lights. Then I throw some water on the dying embers in the fire-place and double-check that the doors are all locked before I head upstairs. I hear the water running down-stairs as Emily gets ready for bed, too.

I spread thick night cream on my face, neck, and scars, then rub what's left of the heavily scented lotion into my hands and feet, and my thoughts turn to Tristan. I saw the expression on Emily's face when she told me a red-haired woman had been stabbed to death in their small commu-nity. She has doubts about her husband.

I do, too. But if he wanted to kill her, Emily Rose would've been dead a long time ago. So either this is all a massive coincidence—which frankly seems impossible—

or he's playing a different game with her. *What's your angle, Tristan?* I assign the question to my subconscious with instructions to work on it overnight.

I climb into bed, pull the blankets up to my chin, and fall asleep to the sound of the snow turning to a driving rain. Rain is good. Rain is better than snow for the utility companies and road crews—just so long as it doesn't end up as ice.

As I drift to sleep, I feel an odd intimacy, almost a bond, with the woman in my guest room, and I wonder if she feels it too. We're strangers, but we share a bone-deep understanding of how a single violent night can change your whole life.

twenty-eight

Emily

As I brush my teeth, Alex's words run through my head. *You can't build a marriage on lies.* In my heart, I know she's right. She's also right that my marriage rests on a shaky foundation of lies thanks to both Tristan and me. I think—I *hope*—his lies are the same as mine: lies of omission, silences that shouldn't be. Somehow this seems less serious than actively lying. This is what I always tell myself to justify keeping Cassie's murder from him.

Still, I'm struggling to wrap my mind around the enormity of all he's kept from me over the years. His troubled childhood. His father's suicide. The fact that he has a brother. What else has he kept from me?

And if Tate is as dangerous and unstable as Alex thinks he could be, there's no excuse for not telling me about him, just in case he turns up at our door someday. Or is there? Could there be a very good reason for Tristan's reticence? A reason I'm not seeing.

I should do what Alex suggests and sleep on this, but instead I pick up the telephone on the bedside table. I need to say good night. I need to hear his voice. Maybe that will untangle this knot in my stomach. I dial his mobile number and look around the tidy, sparsely furnished room while I wait for him to pick up.

"Hello?" He answers with a polite, reserved tone, and I realize he doesn't recognize the number.

"It's me."

"Em? Where are you?"

"I'm calling from Alex's house."

"What's wrong? Are you okay? Why are you there?" He rapid-fires the questions at me.

"I'm fine. The storm hit," I tell him, "and the power went out in the cabin. I'm staying at the farmhouse tonight."

"With Alex?"

There's something in his tone. Worry? No, fear. I say, "Well, yeah."

"Be careful."

"What does that mean?"

He blows out a breath. "She's a stranger. We don't know her."

Well, that's not exactly true, now is it?

"Actually, you probably do know her," I tell him.

"You mean because we both grew up in Windy Rock? I told you, I don't remember her."

I want to say "she remembers you," to see how he responds. But I control myself.

"Her name was different then. She went by Lexi. Lexi Lincoln."

I almost add that she's a few years older than his brother, but I don't want to do that over the phone either.

"Lexi Lincoln," he repeats slowly.

"Yes."

Even if he didn't recognize her when he saw her, her name must ring a bell if the town is as small as they've both said it is.

He says nothing. I wonder if we're about to tip over from lies of omission to lies of commission. Then he removes any question.

"Oh, right. I do know that name. She's a good bit older than me." He pauses. "I have a vague memory that she has some emotional problems. I don't know the details, but I wouldn't take anything she says at face value."

It's simply not believable that he would remember her name and not the fact that someone tried to carve her up.

Especially not when it happened three days before his father killed himself. He's lying.

I rein in my emotions and say, "Well, it was kind of her to let me sleep here. The cabin's going to be really cold."

"You could have built a fire."

I ignore this and chirp, "I made great progress on the book—until the power went out, at least."

"That's fantastic, Em." His voice is suffused with happiness for me. Sheer, uncomplicated joy. It makes me feel gross for doubting him.

"Thanks." Then I remember. "Oh, did you ever hear back from Tyrone—about the man I saw?"

"I did."

I'm silent, waiting for him to elaborate. But the pause stretches out long enough to be awkward before he says, "He's grateful we let him know."

There's something he's not telling me. I know it in my bones. And for the first time, I feel safer being away from him than with him.

I tell myself I'm not being fair to him. I'm emotional from all the wine and soul-baring. It's not reasonable to expect him to bring up his brother on this phone call spontaneously or share what happened to Lexi or his dad.

I fake a loud yawn and say, "Well, I'm pretty sleepy. I just called to say good night."

"I love you more than life, Emily." His voice thrums with energy.

"Love you, too. Good night, Tristan." I wonder if he senses the emptiness in my response.

I nestle the phone in its base and sit on the edge of the bed. The call I'd hoped would assuage my concern has increased it. And I'm forced to ask myself, how well do I really know my husband?

twenty-nine

Tristan

When I hang up with Emily, I'm keyed up, worried Alex will tell her about my family and she'll draw the wrong conclusions. I really don't like the idea of them spending time together. This damned storm could send my house of cards tumbling.

I pull up the weather map and am gratified to see the snow is changing over to rain. Rain means it should be warm enough for Em to return to the little cabin tomorrow and keep her distance from her host. I exhale, relieved. The less Emily interacts with Alex/Lexi/whatever the hell she's calling herself, the better.

It's not that I don't have sympathy for what she went through. Believe me, I do. But I've built an entire life around plausible deniability, and the thought of losing it now is unbearable. I know what my brother did, but I don't *know*. Alex Liu *knows*.

Tate stopped short of telling me point-blank that he attacked Lexi and killed Dana. And I've clung to that. The only crime Tate didn't at least obliquely reference was killing Cassie. Of course, I haven't seen him since that night in Kansas, or I'm sure he would've.

But, he didn't need to. Once I saw the photograph of Emily that ran with the newspaper article about Cassie Baughman's murder, I knew two things: My brother killed Cassie, and Emily had been the intended victim.

Consumed by the thought that Tate would want to finish the job, I moved to Hope Falls. I spent the first semester watching Emily, learning her patterns and routines. When I glimpsed her in the lobby of Dr. Wilde's office building and realized we were both seeing the same psychotherapist, it felt like a sign.

So I engineered to meet her. Not to be creepy, and certainly not to weasel my way into her life. I never planned to date, fall in love with, and marry her. My intention was to keep my brother at bay. But, trite as it is, the heart wants what it wants. And my heart wants Emily. It did then, and it still does.

If she finds out about my history and all the truths I've withheld from her, she'll never believe I was trying to, am still trying to, protect her.

The entire time I lived in Hope Falls, I looked for Tate. Once I started working as a teaching assistant, I accessed the university records, but Tate wasn't working at my school. So I made it a point to get friendly with a guy who worked in the human resources department at Emily's college. They had no record of Tate either.

He was a ghost, a cipher. Eventually, I decided he must've moved on and Emily wasn't in any immediate danger. But by that point, I was in love with her.

I've never stopped trying to protect her. I never will.

Case in point: the moment Giselle Ward's body was found, I understood what her murder meant: Tate was back. So I found a way to get Emily out of town to keep her safe until I could find him and end this once and for all. Now, though, the tightness in my chest makes me wonder if sending her to that cabin on the mountaintop is the worst mistake I could've made.

Worrying about what Alex might tell Emily is a distraction I don't need. I have to focus on Tate. Why would he fake his death and arrange for Dr. Wilde to call our mother? It's clearly a message for me. Unfortunately, I have no idea what it means.

Six months ago

Even through the videoconferencing software, Dr. Wilde's eyes communicated concern. His expression radiated empathy. But his words, despite the soft delivery, were razor sharp. They sliced through me like a knife.

"Tate, isn't it possible your brother doesn't think about you at all?"

I hesitated. Was it? No.

I shook my head. "No," I told him. "You have to understand, he's been trying to get a reaction out of me for more than twenty years."

"Twenty years, hmm. Isn't that when your mother took you and moved away, leaving him behind?"

"Yes."

So I told him my name is Tate, but I'm not pretending to *be* Tate. When we talk, I tell him my real story—Tristan's story—I just swap our names. And leave out a few details.

He squinted at me. "Do you think he's jealous of you?"

I thought about it. "No. Not jealous, exactly. I think he knows I've had a better life than he has. But I also think he understands that's not my fault. He's bitter, but not toward me." *I hope.*

"Toward your mother?"

I sighed. "Maybe. He should direct his anger toward our father. Or the social conventions that let an entire town turn a blind eye to an abuser."

"Perhaps." Dr. Wilde steepled his fingers, and I wondered if some program taught this body language or if therapists just settled on it naturally. "But it's difficult to hold abstract concepts accountable for our pain. And a dead man, a town? These aren't real. Not in the way the mother and brother who abandoned him are."

I bristled at the framing—I was *nine*, I didn't abandon anyone. But I didn't go there. I only had thirty minutes, after all. I needed to focus.

"We've talked about whether I have an obligation to try to find him, and I know you say no. But ..."

He leaned forward. "What, Tate?"

"What if he's gearing up to hurt someone again? Or worse?"

His eyes flashed. "Do you have actionable information? Evidence?"

We did this weird dance every so often, Dr. Wilde and I. Ohio law required him to report it to the authorities if I told him my brother intended to harm or kill a specific identifiable person. But anything I told him about past actions was privileged, off-limits unless he was subpoenaed by a court. So, anything I tell him about things my brother's done—or that I think he's done—is confidential. What he's *going* to do, that's a different story.

"Well, no."

He gave me a long-suffering look. I ignored it.

"It's cyclical. Every seven years."

"Hypothetically, who is he going to attack?"

"I don't know. A woman. In her twenties. With red hair."

"Cassie Baughman was a blonde," he countered.

I huffed. "Don't fight the hypo."

It's a turn of phrase I've picked up from the prosecutors I work with. Lawyers call it 'fighting the hypo' when you resist the facts of a case as stated.

He rolled his eyes. I was pretty sure they didn't teach him *that* body language in school.

"If you told me he was going to hurt a specific, named person, I'd call the police. If you truly believe he's going to hurt someone, soon, but you don't know who or when, you might want to try to contact him. Not because you're obligated to, because I don't think you are. But because you want to stop him. It's valid to act because you want to, Tate, and not just because you have to."

It sounded so obvious when he puts it that way. That was his job, after all—to cut through the bullshit and expose the truth, the heart of the matter. But he was wrong to think I secretly wanted to find my brother. I'd do it if I had to—if the law, or morality, or my psychotherapist told me I must—but I couldn't justify exposing my life, my wife, to the monster that was my brother if I didn't have to.

This was, I knew, the same calculus that my mother had used when we basically fled from Maine. She hadn't *wanted* to cut ties with her firstborn. But her safety, and, at that time, mine had required her to do so.

I left the session with Dr. Wilde resolute in my decision *not* to connect with Tate.

Six months later, Giselle Ward's neck will be sliced open, resulting in the complete transection of her carotid artery. The fully severed artery will cause a massive hemorrhage. Her death will be nearly instantaneous. And it will be my fault.

thirty

Emily

I wake up to drumming. It takes a minute for it to sink in that the noise is hard rain pelting the windows. I turn toward the sound, which is when I realize I'm not in my bed, not in my house. I panic for a moment, then I recall the events of last night. I'm at the farmhouse, Alex's farmhouse.

I rub the sleep from my eyes and look around for a clock, but there isn't one on the bedside table. A glance at my fitness watch tells me it's a few minutes after seven. I bolt upright, my heart pounding, not from fear, but from amazement. I have literally not slept past 4:51 AM in seven years. I can't believe I did it here, of all places. I spend a few minutes trying to work through the psychological meaning of this breakthrough and ultimately decide it's a question for my next therapy session.

Ridiculously refreshed from the two hours and twelve minutes of extra sleep, I stand up and stretch, then walk over to the window, cracking my back and hips with a series of satisfying pops as I go. I pull aside the curtain. It's pouring. Yesterday, for all the wildness of the blizzard, the world was white and beautiful, pristine under the heavy blanket of snow. Now the snow is a melting grayish slush, wet and raw. I hate the rain.

I turn from the window and pad down the hallway to brush my teeth and splash some water on my face.

Alex is already in the kitchen, slipping a blue enamel dish into the oven. Freshly brewed coffee sits in the carafe.

"Good morning."

"I made a quiche," she says in a bemused voice.

Then she throws me an embarrassed, baffled look over her shoulder as she shuts the oven door. "I don't know why. I've literally never even thought about making a quiche before today. I feel like a 1950s housewife."

"It smells wonderful," I tell her.

She ducks her head and smiles. "Dried herbs from my garden."

I consider her for a moment. "So you grow your own food? And preserve it?"

"Some. I have a vegetable garden. I can. I pickle. I jar jams and sauces. I dry herbs."

"It must be satisfying to be so self-sufficient."

"It's something to keep me busy." She deflects my admiration deftly.

"So you don't work?" I wince at how that sounds and hurriedly add, "I mean, I know you rent out the cabin. That's work."

She laughs. "No, it's okay. I don't have a job. I live pretty simply. A lot of what I need, I make. Or I barter for it. My biggest expense is books, but I get those used and swap with some folks in the valley." She shrugs. "And, you're right, I have the rental income. I don't have to be so frugal—Robert earns a good salary. But we're saving most of it."

The first real smile I've seen lights her face, softening the hard edges of her jaw.

"What are you saving for?"

She waves a hand. "It's stupid."

"I want to know. Tell me."

I grab a chair and she hands me a mug of coffee. She retrieves a notebook from the counter and slides it across the counter. I trap it under my palm.

"We have a bucket list for when Robert retires. He's a military linguist and his work has taken him all over the world, but I haven't gone along. So when he's done in two years—actually twenty-one months—we'll sell the farm, get rid of most of our stuff, and become global nomads. We'll travel around, see all the things I've read about or places he's seen in passing in a blur during a leave. We're going to experience the entire world together."

As I page through the notebook taking in the places, events, and ideas scribbled in cramped blue ink, I get swept up in her excitement. "That's amazing."

She flushes. "It seems silly sometimes."

"You're going after a dream. That's bold, not silly."

She pours herself a cup of coffee and joins me at the table. "What's your bold dream?"

"Oh." I sip my coffee and think. "I suppose I'm doing it. I've always wanted to write and I'm living that dream. Maybe it's not as exciting as globe trotting, but I have a rich interior life," I say lamely.

She gives me a steady look. "Tell me about the book you came here to work on."

"I don't really talk about works in progress."

"Is that a superstition?"

I scrunch up my nose and try to figure out how to explain my process. "No, it's not that I think it's bad luck to talk about it. It's that I don't know the story until I'm finished writing it. I discover it as I go. So what I tell you now might not be the way the story ends up."

"It's okay. I won't hold you to it," she says with a laugh.

For most of my books, I wouldn't be able to do this, but this one's different since it's a retelling. "I'll give it a shot. My agent has a client who's a huge romance author. People tattoo her characters' names on their butts and name their cats after her. There are tours of the town she sets her books in."

She nods. "I think I know her. Jillian James, right? The one who bought the bookstore?"

"Right. So, you know, she's a force unto herself. Jillian had this idea to have twelve authors each retell a fairy tale. She'll release the books over the course of a year. And I was invited to participate."

"So it's a romance?"

"No, mine isn't a romance. It's women's fiction, which is what I usually write." I paused. "Actually, this one's a little dark for me."

"Frankly, I'm surprised you don't write noir given your past."

This is an echo of our conversation about true crime. But it's just not in my nature. I shrug. "My books are all about relationships. In this book, the relationship is a friendship. It's based on *Maid Maleen*. It's an obscure German fairy tale, not one of the famous ones."

"Right, the princess who's put in the tower for seven years and her father forgets about her."

My jaw hinges open. "Literally nobody, including my agent and Jillian, has ever heard of *Maid Maleen*."

It's her turn to shrug. "I read everything," she tells me.

"Then you know the plot. In the Grimm brothers' version, she's in love with a prince, but her father wants her to marry someone else. In the original version, there is no king-approved suitor. Her father just doesn't like the one she has, so he puts her in the tower to break her spirit."

"He builds a windowless tower, sends up seven years' worth of food and drink, then seals Maleen and her lady-in-waiting inside," Alex adds.

"Right. Maleen has a choice. Her lady-in-waiting doesn't."

"Does her maid even have a name?"

"Not in the fairy tale. I named her Ruth."

"Are you doing the part where the prince futilely rides around the tower on a horse calling Maleen's name?" she asks with a laugh.

"I'm on the fence. It *would* be an effective way to show how useless the prince is. He's not capable of rescuing her. But he's not essential to my story. So, probably not."

She nods with what seems like approval.

"Anyway, seven years go by, the food runs out, but nobody comes to let them out of the tower. They've been forgotten. So they have to rescue themselves." She's still nodding along, so I speed it up. "And, you know, in the fairy tale, when they dig themselves out with the butter knives after three days, that's basically the midpoint of the story."

"Right. They free themselves and find the kingdom in ruins. They travel to another country, which happens to be where the hapless hero lives."

"Then Maleen's working in the kitchen, and the prince's new bride forces her to be a stand-in at the wedding. When Maleen drops enough hints that the prince realizes who she is, the other woman orders her execution. Then, *she's* killed, and Maleen and her guy live happily ever after."

"As any good princess should," she says in a wry tone.

"Yeah, well, I'm not doing any of that. My story is called *The Tower*, and it focuses on the seven years Maleen and Ruth spend in captivity. The climax is their escape. The book ends when they get out."

"Why?"

I consider her question for a moment. I haven't written the ending yet, but I know what I want it to be. "I guess because life doesn't always have a tidy, happy ending. I want Maleen to have a new beginning off the page. And Ruth, too. Did you ever notice that, in the original, once they reach the new kingdom, we don't hear anything more about the lady-in-waiting? Where'd she go?"

Alex furrows her brow. "I never thought about it, but I guess we don't. That's pretty harsh. She gave up seven years of her life for this woman. Maleen gets her prince and Ruth gets shafted."

"Exactly. I like to think she was smart enough to cut ties and move on, but we don't know. In my book, they both get their freedom. But most of the focus is on the seven years they spend together in that tower and the effect that has on them." I suddenly feel exposed, vulnerable, talking about this. "Anyway, that's the story."

What I can't bring myself to explain is that I can't brush aside the seven years to focus on a reunion with the prince because I'm fascinated by other questions: How did the experience of being locked up in the tower change Maleen from someone who was passive and obedient to someone who dug her way out of a tower using a bread knife? How did Ruth change during that time? The captivity changed them, but they probably also changed one another.

Alex says aloud what I've been thinking, "Seven years in the tower changed both of them."

We exchange a look.

The towers she and I have been trapped in have likely changed us, too.

The ding of the oven timer saves me from having to respond.

We devour the quiche, which tastes as amazing as it smells. Then, while we're clearing the table, I say, "Oh, I used your phone last night."

"Oh?" her tone is light and casual, and she doesn't turn away from the sink, but her shoulders stiffen. "That's lucky. It's out now."

"Wait, the phone lines are down?"

She jerks her chin toward the phone. "It was this morning. You're welcome to check." She pauses. Then,

"Who did you call?"

"I wanted to say goodnight to Tristan."

She shoots me a sidelong glance. "You didn't."

"I didn't tell him about our conversation. Except ..." I trail off and turn to the window to watch the rain slide down the pane.

"Except?" she prompts.

"Except I mentioned that he would have known you as Lexi Lincoln."

"What did he say?" Her voice is low.

I turn to look at her. "He acted like he didn't recognize your name immediately, which I find hard to believe—given what happened."

She locks eyes with me. "There's zero chance that he didn't remember me right away, Emily."

"I know. He lied to me."

Anger flashes across her face, and I'm glad I left out the part about her being untrustworthy and emotionally disturbed.

"Do you think he'll do something?"

"Do something?" I echo, confused. Then I realize Alex isn't angry, she's afraid. She's afraid of my husband. "No, of course not."

She doesn't look convinced. "What's your next move?"

"Nothing until I get back home. Maybe a joint counseling session so we can talk about these things because he obviously doesn't feel comfortable confiding in me—

not about you, or Tate, or his dad's suicide." Saying the words aloud is like a gut punch.

"I hope you didn't make a mistake by telling him."

I regret bringing it up with her—not bringing it up with him. He's my husband. *Of course,* I told him. I ignore the little voice that reminds me of all the things I *haven't* told him.

I clear my throat. "I need to work on my book today. Do you think there's any chance the power came back on at the cabin?"

"Doubtful. It's not as if the switchover from snow to rain magically healed the lines. And even though it's warm enough that it's raining, there's a good chance the mountain road iced over last night. I wouldn't expect to see a utility crew out here for another day or two."

I blow out a frustrated breath.

She continues, "The good news is, according to the weather on the radio, the storm is moving on. The rain should stop by this late afternoon."

"Great" I say weakly. I can block out the world—the weather, Alex, Tristan, all of it—and re-immerse myself in my story.

"I can show you how to make a fire. Or you're welcome to work here, where you can charge your laptop."

"I appreciate the offer, but I should go back to the cabin before I overstay my welcome. But I would be grateful for the fire-starting lesson."

"Suit yourself."

We finish washing the dishes, then I have another cup of coffee and pack my bag. We lace our boots, pull our hoods up, and head out into the downpour. We stomp through the slushy snow to the cabin, trying to avoid the fallen tree limbs that litter the path. I'm glad that the ground is mushy and mucky, and not icy—yet.

When we reach the cabin, we jog up the stairs to the porch and I dig into my parka for the key. "Give me a second."

"Are you sure you locked it?" She's frowning at the front door.

"I'm positive," I tell her as I fish out the key ring.

"Well, it's unlocked."

She pushes the door open, stomps the slush off her boots and walks inside. She heads straight for the fireplace. I guess she's as eager to be rid of me as I am of her.

I trail behind her. "I know I locked it."

I have a specific memory of juggling the bag with the wine bottle and the food and my laptop bag all onto one arm so I could pull the door shut and lock it with my free hand. I don't tell her this because I know it will make me sound defensive.

She gives me a long look, then shakes her head. "Sure you did," she mumbles before gesturing toward the kitchen. "I'll show you how to get the fire started. There should be a gas lighter in the drawer by the stove."

I swore I left it on the hearth. "I had it out last night. It's not over there?"

"Nope."

I must've put it back in place on autopilot. As I'm passing the little writing desk on my way through the living room to the kitchen, something on the floor glints in the sunlight, catching my eye. I crouch to pick it up. It's a sliver of glass.

Puzzled, I scan the floor for more, but it's just the one shard. Then I see it. The corner of a rose gold rectangle peeks out from beneath the sofa. I pull it toward me.

"Shit."

She turns. "What?"

I raise my phone to show her the smashed glass. "My phone's broken. I left it here last night because I don't have a signal. I left it plugged in even though I know it wasn't charging. Habit, I guess."

She leaves the hearth and joins me at by the couch. "That stinks."

The charger is still plugged into the wall outlet, the cord dangling loosely.

"I don't even understand how it fell off the desk. The wind maybe?"

She gives me a strange look. "The wind didn't blow your phone halfway across the room through a closed window. Maybe you bumped it with the bags when you were walking through?"

"No." I shake my head. "I packed up my desk first. Then I got the food from the kitchen and put on my coat. I didn't go this way. I came down the hallway." I point to the hook where my coat was hanging.

She follows my finger then her eyes cut toward the front door. "And you're *sure* you locked the door when you left?"

"I'm positive."

Our eyes lift to the ceiling, and I know we're both thinking the same thing.

She stands and gestures for me to follow her upstairs. I hold up a finger. *Wait.* Then I creep out to the kitchen and grab a knife from the block on the counter.

When I return to the living room clutching the knife, she whispers, "I'll go first."

"Or we could leave?" I whisper back.

She raises an eyebrow and shoots me a look. I sigh. It was worth a shot.

As we tiptoe up the steps my heart thumps. I brace for the creak or squeak that will give us away, but we're as silent as thieves. My left hand on the banister is slick with sweat. I clench the handle of the knife more tightly in my right so I don't lose my grip.

We reach the second floor and she moves quickly from room to room. I'm a step behind her. The rooms are empty.

"There's no one here."

"Anymore," I say.

She gently removes the knife from my shaking hand. "The simplest explanation is usually the right one, Emily."

She heads for the stairs and I follow her, not willing to let it go.

"Do you honestly think the simplest explanation is I somehow wandered from the hallway to the desk, accidentally knocked my phone to the ground hard enough to break it without noticing, and have a false memory of locking the door when I left? That might be the most convenient explanation, but it's certainly not the simplest. The simplest explanation is after I left, someone broke in and smashed my phone."

"Why?"

"Why what?"

She turns and looks at me from the bottom of the steps. Her expression is one of genuine curiosity. "Why would someone do that? And, more to the point, who would do that?"

We go into the living room. She sits on the couch. I take the chair near the desk and try to gather my thoughts. I didn't expect her to believe me. I was prepared for her to dismiss the idea the way Tristan tried to get me to believe it was an animal, not a person, in Lashina and Ty's garden. But she's just watching me, waiting for me to answer.

"I don't know why," I begin slowly. "But it's happened before. In the weeks before Cassie was murdered, I kept thinking someone had been in our apartment. Things were out of place. Nothing was ever missing but just things weren't where they belonged; they'd been moved."

She draws her eyebrows together and her face takes on this pinched expression. Then she says in a quiet voice, "That happened to me, too. It started a month or so before I was attacked. It got so bad I worried I had a cognitive impairment."

My pulse is a jackhammer and my mouth goes dry. "And the smell?"

She blinks. "Smell?

"There was this distinctive scent—kind of spicy, kind of sweet. Sandalwood. It's used in cologne, perfume, candles, all sorts of stuff. I smelled it everywhere—in our apartment, in my car, empty classrooms. Then after Cassie died, it went away."

"You think it was him?"

Him. She means Cassie's killer. And I do.

"I always wondered. I definitely have an association with the scent. The first time I spent the night at Tristan's, he lit a candle that he picked up from a little shop in town. The smell made me so sick."

"Sandalwood?"

"Right."

"That's a pretty big coincidence for him to have a candle with a scent that triggers you. Don't you think?"

"You don't think it's a coincidence?"

"Do you? Honestly?"

She watches my face while I work through it.

"It has to be. He didn't know about Cassie's murder, and he couldn't have known about that scent following me around. And even assuming for the sake of argument that he somehow found out, why would he deliberately try to throw me off balance on a night when we were taking our relationship to the next level? It doesn't make any sense."

She bites down on her lip hard enough that a drop of blood surfaces.

"Just say it," I tell her. "Whatever you're going to say, say it."

"You're right, it doesn't make any sense. *If* Tristan's who you think he is—a good guy who loves you who isn't involved in any way in the attack on me, your roommate's murder, or this latest murder in your town. *But* if, like you say, we don't rely on the most convenient explanation, but go to the actual simplest one, then your husband's not who you think he is."

I sit on my hands to hide the fact that I'm shaking again. "We've been over this. Tristan was nine when you were stabbed."

"I'm not necessarily saying he's a killer. Maybe he's a gaslighter, a stalker, a sociopath. Or just a garden-variety dick."

"Oh, come on, Alex. So, what, you think he's hiding in the woods, watching us? Getting off on this? He's the one who moved the axe, broke my phone? He's in Pennsylvania."

"Maybe he is, but we don't know where Tate is."

This is true, but it feels like a huge stretch. I give her a close look. "There's something you're not telling me."

Now she's shaking, and that's frankly more terrifying to me than anything that's happened so far.

She swallows hard. "Remember you said you smelled it—sandalwood—on my blanket?"

"Yes."

"I didn't know what you were talking about. I didn't know the name of the scent. But I took a nap on the couch yesterday, and I pulled the blanket up over me. When I was falling asleep, I smelled something that stirred a memory in me. I didn't know what it was then. But I've smelled sandalwood before, too. A long time ago. When I lived in Windy Rock."

The full weight of what's she's saying hits me.

"We don't know where Tate is," I repeat her observation.

We both turn to look out the window toward the rain-lashed woods.

thirty-one

My stomach growls. I ignore it. I skipped breakfast and started poring over the case files as soon as I came downstairs this morning. The ticking clock in my head grows louder with every passing moment. I don't have time to eat. My stomach protests—more loudly this time—and I glance at my watch. I've been at it for four hours. Twenty more minutes, I promise myself. Then I'll take a break and scarf down a sandwich or reheat some chili.

My appetite appeased by the prospect of food, I turn back to the documents spread out on my desk. And as if on cue, my cell phone chirps. My inclination is to ignore that, too. But it could be Emily. I turn it over to check the display: *Mom.*

"Sorry, Mom," I mutter to myself as I send the call to voicemail.

She's texted several times, asking if I've heard from the authorities in Ohio about Tate's remains. I haven't, of course. Because I haven't contacted any authorities in Ohio. I guess my terse *'not yet, will keep you posted'* responses are wearing thin.

I'm not unsympathetic. She genuinely believes he's dead, and I'm sure she wants to make whatever final arrangements one makes for one's disowned, emotionally disturbed child. But I have other priorities at the moment. Like the fact that Emily's holed up with a woman Tate almost certainly tried to kill and the fact that there is literally nothing at all in these files that tie Tate to either the Ward murder or the Rowland murder. I exhale through my nostrils like a bull. My brother's smart, but I refuse to believe he's outplayed me this adeptly.

"I don't know where Tate is, but I know damn well he's not in a morgue in Ohio." My words echo in the quiet house.

If I can't find evidence Tate killed these women, I'm going to have to find Tate himself. I could call Dr. Wilde. It would be a logical starting point since he's the one who was informed of Tate's alleged death.

That's a nonstarter, though. Since he thinks *I'm* Tate, I'd have a lot of explaining to do. And if I come clean about who I am, then he'll want to discuss my six-year-long deception, and I don't have time for that right now. Besides, Tate's probably the one who called him and told him Tate Weakes is dead.

Unless Tate has a partner. I've wondered off and on through the years whether he teamed up with a partner because he sure seemed to want one. Of course, he might think murder is the sort of thing you keep in the family. In which case, when I turned him down, he'd have kept flying solo.

I do a few more public records searches for 'Tate Weakes' but nothing pops. It's been a consistent theme: he's like a ghost. He's not a registered voter in any state that I've searched, doesn't have a drivers' license, doesn't own a home, doesn't have utilities in his name. It's as if he doesn't exist. He could have a fully papered alias, but more likely he sublets a place, utilities included, for cash, uses prepaid gift cards when he can't deal in cash, and trades services for goods when he can.

Time for a break. I push back my chair and head to the kitchen. After staring into the open refrigerator for a full three minutes as if it contained the secrets of the universe rather than some leftovers and sandwich fixings, I settled on eating two heaping spoonfuls of peanut butter straight from the jar, as unsanitary as my wife thinks that is. What Emily doesn't know won't hurt her, I tell myself as I return the jar to the pantry, wash down my 'lunch' with a swig of lukewarm coffee, and return my butt to my desk chair.

What Emily doesn't know *could* hurt her. The thought sparks an idea and I switch tacks to research the one murder I haven't gone back over: Cassie Baughman's. I pulled her files a few times over the years while I was working at the crime lab and did the same thing I did with Giselle Ward's file. I took pictures of the documents with my phone, transferred them to my home computer, and printed them. Forwarding myself the Rowland file via email was a risk, but I was too concerned about losing access to the materials to worry about leaving an electronic footprint.

I've got the file folder labeled '*Appliance Warranties and User Manuals*' halfway out of my desk drawer when I freeze. The prosaic label ensures my wife will never open the folder, and the thick file does contain a sheaf of manuals for items as diverse and uninteresting as our hedge trimmer, toaster oven, and the furnace. I just happened to hide the gruesome file documenting the murder of Emily's roommate and closest friend behind the manuals. Instead of opening the folder, I shove it back into its spot and slide the drawer closed.

An unanswered question scratches at my brain like a dog at the door, demanding to be let in.

I emailed myself the cold case file because I'd been unceremoniously sidelined from the Ward investigation. I've concluded I didn't contaminate a sample—I'm too careful. Someone planted my DNA at the scene. If I rule out the crime scene team, that someone is Giselle Ward's killer. Tate. He would obviously benefit the most from sidelining me.

But I can't work out why he would go through the trouble of getting me kicked off the case only to turn around and fake his death. What's the angle? I tip my chair back onto its rear legs and stare up at the ceiling. Why would Tate want me off *and* want me to think he's dead?

The answer smacks me in the face and I return my chair to the floor with a thump. He's going to finish what he started seven years ago. A scream rises in my throat and I push it down. I scrabble for my phone and redial the number Emily called from last night. Alex Liu's landline.

Come on. Answer.

The phone doesn't ring. Instead a steady, rapid busy signal beeps in my ear. Service must be out.

I swear loudly and hang up, jabbing at my contacts list to call Em's cell phone. I know there's virtually no chance she has coverage, but I have to warn her that Tate is coming.

I grab my keys and run toward the garage but before I'm at the door to the attached garage, the doorbell rings at the front of the house.

I have half a mind to ignore it, and later I'll wish I had. But I don't. Instead, like the fool, I dutifully turn on my heel and walk toward the front door. I pull it open and blink at the man standing outside.

"Graham, this is a surprise."

Graham Stone's smile is tight, and I glance over his shoulder to see two black and whites idling in the street. My pulse quickens. Surely he's not going to arrest me for forwarding myself a file. Yes, it was a breach of protocol, and technically it's a crime. But this seems excessive.

"Tristan." His voice matches the smile—clipped, terse.

"Is something wrong?"

"I think you know it is."

So this *is* about the file.

"I shouldn't have done that. I'm sorry. Come on in."

The bewildered look he throws me confuses me.

"You're sorry?" His tone is laced with disbelief.

"Yeah, I'm sorry. That was wrong."

He looks behind him, like he's about to call for back up. "It's more than just wrong. It's heinous."

Heinous, really?

"I forwarded myself a file. It's not a capital crime."

"You forwarded yourself a file?" he repeats blankly.

"Yeah, I forwarded myself a copy of the Dana Rowland file when you asked me to forward it to you. I thought I could work on it while I'm here waiting for you to clear up whatever misunderstanding got me kicked off the Ward case."

"I'm not here about a file, Tristan."

"Then why are you here?" My eyes flick back to the police. "And why did you bring them?"

"Son, you're gonna need to come down to the station with us."

"Why don't you tell me what this is about?"

He exhales heavily. "I convinced them to let me talk to you first. Don't make me regret it. We need you to clear up some things about your brother."

My stomach hits the floor and I grip the edge of the door with both hands. This is it—the moment I've been dreading my entire adult life. Tate's crimes have caught up with him, which means they've caught up with me.

"My brother," I stall.

"Yes, your brother. Tate Weakes."

"I can't answer any questions about Tate. We've been estranged for twenty-one years. Since I was nine." I flash him a tight smile of my own. "I don't know where he is."

A detective I recognize from cases I've worked comes around the corner from the narrow alley between our place and Lashina and Ty's house. His name is Dunn or Dane, something like that. He must have been standing just out of view, listening.

"We know where he is," he informs me in a grave voice.

"You do?" This is comforting news. If they have Tate, Emily's not in danger.

"Yes, we found his body in the parking lot behind the gym you frequent."

"His body?" I repeat.

Graham sighs heavily. "Your brother's dead."

I almost snark, *Again?* But I control myself and, instead, say, "Is that right?"

The two men exchange a look.

"That's right," the detective says. "And you'll never guess what we found."

"Well, it's got to be something that ties him to Giselle Ward's murder. Right?"

Surprise sparks in Graham's eyes. "What?"

I exhale heavily. "I ordered that cold case file from Arizona because I have a theory that Giselle Ward and Dana Rowland were murdered by the same person."

"I know. We talked about this."

"What I didn't mention is I suspect my brother was that person. I guess I'm right. Did he kill himself? It's just like him to take the coward's way out."

Another unreadable look passes between them before the detective says, "No, your brother didn't kill himself. Frankly, I'd have expected a better cleanup job from you."

"What?"

"Just do it already, Dunn," my boss says.

"Tristan Rose, you're under arrest for the murder of Tate Weakes and Giselle Ward. You have—" The detective's winding up to read me my rights when he interrupts himself and turns to Graham. "Should we add Dana Rowland?"

"Better run it by the DA."

My brain takes a minute to catch up with the words. When it does, I panic. "No. This is a mistake."

"Tristan, don't make this harder than it has to be."

"I didn't kill anyone." My voice goes high.

"Your gym bag was lying beside him."

"No, see, that's not possible. My gym bag's in my car. Come on, I'll show you in the garage," I babble.

My law enforcement training is screaming at me. I know better than to invite the authorities into my home or to volunteer any information. I *know* I need to lawyer up. And yet, I honestly believe I can explain this away. Graham knows me. He likes me.

Dunn shrugs. "Fine. I'm gonna have to cuff you, though, Tristan. You understand."

As a point of procedure, I should already be hand-cuffed if they're arresting me.

Still, it seems ludicrous. But I'm eager to appear reasonable, so I extend my wrists obediently. He gestures toward the patrol cars, and the pair of uniformed officers from the lead car exits their vehicle and joins the unhappy little gathering on my front stoop. Dunn slaps the cuffs on me and keeps a hand on my arm as I lead the group through the house to the garage.

Graham opens the door and I instruct them where to find the bag. My boss and the detective flank me, while the officers pop the trunk and search my car.

"There's no bag here, sir," the female officer says as she slams the trunk shut.

"It has to be there. I haven't taken it out since ...." I try to remember.

"Since when?" Dunn asks.

Since my appointment with Dr. Wilde, I think.

Instead I say, "I want an attorney."

"That's a good idea because you didn't ask us what we found in the bag."

I already know what they found—my gym clothes and a tablet wrapped in a towel. No big deal. I shrug.

Graham shakes his head. "I wouldn't be quite so cavalier if I were you. We're probably going to be able to match that knife to Giselle Ward's wounds as well as your brother's."

A knife?

My knees buckle. Detective Dunn grabs me before I hit the cement floor.

Over the years I've feared, pitied, and hated my brother. I suppose at one point, when I was very young, I might even have loved him. But now I realize I've underestimated him.

Tate has outplayed me with a final master stroke. He's set me up for the murders he's committed, killed himself, and set me up for murdering him, too. I'm trapped.

part iii. escape from the tower

She took the bread-knife, and picked and bored at the mortar of a stone, and when she was tired, the waiting-maid took her turn. With great labour they succeeded in getting out one stone, and then a second, and a third, and when three days were over the first ray of light fell on their darkness[.]

—*Maid Maleen,* as retold by the Brothers Grimm

Ruth and Maleen exchanged a long, knowing look. All their patience, all their waiting and acquiescing, and all their prayers had done nothing. It had only condemned them to a certain death.

They bowed their heads, defeated.

Unless, Ruth thought with a sudden spark,

they shook off the mantel of obedience. Unless, she thought, they rescued themselves.

Her gasp caught Maleen's attention, and the princess raised her head. They locked eyes. Maleen's warm hazel eyes and Ruth's cool, gray eyes, the only eyes either had seen in seven years, the eyes they now knew better than their own.

Ruth nodded toward the dulled and dusty bread knives. They had once shone, a brilliant pewter. She stretched out her hand around and wrapped it around one handle.

Maleen lowered her chin, grasped the other knife, now oxidized green.

Together, they strode across the cold stone floor to the tower's thick outer wall.

—*The Tower,* by Emily Rose

thirty-two

`Alex`

As difficult as it is to believe that Tate is hiding somewhere on the property, it's the inescapable conclusion. Someone moved my axe, someone broke into the cabin and smashed Emily's phone and took the lighter. And, this is the part I really don't want to accept—whoever they were, they were inside my farmhouse, too. They must've been. Either that, or Emily's lying about the sandalwood scent.

I glance at her, still shivering, still staring out the window into the woods that surround the cabin. The rain changed over to an icy sleet a while ago. We should have left, headed back to the farmhouse as soon as we realized the cabin had been broken into. But she was in no shape for even a short walk. And I'd rather support her through a full-blown panic attack in here than out in the storm.

But I'm getting antsy. She's through the worst of it, and I want to get out of here. The farmhouse isn't more secure. I know this. But my desire to hole up there isn't based on rational thought. It's my fortress. I *feel* safe there. Although I'd feel a hell of a lot safer if I'd thought to stop and get the gun out of the safe in the guest room. It's been locked away for so long, that I'd nearly forgotten it was there. It doesn't matter now—I can't leave Emily here alone to go back and grab it.

"We need to be smart," I say aloud. It's for my benefit —to remind myself not to allow my emotions to take over. But the words also calm the quivering mess of a woman to my right.

She wipes her tear-stained face, squares her shoulders, and raises her chin. "You're right." Her voice, while not loud, is steady.

Relief courses through me. If she can pull herself together, and keep herself together, we have a chance of getting out of this nightmare alive. After all, there are two of us and only one of him. *Unless his brother's out there with him,* my traitorous mind whispers. No. I can't even go down that road. Tristan's in Pennsylvania. His wife seems certain, and I have no real option other than to believe her.

"Okay, let's think this through," I say.

She turns to face me. "Can your truck make it down the mountain in this weather?"

No, I think. I know it can't. By now the road is definitely iced over and that mountain is treacherous under the best of conditions. I would never attempt the drive in these conditions, not in a million years.

"Maybe," I lie. I absolutely *should not* try to make the drive. But what option do we have? Wait for him to show himself and kill us both? I didn't survive twenty-one years ago just to sit around and let him kill me now.

She blinks as if she'd been expecting a different answer. "Really?"

"Maybe," I emphasize.

"I'd rather die by going over the side of the mountain than be stabbed to death," she says calmly—too calmly.

I counter with a joke, "Are you suggesting a Thelma and Louise pact?"

She answers me seriously. "It's preferable to the alternative."

That snaps me into action. "No. No way, Emily. Listen to me. We can get out of here safely. All we need to do is make it to the first house in the valley. I know the family. They'll help us."

She manages a wobbly smile. "Then what are we waiting for?"

We bundle up. She leaves her laptop but grabs the chef's knife again. I snatch the fireplace poker and join her at the door.

"Ready?" I ask.

"Ready."

I push open the door and step out onto the porch. The sleet has turned to solid ice, and I grip the railing tightly with my free hand as I mince my way down the ice-slicked steps to the yard. The ice pellets sting as they bounce off my exposed skin. I wince and turn to watch her gingerly descend the stairs.

We follow the gravel drive for as long as possible. It provides some traction even though it's not the most direct route to the barn where the truck is parked. Reaching the end of the drive, I step onto the wet grass and immediately lose my footing.

"Careful, it's slippery," I call to her as I right myself.

We shuffle across the yard like penguins. Our progress is torturously slow. My heart pounds and my hand aches from gripping the poker. We're exposed and vulnerable. If he's watching us, now, he might be tempted to charge us.

I swallow and force myself to resist the urge to run. That'll only end up with me on my ass. Through the driving ice, the barn comes into view over the rise. We're almost there. I push aside the thought that once we get there, we're hardly out of danger. The drive to the valley is going to be hair-raising, at best. I don't allow myself to think about the worst-case result.

I turn to check on Emily's progress. She's about ten feet behind me. Her head is lowered like she's watching her step as she inches along. Every few steps, she stops and wipes the moisture from her eyes. Her mouth is set in a firm line.

She must feel the weight of my gaze because she looks up and flashes me a thumb's up sign. I smile and hope it's encouraging because it feels like a rictus. Then I turn back to the barn, checking for movement in the woods from the periphery of my vision.

Finally, we reach the barn. Breathing hard, I stretch out my hand to unlatch the door and freeze.

"What's wrong?" she pants.

The words lodge in my throat and it takes a moment to choke them out. "The door's not latched."

"Maybe the wind blew it open," she says hopefully.

"Maybe." I doubt it, though. The door was secure. I checked before the storm began.

My pulse hammers in my throat as I push open the door. Raising my poker overhead, I creep forward, terrified of what—or who——might be waiting inside for us. As I step out of the ice storm and into the dim barn, I clutch the poker harder and wait for my eyes to adjust. When they do, I have to stop myself from sinking to my knees.

"No."

thirty-three

Emily

"No," Alex whispers.

I step forward to stand beside her in the darkened barn. I follow her gaze, but between the water running into my eyes as the ice on my hood melts and drips down my face and the darkness inside the structure, I'm not sure what we're looking at. I can tell from the slope of her shoulders that whatever it is, it isn't good.

I take another step closer to the truck, and my heart drops into the pit of my stomach as I see what Alex saw. The front tires are flat—completely flat. I walk to the back of the vehicle on shaky legs and confirm that the back tires are flat, too.

Alex is frozen to the spot, staring.

My mind races. I'm about to ask how this could have happened when I see the rubber flapping in the cold wind that gusts in through the open barn door. Someone has taken something sharp, probably a big kitchen knife like the one I'm holding, to the tires. Any hope that this is just bad luck vanishes.

"He did this," Alex rasps in a hoarse voice.

Suddenly, the warm, dark barn feels less like a shelter and more like a tomb. I run around to the front of the truck to stand as close to Alex as I can.

"He could still be in here," I whisper back.

The muscle in her cheek twitches, but she says nothing. Instead, she removes the flashlight from the pocket of her parka and turns it on. The beam is bright in the dark interior. She slowly arcs it across the wall and then back, stopping at each stall, every corner, before turning it up to the loft.

He could be hiding up there, I think, pressed down flat against the floor. But I'm not about to suggest mounting the ladder and climbing up to the hayloft to find out. I keep my eyes fixed on Alex's drawn face.

She clicks off the light and pockets the flashlight. She closes her eyes for a moment and gives her head a small shake before raising her gaze to mine. "It was probably a suicide mission anyway."

I thought as much, but at least it was something we could *do,* an action we could take, instead of sitting around waiting to be slaughtered.

"So ... do you have a spare?" I ask stupidly.

She gives me a sympathetic look. "Yeah, I have one, not four. And before you ask if I have another vehicle, I'm neither foolish nor brave enough to try to drive a tractor down an ice-covered mountain."

"So that's it. We're trapped." My voice shakes.

After all this time I've spent wondering when Cassie's killer would finally catch up with me, he finally has. The fact that it's my brother-in-law is more than my frantic, frightened mind can grasp.

Alex's eyes narrow.

"What?"

Her gaze darts around the barn, and I realize she's not entirely sure we're alone either. She gives an imperceptible shake of her head and motions for me to follow her outside. Just moments ago, I was so relieved to be inside. I never would have imagined looking forward to being back out in the elements. But I eagerly trail out of the barn behind her.

She stops and latches the door. We both know that if he's in there, it won't stop him. But it might slow him down.

She speaks in a low voice. "There's no guarantee, but if we go back to the farmhouse and up to my attic, we might be able to make a call. Sometimes I can get a cell phone signal if I hold my phone out the window."

"How do you live like this?" I blurt.

When her eyes meet mine again, they're full of dread and sorrow. "I thought it was protecting me. I never dreamed it would endanger me."

A long silence passes between the two of us and then I say, ever hopeful, "Well, maybe the landline is back. I mean, it was working last night when I called Tristan. Maybe—"

"Maybe." She gives me a gentle look. "But don't get your hopes up. The ice weighs the lines down. It's even worse than the wind and snow. Still, you're right. There's a chance. There's *always* a chance. So we can't give up."

On an impulse, I shift the butcher knife to my left hand and grab her left hand with my right. I squeeze, and she squeezes back. Then we run as quickly as we dare, using a little Charlie Chaplin stride to cross the slick grass. Once we hit the gravel in front of the farmhouse, we drop hands and run flat out, no longer worrying about falling.

Alex has the key out and is turning it in the lock even as we reach the front door. She pushes it open with her shoulder and we race inside.

"Emily, lock it," she shouts.

I throw the bolt, and she picks up the phone in the kitchen. Then she turns to me and shakes her head. No signal. She reaches into the top drawer of the desk up against the kitchen wall and grabs an old flip phone. "Come on."

She gestures for me to follow her and we race through the house to the stairs, pound up the stairs, and past Alex's bedroom to the end of the hall. There's another set of stairs. We race up them. My heart threatens to beat out of my chest.

At the top of these stairs, a door leads to yet another narrow stairwell. I clamber behind her up the steep stairs to the attic, where yet another door stops us. There's no landing, so I stand on the step beneath her while she struggles with the door.

"It sticks. The paint swells when the humidity rises." As she explains, she gives the door a hard bump with her hip.

It doesn't budge. Just as I'm about to let the wave of defeat engulf me and sink to the ground, Alex throws her whole body at the wooden door and it jerks open.

"Come on." She grabs my hand and yanks me into the cold, drafty attic.

thirty-four

Tristan

I shift my weight in a futile attempt to find a comfortable position in the molded plastic seat. Still, I'm grateful for my grim surroundings. Graham pulled some strings to get me into an interview room and not a holding cell. It's probably only a matter of time before I'm behind bars, but I'd like to delay that for as long as possible. Apparently, my boss would, too.

The officer who booked me did, however, take my watch, and the clock on the wall is stuck at ten minutes to eight. It could be intentional, an effort to disorient people. Or it could be a dead battery. As a county employee, I'm leaning toward the latter. Whatever the reason, though, it *does* disorient me. I don't know if I've been in here for twenty minutes, two hours, or some amount of time in between.

I turn my gaze away from the infuriating stopped clock and crane my neck up to study the water stain on the ceiling tiles and wonder if it's evidence of a budgetary issue or a Rorschach test. I'll know for sure when someone asks me what I see.

The door opens and Detective Dunn comes into the room. He doesn't care what I see in the stain. Instead, he says without preamble, "Give me your arms."

I obediently lift my wrists, and Dunn unlocks the cuffs.

"Thank you." I rub my raw, red skin and then turn circles with my wrists to get the blood flowing again.

"Don't thank me. Captain's orders. I'd leave you cuffed like any other suspect."

"I understand." And I do. The system really only works if everyone's treated the same in the eyes of the law.

Dunn narrows his eyes. "That right?"

"Sure, even though I'm presumed innocent and, in this case, actually, factually innocent, there are procedures to be followed. I can respect that you don't want to give me any special treatment just because I work at the crime lab."

"So you want me to put the cuffs back on?" He smirks.

I have nothing to lose by being honest. "No, I like the special treatment. But I understand why you don't."

He nods a couple of times. Then he twists his mouth to one side. "You know, you have a good reputation around the station. The book on you is that you're a straight shooter and a talented analyst. But being good at your job doesn't mean you aren't a murderer. And I gotta tell you, man, it doesn't look good for you. The evidence is compelling."

"Show me what you have. If I see it, I can explain it."

"Maybe you could." He gives me a shrug. "But I can't do that because you lawyered up."

It's my turn to look skeptical. "Surely you didn't come in here to do a good cop routine to get me to talk. At a minimum, you need a bad cop, too."

"Nah, man, it's not like that. Your lawyer's on her way. But if you have an explanation for this, I would love to hear it."

"And you will," I tell him, "when my lawyer gets here."

The detective shakes his head as he leaves the room. "Suit yourself."

The door locks with a loud click, trapping me inside. I may be sitting at a conference table with free use of my limbs rather than on a metal bunk behind thick bars, but there's no mistake. I'm not free to go.

I stare up at the water mark a while longer and finally decide it looks like a boat sailing on turbulent seas. I tip the chair back on its back two legs and continue to focus on the boat. It reminds me of the whale-watching cruise.

Three summers ago, Emily and I spent a week on Cape

Cod. As a surprise, she booked the excursion—a private charter with a local naturalist to see the whales up close. The morning sun streaked the sky pink, the water shimmered, and the sea spray tinged my takeout coffee with a hint of salt. Emily's cheeks were flushed, her eyes were bright, and her wavy red hair was windblown. We held hands, stared out at the endless blue water, and just breathed. And, despite it being peak migration season, we didn't see a single whale. When we returned to the pier, Captain Mark tripped all over himself apologizing for the whale-less nature of our trip and tried to refund our money. But Emily and I waved him off. We didn't need a pod of whales, we had each other.

And we still do. This realization gives me a sense of calm despite my shitty situation. My estranged, deranged brother is dead, which means Emily is safe. While being accused of murder is less than ideal, I can fix this. There's no way Tate's getting the better of me. For one thing, I'm alive and can adjust my strategies as needed. Tate played his last hand before he died.

I am surprised he didn't stick around to watch his plan play out. I'd expect him to fake his death, but the police and Graham have seen his body. Killing himself to frame me is a level of commitment I didn't expect. I know he hated me, but I didn't realize he hated me *that* much.

Footsteps sound in the hall. I tip the chair back down to the ground and watch the door, waiting for Loretta Simmons to walk through it. Calling Loretta my lawyer is a stretch. But I *am* her parents' next-door neighbor, and I've seen her in action in court. She's a young, hungry criminal defense attorney. She's exactly what I need.

I straighten my back and prepare to greet her. But when the door swings open, it's not Loretta who's standing in the doorway. Instead, my boss eyes me balefully, clutching two styrofoam cups.

He flashes me a smile. I don't return it.

"Where's Loretta?"

Graham nudges the door closed and plunks down in the chair across from me before answering.

"She just called. She's stuck in traffic. Four-car pileup on the expressway."

He slides one of the cups toward me. "Thought you could use some terrible police station coffee."

I consider making a joke about the coffee, comparing it to paint thinner or varnish remover, but I don't. Instead, I cock my head and give him a disbelieving look.

"You can't seriously think I'm going to touch this cup so you can use it to gather DNA evidence. Did you forget who you're talking to?"

He blinks, but his face gives away nothing. "Did *you* forget we have a sample of your DNA?"

I haven't, of course. But I also know how this works. The more they collect, the better.

"Still. I'm not thirsty."

He shrugs. "Suit yourself." He raises the cup to his lips,

takes a sip, and grimaces. "Actually, good call. Jeez, this sucks."

I chuckle, then I lower my chin and give him a close look. "What do you want, Graham? You're not going to get to a confession out of me by pretending to be my friend."

"I am your friend."

I let that pass. "You can't trick me into confessing. For one thing, I know all the tricks. For another, I didn't kill anyone. So there's nothing to confess to."

He abandons the coffee and rests his forearms on the table, leaning across to peer at me. "That isn't entirely true, though, is it? You may not have killed anyone—although, the evidence is what it is, Tristan, and it's going to be hard to explain away. But you know *something*. You've said as much. At your house you claimed you suspected your brother of the Ward and Rowland murders. So what did you do? Withhold evidence? Tamper with it?"

"Of course not."

"You were working together, weren't you?"

"No." My voice is forceful. Then the thought —hitting me with the force of a gut punch. Despite Tate's repeated overtures, I wasn't working with him. But what if he did have a partner?

I must gasp or grunt because Grant peers at me. "What?"

I ignore him. My mind races. If Tate was working with someone else, then Emily could still be in danger. No. If that's true, she *is* still in danger. The truth unspools in front of me like puzzle pieces snapping together.

"Tristan?"

I can't wait for Loretta. "How'd you find Tate's body?"

"I told you. He was in the parking lot behind the gym."

"Not where. How? Did someone stumble over it? Who called it in?"

He narrows his eyes. "I'm not sharing details of the investigation with you. Like you said, you know how this—"

I pound my fist on the table, and he flinches.

"We don't have time for this, Graham. I think Emily's in danger. Who called it in?"

He bites his lip for a moment, then shakes his head. "I shouldn't be telling you this."

I hold my breath and say nothing, letting him get there on his own. I can't still my jittering leg, though.

"We got a call to do a welfare check. Tate's therapist, a Dr. Wilde, was worried because he didn't show up for his last video appointment, and he couldn't reach him."

Wilde told my mother the police called *him*. He also told her that Tate was in Ohio—or at least let her believe it.

"When?" I croak.

"This morning. He didn't have a home address, but he said Tate worked at a local gym. So we sent squad cars to all four gyms. We found him behind the Sweetwater Sweat Spot. What's going on, Tristan?"

"I need you to call this number." I rattle off the digits for Alex Liu's landline while he stares at me.

"Graham, please. I need you to warn Emily."

"Warn her about what?"

"Make the call. Tell the woman who answers that Emily's therapist is coming to kill them."

thirty-five

The attic smells like cedar and must. The rafters are exposed, and some of the floorboards are as well. Wood paneling covers the walls, and old furniture, boxes, trunks, and bins are scattered apparently haphazardly throughout the space. There's a wooden framed standing mirror propped in one corner and an old vanity. And there's one round window, the kind you might see in a beach house. It seems out of place in a farmhouse in the North Carolina mountains. But I imagine with the peaked roof, it was the best shape the builder could come up with.

"If I have a signal, it'll be over here." She rushes to the portal window, and I follow.

The tang of sweat and fear rises from her skin, and I'm sure my own perspiration-slicked body is giving off a similarly metallic scent. I peer over her shoulder, squinting at the gray light streaming in through the window while she bends her head over the flip phone.

"No bars." She raises her head and squares her shoulders. "You're taller. Open the window for me." She points, and I see a crank mechanism. I flip up the lock and turn the crank. The window opens to the side and cold rain trickles into the attic.

Alex stretches her arm out and holds the phone outside, pointing it toward the sky. She tilts the screen back toward the room so that we can see. We both let out a hoot of triumph. There's a bar. Only one, but it's there.

"You can call emergency services even if the tower is out, right?"

"As long as we have a signal, yes."

She pulls her arm back in and hits the button for nine. The signal is so weak that I'm not sure it'll go through. I close my eyes and pray.

A tremendous crash of glass echoes through the downstairs and the slam of the door shakes the house. I open my eyes and meet hers, my heart thumping. He's come for us.

"Hurry up. Call," I urge.

Alex's finger shakes as she hits the one, then she clicks her tongue. "Lost the signal."

She rises on her toes and holds the phone out through the open window to try again.

"Lexi, Emily, come out and play," a male voice calls from below.

Alex starts, and the phone falls from her hand onto the pitched roof.

"No!" Her scream is anguished.

Nausea rises in my throat. My pulse races.

"You want to play hide-and-seek? Ready or not, here I come," the man bellows.

Alex is leaning out the window, her feet dangling off the floor as she scrabbles for the phone.

"I know that voice," I murmur to myself.

Alex cranes her head over her shoulder, still half-out the window. "Tristan?"

I shake my head. "No, but I know it. I *know* I know it. Does it sound familiar to you? Could it be Tate?"

"I don't think so. But I don't know. It's been so long."

"Whoever he is, he knows us."

She drops her feet back to the floor and lets her head fall back against the wall, staring wide-eyed at the beams above. "I can't reach the phone. It's over."

Her stricken expression chills me. My throat closes. This is it. I've been waiting for the other shoe to drop for seven years. And now it has. I slide down the wall and let the kitchen knife slip from my hand. Then I wrap my arms around my shins and rest my forehead on my knees. There's no hope left.

A scene plays out in my mind. It's my scene, the one I've had planned for my book. The scene where Maleen and Ruth come into their power. Now expanded, fleshed out by my visceral understanding of what the two women felt.

Maleen rent her hair in despair. "It's over, Ruth. The food is gone. We have enough water for one more day. We've been forgotten, left to die in the windowless tower."

Ruth raised her head, a defiant gleam in her eye. "You may be content to curl up and die here, but I'm not. I may die, but I'll die trying."

Maleen's laughter was harsh. "Trying to do what?" She gestured around their prison. "How do you intend to escape this tomb?"

*Ruth's determination faltered under the weight of Maleen's statement. And this—more than the lack of food, more than the knowledge that their deaths by starvation would be slow and painful, more than the pain of abandonment—terrified Maleen. Ruth had always, **always**, been the strong one. The capable one.*

Now, though, Ruth blanched. She sighed and hung her head. "You're right. It's over."

And these words lit within Maleen a hidden flame she didn't know she possessed. Fire burned low in her belly, and her voice was hot when she grasped Ruth's shoulders. "No. Look at me."

Ruth raised her head, tears shining in her eyes. "Your prince has forgotten you. Your father is most likely dead. If anyone remembers we're here, they no longer care. Nobody's coming to save us, Maleen."

Maleen dropped her hands from Ruth's shoulders and covered her face with her hands, the fire doused.

But Ruth scanned the dim interior of the round room, falling at last on the dull bread knives resting on the empty, dusty platter. She snatched up the utensils and pressed one into her friend's hand, which hung limply at her side.

"What am I to do with this?" Maleen scoffed, laughing without humor.

"You're right. Nobody's coming."

"So we save ourselves." Maleen straightened her shoulders, gathered her skirts with her free hand, and knelt before the wall. She ran her fingers over the smooth, cold surface until she felt a seam. Then she took her silver knife and began to dig.

I lift my head and give Alex a fierce look.

"No. We're not going down like this. We can't. We haven't survived all the shit we've survived to sit here waiting to die in an attic."

I grab the knife off the floor, pull myself to my feet, and cross the small attic to stand in front of her. I take her by the shoulders and give her a gentle shake. "There are two of us and only one of him. Come on, Alex. You have a bucket list to work through. I'm pretty sure this isn't on it."

Alex holds my gaze for a moment, or maybe an hour. It

feels interminable. Then a slow smile spreads across her lips. "Actually, killing the bastard who attacked me *is* on my bucket list."

She grabs the poker that she rested against the wall when she tried to get a signal and grabs my free hand. We raise our interlocked hands overhead.

There's so much to say, but none of it matters. Or maybe I don't know how to word it. Before I can settle on an appropriate final statement, Alex drops her hand.

"Come on," she says, suddenly reinvigorated. "Push everything you can against the door." She points to a large rubber bin. "It's full of books. It's heavy. Help me."

Grunting, we lay down our meager weapons and drag the bin full of books across the floor and against the door. We pile boxes, a rocking chair, an old set of blinds, snow shoes, everything we can think of, against the door. As we do, the taunts continue. The voice grows louder, coming closer, and then we hear the footsteps on the attic stairs.

My heart flutters so rapidly it feels like there's a bird trapped in my chest. Alex picks up the knife and the poker and thrusts them both toward me.

"What are you doing? Keep that." I try to push the poker back toward her.

"I'm going to go out on the roof."

"No, you can't. We're going to fend him off— together."

She hesitates, and I read in her expression what she won't say. She doesn't think I have the will to do it.

But what she says is, "Three digits, Emily. If I can grab the phone and call 911, we can take him down while help is on the way. Just in case."

She definitely thinks I'll freeze or fold in the face of danger. Sadly, she may not be wrong about that—but she *is* wrong about this plan of hers.

"You'll fall," I protest. "The roof is slick."

"I won't," she promises.

"Alex, don't," I say.

Alex grips me by the shoulders and stares hard into my face. "I have to."

"We have a plan." I gesture with the weapons.

"We have to try everything. Now, come on, I need you to boost me out the window. I'll be back in a flash and we can kick this guy's ass."

I don't like it, but I do it. I set the poker and knife aside as she gets a running start, grabs the rounded window frame, and hoists herself up so that her head and torso hang out the porthole-shaped window.

"Ready?" I ask.

"Ready," she calls back. Her voice is thin, ripped away by the wind and rain.

I grab her shoes and push forward. I don't want to look, but I do. She slides down the roof. She's moving fast, too fast, but she still manages to grab the phone on her way.

It's a Pyrrhic victory, though, because she's still sliding, headed for the eave and, then, I know, the ground.

"No!" I squeeze my eyes shut and wait for her to scream as she plunges over the side of the roof.

There's no scream. Instead, there's a loud thump followed by soft cursing.

Against my better judgment I open my eyes to see her lying against the gutter, twisted now from the impact. She looks up and flashes me a triumphant grin just as the pounding on the door starts.

"Knock, knock."

I say nothing, my head swiveling from the door to the window. Alex starts to crawl back up the roof, the phone firmly in hand.

The pounding continues. "I said, knock, knock."

I know this voice, I'm sure of it. But I still can't place it.

Finally, I croak, "Who's there?"

A high, long shriek fills my ears. I turn back to the window in time to see Alex sliding backward down the roof. She gathers speed, busting through the crumpled gutters, flies over the edge, and drops from view.

thirty-six

Icy rain pelts my neck as I lay facedown in the frozen mud. When I press my hands to push up, pain lances through my right shoulder. I collapse, panting.

*Stupid, stupid, **stupid.***

I was so sure I could grab the phone, call for help, and get back into the attic. Now the phone is as broken and useless as I am. It lies, its screen smashed and dark, in the mud near the edge of the lawn.

My pulse thrums in my neck. I gather my strength and will myself to try again. My right arm quivers as I tense it to straighten it. Another bolt of stabbing heat tears through my shoulder, and I hear the crackling of bone grinding on bone. I grit my teeth and force myself to turn onto my left side. Sweat beads my forehead, my stomach lurches, and bile rises in my throat.

I support my full weight with my left arm and push myself to a seated position. Clumsily, I make my way to my knees, ignoring the throbbing in my right shoulder. But when I try to stand, I don't even make it halfway up before collapsing back to the ground in a heap, my right ankle pulsing as pain shoots up my leg. I can't walk.

I'm trapped. Helpless. Unable to rush to Emily's aid. I turn my gaze up to the attic, half-expecting to witness the attack on her play out in front of the round window. But I can't see anything through the stinging, wintry mix of sleet and sheets of rain.

A hot pulse of anger slices through my agony and despair and with it, a shard of fragmented memory emerges—the first sliver from the night I was attacked two decades ago working its way to the surface like a splinter that's been embedded deep in my skin.

Tom Weakes' face pressed against glass. My window. He's always been creepy, too familiar. And now he's watching me.

I scream. His eyes widen, and for a heartbeat I think he's reacting to my shriek. But his expression conveys horror, not arousal, and his gaze is over my shoulder.

I turn to see what he sees and—the scene dissolves, replaced by the light gray mist that always fills my mind when I try to remember the attack.

But the emotion from that night remains. In that moment, twenty-one years ago, when I turned to see … whatever I saw … I didn't feel fear. I felt rage. Heart-pounding, gut-twisting rage. The same rage that propels me forward now despite the exquisite, excruciating toll it exacts.

I crawl. Each movement sends a jolt of electric heat through my body. I swear, I sweat, I cry, but I keep going. My left hand claws the earth as I drag myself toward the steps, my busted shoulder and mangled ankle bumping uselessly against the hard ground. But I keep inching forward.

Tristan

"Go find Graham. Please, Loretta. I need to know if he got ahold of Alex Liu."

My attorney gives me a concerned looked. "Tristan, we need to focus on these charges. They're serious."

"Emily's in danger," I insist. "And so is Alex."

Loretta takes off her glasses, polishes them with her sleeve, and returns them to her face. Then she peers at me, owlish and alert. "Tell me again what you think happened."

"I know what happened." My voice is raw. "My father was a voyeur. Tate, too. But watching wasn't enough for Tate. He … escalated."

"To attacking women."

"Killing them."

"Including your wife's college roommate years ago?"

"Cassie. Right. And a woman in Arizona. Before that, the one who started it all, was Alex Liu. But she survived." I can see the question forming in her mind and answer it before she asks. "With no memory of the attack."

She considers this. "And Tate's dead now, but you didn't kill him."

It's a statement, not a question. I nod in agreement anyway. "I think Wilde killed him. Tate got close to him somehow. And now Dr. Wilde is—" My throat closes around the words.

She waits.

"—finishing what Tate started," I choke out. Then I stalk back to the table and press my palms against the cold metal surface. My gut twists. "Tate wanted a partner."

Before I can go on, the door bursts open. Detective Dunn, trailed by Graham, rush in. Their expressions are grim.

"Did you speak to Alex?" I demand.

Graham shakes his head. "The storm knocked out her landline."

I clench my fists.

Dunn clears his throat. "I contacted the local PD. Their 911 service received a call from Alex Liu's mobile."

"What did she say?"

"There was nobody on the line when the call came through. The operator tried calling back, but there's no answer. Either she lost her signal or her phone died."

"Or she died. Do something."

I hear the pleading tone in my voice and I hate it. I hate being helpless, trapped here hundreds of miles away while Emily's in danger. I can't rescue her. The only thing I can do is convince the authorities to take me seriously. A bleak comparison springs to mind: I'm like the characters in her manuscript—trapped in a windowless room, lacking agency.

"First responders are on their way, Tristan," Graham tells me levelly.

"How long until someone gets there?"

"Emergency vehicles are ten minutes out." Dunn hesitates. "But it could be longer. The mountain roads are slick."

My stomach lurches. "That might be too late."

"Emily's a smart woman," Loretta says. "If she and this Alex woman already called 911, they know something's wrong."

"Wilde's been her therapist for years. He knows how she thinks. He'll be able to anticipate her every move—if she even realizes she can't trust him, which isn't guaranteed."

Loretta pauses, lets this sink in. Then she counters, "If what you say is true, Alex Liu is a survivor. Emily isn't alone."

Alex was lucky. And everybody's luck runs out sooner or later.

Emily

A sharp crack splits the air. The rocking chair, stacked precariously on the pile of boxes barricading the door, slides an inch to the left.

My gaze darts to the window where Alex vanished, then back to the door. My worry for her wars with my fear for what will happen when my luck runs out and the door gives way. Trapped in this attic, I can't do a single thing to help her. I have to save myself if I'm going to have any chance of saving her.

Another crack, and the rubber bin full of books shifts. A sob rises in my throat.

"Fee-fi-fo-fum," the voice sing-songs from the other side. More splintering sounds follow, and the door frame buckles. "I smell the blood of—" A pause. "Well, you know how it goes, Emily."

That voice. So familiar, yet somehow wrong. Distorted,

like it's a bad cell phone connection. Is it Tate? Maybe I recognize him because he's my husband's brother, but it's off, wrong, because it isn't Tristan?

Maybe. Whoever it is, the menace underlying the old nursery rhyme sends a shiver through me. I back away from the door, gripping the poker in my sweat-slicked hands. My shoulders smack the wall beneath the window. Cold air whistles through the open window. I almost turn to look, to see if Alex has miraculously stood up and escaped. Saved herself.

I hope she has, but I don't check. I can't think about Alex now. I have to focus. Have to—

The rubber bin topples. Books cascade across the floor like dominoes. The man outside laughs. And suddenly I know why I recognize the voice. It's not Tate. It's Dr. Wilde. My throat goes dry.

Dr. Wilde.

The man who helped me process my trauma, who guided me through my darkest moments after Cassie's death. The one person who knows my every fear, every weakness, every vulnerability. I've bared more of myself to him than anyone, including my husband.

Another crack. The barricade shudders.

"Your sessions were quite illuminating, Emily." His voice, despite it all, maintains his professional warmth. "All those hours discussing your novel and what it meant to you. A woman trapped in a tower. How autobiographical."

I grip the poker until my knuckles turn white. My mind races. Every revelation about my past, every breakthrough about my anxiety, every piece of understanding I gained about my past gave him a blueprint. An operating manual that he can use now to manipulate me, torment me.

Fuck that.

The words explode inside me. I won't let him. I can use his knowledge of me against him.

I stiffen my spine, solidifying my resolve, as the door frame splinters. Through the widening gap, I catch a glimpse of him. The familiar face that nodded sympathetically across his desk while I sobbed about Cassie is now twisted into a distorted mask of violence.

thirty-seven

Alex

A crash sounds from above. I can't tell if it's thunder, a tree branch splitting, or the attacker in my attic. My throat closes. I need to hurry. Through sheets of icy rain, I drag myself toward my front steps, my useless right arm trailing in mud. Each movement sends fresh agony through my shoulder, but I keep going. I have to. Emily is trapped up there with—someone. The same someone who hurt her before? The same someone who hurt me? *Tate.*

The cold rain soaks through my clothes, and another memory emerges. I'm not in North Carolina.

I'm in Maine, in my apartment lying on my floor, my body

broken and battered. The storm lashes through my shattered slider door, and Tate Weakes stands over me with a hunting knife. Hot blood—my blood—drips from the blade onto my exposed collarbone. His expression hovers somewhere between pleasure and disgust.

I gasp at the strength of the memory, then turn and retch into the mud. When I finish and wipe my mouth with the back of my hand, the scene is still spooling out in my mind.

Tate's not looking down at me, he's staring out my window, his eyes locked on something. No, someone. I can't turn my head or lift myself to see what he's looking at, but I know. It's his father. Tom was watching.

Sharp pebbles of gravel from the driveway bite into my palm as I pull myself forward. Twenty feet to the steps. Might as well be twenty miles. But I won't stop. Won't give up. Won't be helpless again.

I grit my teeth and dig my fingers deeper into the earth. Fifteen feet now. Fire radiates from my useless shoulder, and my ankle throbs with each bump against the ground, but the pain pushes me forward.

A scream pierces the storm's howl.

Emily.

I force myself to move faster, ignoring the grinding in my shoulder. If I can just make it to the guest room. To the locked box in the closet. To the weapon inside.

Emily

Dr. Wilde steps over the splintered wood into the attic and his homicidal mask melts away. He looks the way I remember him. Kind, serious, attentive. For a fleeting moment, I feel safe, relieved.

I shove the emotion away. I'm not safe. I have to remember that. I can't allow him to lull me into a feeling of false security.

"What ... why are you here?" My voice shakes. I let it.

"I need to finish this."

I swallow, my eyes locked on his. "Finish what?"

He pauses, considering his answer. He takes a step toward me.

I force myself to stand still—as if I've frozen.

We've been over fight, flight, fawn, freeze dozens of times in our sessions. He knows my trauma response as well as I do. I freeze.

The only way out is to let him think I'm paralyzed with fear—and then fight. It's the only chance I have.

He takes note of my stiff posture and a hint of a cruel smile flashes across his mouth before he answers.

"Your husband has been protecting you," Dr. Wilde says in the same measured tone he uses in our counseling sessions. "From his brother. From himself. From the truth. From your destiny, Emily."

"My destiny?" I croak.

"Yes. You have to die."

He says it without emotion—like it's just a fact.

"Why?"

"To close the circle."

"I don't understand."

I don't actually care what reasoning his diseased brain has latched onto, but I need to keep him occupied while I use my peripheral vision to scan the attic for a weapon. The poker and knife rest against the wall near the window, tantalizingly out of easy reach—I'd have to dart past him to get to them. There's a framed print resting against a chest, a box labeled ornaments, and a stack of bins. Nothing that will protect me from the blow of an axe, if that's his plan.

Involuntarily, my gaze falls on the axe.

He looks down at the tool in his hands as if he's surprised to find it there.

Then he gestures with it, carving an arc through the air. "I've been treating Tristan."

I stare at him. "My Tristan?"

He nods. "For years. For as long as I've been treating you."

For a long moment, I consider this, then I shake my head. He has to be lying. "That's not possible. Isn't that—?"

"A conflict of interest. It would've been if I'd known, but he lied to me. He told me his name was Tate Weakes. For years, I didn't realize you were married to him. He used his brother's name, but his own story. I was helping him work through his guilt and trauma."

Heat surges through my chilled body, and my vision swims, as I try to process what he's telling me. "What trauma—his dad's death?"

"In a way, yes. But more than that, the fact Tristan knew, or at least, suspected that his brother had ... urges. That knowledge shaped the trajectory of your husband's life."

As curious as I am about this statement about Tristan, I focus on the urges.

"Urges? Tate attacked Alex, didn't he?" I venture.

He nods. "Yes, Lexi was his first attempt. It's not unusual for a killer to botch the first attack. After that, he honed his methods. He practiced and improved for seven years before his second attempt, which was successful."

The admiration in his voice turns my stomach. Bile rises in my throat and I force it back down.

"I don't understand. If you thought Tristan was Tate, how do you know what the real Tate did?"

He smiles. "Tate was smart. Smarter than anyone gave him credit for. He knew what Tristan was doing—not with me, not at first. But with you."

"Me?" I squeak.

He nods. "We'll get to that. After all, you're at the center of it all." He gestures again with the axe.

I really wish he'd stop that.

"What is Tristan doing with me?"

"I told you, he's protecting you."

"From what? He doesn't know about Cassie, or my anxiety. He doesn't know any of it," I insist.

He paints me with a pitying look, as if he hates to be the one to break it to me. "He does, Emily. He's known from the beginning. He knows everything—more than you do."

"No." I shake my head.

"Yes. As soon as he heard about Cassie's murder, he suspected Tate killed her." His eyes gleam. "And he knew you were the intended victim." He gestures to my hair. "You fit the type—not her. And he always thought Tate would return to finish the job."

"He *knew*?" My mind spins. My knees threaten to buckle. I'm sweating and on the verge of hyperventilating.

"I ... have to sit." I sink to my knees.

Dr. Wilde nods. "It's a lot to process, I know. Your marriage, your life together, is built on a foundation of lies. To be fair, though, you've withheld your truth from him, too."

His words barely register. But something else breaks through the noise buzzing in my head. Not about Tristan, about Tate.

I look up at Dr. Wilde. "You talk about Tate in the past tense."

He tuts. "It couldn't be avoided."

Fear twists my gut. "What couldn't?"

"I had to keep him quiet so I could finish my work."

"Your work?"

"He tracked me down, and at first, I genuinely thought I could help him understand his compulsions. I was so sure I could ..." He trails off, then shakes his head. "I was arrogant. I thought I was studying him, analyzing him. But he was studying me. He used me, Emily, and I failed to see it."

My chest tightens. I thought I was frightened by his rage when he broke down the door. But the clinical detachment in his voice terrifies me.

Finally, I squeak out, "What did you do?"

"What he couldn't do himself anymore. What he'd been grooming me to do." His professional mask slips, revealing something lost and confused underneath. "I didn't understand at first, why he chose me. But he knew. He saw how fascinated I was by you, by Tristan, and, of course, by him. He used my interest to pull me in. By the time I realized what was happening, I'd already helped him plan Giselle's death." He gestures helplessly with the axe.

The impulse to freeze for real is almost too much for me to fight. I'm numb. I can just sit here. Let whatever's going to happen, happen.

What am I fighting for, anyway? My marriage is a lie. And I've already lived a longer life than I deserve. I should have died seven years ago.

A sob rises in my throat. "You helped him?"

"Not directly. I thought he was telling me about his

past crimes. But he was planning his future crimes." Dr. Wilde's voice is almost reverent. "There was an art to it, you know. How he selected his victims. The red hair, the timing, the storms, the brutality of the attack. There's a pattern, a methodology. His work deserves to be understood."

I want to keep him talking, but I'm suddenly incapable of forming words. I make a noise that could mean anything. It does the trick.

He runs his hand along the axe handle. "But Tate became unstable. Giselle fit the pattern, but she wasn't the goal. She was a means to an end, a way to frame Tristan so he could get to you. I couldn't let him do that."

Maybe there's hope. "Because you wanted to protect me?"

Please say yes. Please, dear God, let him say yes.

"No." He laughs derisively, scoffing. "Because he was going to expose himself before I completed my study of his pathology."

"So you killed him." My voice is high, strained. I don't recognize it.

"I didn't mean to. Why would I? My only goal is to preserve his legacy. To make it mean something." He searches my face, his tone pleading for approval. "You understand about legacy, don't you, Emily? That's what your book is about, after all—making sense of trauma, finding meaning in pain."

This son of a bitch. How *dare* he compare my work to

murder. A hot flame of anger licks at my belly. I grab hold of it, hang on to the fire. I need it.

"So, what? You argued and somehow you came out on top in a fight with a serial killer?" I lace my words with disbelief, hoping to rattle him even a fraction as much as he's unmoored me.

He eyes me impassively. "I knew how to use his base impulses against him. He may have been an artist, but I'm a scientist—precise and accurate."

I suppress a shiver.

"Your role is crucial to the conclusion," Dr. Wilde says, his tone shifting to the clinical one he uses to explain therapeutic concepts. "The symmetry is incredible. Here you are with the only other survivor of one of Tate's attacks." He glances over my head at the window, then back to me.

His expression chills me. When I speak, my voice quavers. "What?"

"I'm afraid the narrative requires your death to be self-inflicted. Your guilt over surviving when Cassie died, your writer's block, the discovery of who Tristan really is, it all builds a compelling psychological narrative for suicide."

"I'm not going to kill myself," I tell him.

Something flickers in his eyes. "You have to. You of all people understand story structure. The climax only resonates if you kill yourself. It ties it all together."

"I don't want to die, Dr. Wilde."

I see a flash of what Tate must have seen. Loneliness, disconnection, the desperate need to matter. "I'm sorry, but it's the only way. Otherwise, my work will lack value. But, you won't be alone. I'll be right here with you."

"No." It comes out as a plea, but I mean it as a vow.

His expression hardens. "Enough of this, we need to proceed. The storm provides the perfect backdrop."

"What about Alex?" I stall, terrified I already know the answer.

"If she's not dead already, she's likely badly injured. She'll be easy enough to finish off. An unexpected bonus, really."

No. I won't let him get to her. Not after all she's already been through.

Alex

I nearly pass out after the crawl up the steps. I collapse on the porch, shaking and panting, and gather my waning strength to hang onto the doorknob and pull myself to my knees. The unlocked door swings open and I fall across the threshold, trembling and sweating.

But I'm inside. I can do this. I have to do this.

I drag myself toward the guest room. The doorway looms impossibly far away. Above, the low rumble of voices comes from the attic. Two voices. Emily's still alive.

The knowledge gives me a burst of adrenaline. My fingers scrabble for purchase in the cracks between the cold floorboards as I pull myself forward and push the door open.

I no longer feel my pain. I *am* pain. Bright, white, all-encompassing pain. It doesn't matter. I'm so close.

I army crawl with my left arm and leg to the closet door and yank it open with clenched teeth. The closet, two floors, is directly beneath the attic, and the voices are louder, clearer, here as they travel through the ductwork.

The man isn't Tate. And he's not Tristan. That much I can tell. But whoever this prick is, he was working with Tate, and he's telling Emily she has to die.

The box is in view now, high on the closet shelf. My vision blurs and a thousand tiny pinpricks of light explode as I lean against the wall and push myself to my feet.

I catch a sidelong glimpse of my profile in the mirror affixed to the closet door and gasp, heart thumping because, for a moment, I think someone's in the room with me. I turn and study my reflection. Blood mats my hair, dirt streaks my face, and my right shoulder juts out in a grotesquely distorted hump. But I'm fixated on my eyes: they stare back at me with the same haunted look I remember from the weeks and months immediately after I was attacked.

In the attic, Emily sobs loudly.

I tear my gaze away from the mirror. I prop my right leg against the wall, trying to keep my weight off my ankle, as I stretch up onto my left toes, grit my teeth, and try to reach for the safe on the shelf with both arms. It's no use. My right arm goes no higher than my damaged shoulder. I fall back to my heels and lean against the wall to steady myself so I can try again.

I push off from the wall and reach for the shelf again. My right arm dangles uselessly as I wrap the fingers around the handle of the heavy gun safe and pull it forward to the edge of the shelf.

I tip it toward me and let gravity do the work while I hang on tight. My arm wrenches down like the rectangular box weighs a thousand pounds. I stop it inches before it hits the floor and lower it gently. Then I kneel, my busted right ankle splayed to the side, and fumble with the lock with my stiff, cold fingers.

Overhead, the thud of quick footsteps and a loud thump sound. The beginning of a struggle? I curse under my breath, miskey the code, and have to start over. I race through the sequence again, my ears trained on the ceiling above my head. Finally, I enter the right digits and the lock opens with a click.

I yank the lid open and lift out the gun. It's heavy in my shaking hand. It's loaded, I know. Robert insists I keep it locked away. Our compromise is that I do so with a magazine loaded, the bolt action locked open, and the safety engaged.

I wobble to my feet, rack the bolt to chamber a round,

and I flick off the safety. Given my condition, I'll never make it upstairs in time.

I'll be lucky to get off one shot before I collapse. One shot to create a distraction and give Emily a fighting chance. Shooting blind, through two floors of solid wood, I'm unlikely to hit either of them—but there's no way to guarantee it. My finger finds the trigger and I hesitate, weighing the risk.

Another scream pierces the air, making my decision for me. I aim up at the far corner of the closet ceiling and steel myself for the pain of the recoil. I squeeze the trigger.

thirty-eight

Tristan

The thick silence stretches over the interrogation room. Loretta chews the lipstick off her lower lip. Graham cracks his knuckles. I listen to the thump of my heart in my chest. I'm about to give voice to my fear that I led Tate to Dr. Wilde. I'm responsible for Giselle Ward's death, even if I'm not legally culpable. And if anything happens to Emily or Alex, their blood will be on my hands, too.

My throat closes at the thought of Emily. My wife, my world, my heart. If Wilde hurts her—

Dunn's radio crackles. He's been patched into the police department's encrypted channel in North Carolina.

"Officers on the property. Single shot fired from within the house."

Shot fired? By the police? Wilde? One of the women? The clipped, cryptic message causes a frenzy of synapses to fire in my brain.

"I can't lose her," I croak. I squeeze my eyes shut and pray—if repeating *please, please, please,* can be considered a prayer.

Emily

"The window, Emily. It's time." His voice is flat. So is his expression.

I shake my head. "I can't."

"The note's already written," he tells me like that's what's holding me back. "It sounds just like your voice. I studied your books, you know? On top of all the trauma and guilt over Cassie's death, when you found out Tristan killed Tate, it was too much. The last straw."

"Tristan?" I shake my head, bewildered. "You said you killed Tate."

"Of course. But I can't be arrested. I have more work to do. Framing Tristan was too good to resist. He'll go down for Giselle Ward's murder and his brother's. There's a poetic justice in that, don't you think?"

I don't answer the question. Instead I ask one of my own. "Work? You mean, therapy?"

The professional mask cracks. "No. Tate helped me understand that watching isn't enough. Observation without participation is meaningless." His eyes are fever-bright now. "This will be my contribution to the field. My legacy."

The words hit me with force. He plans to continue to kill. Not just me and Alex. He's going to pick up where Tate left off. A new monster emerging from the ruins of so many shattered lives. I stumble backward, tripping over the framed picture near my feet. It falls heavily to the floor, and the glass cracks. Splinters tinkle out in a small pile.

He tuts at the mess. Then his expression hardens. "It's time to jump."

"I can't," I tell him. "I can't move."

He sighs heavily. "The freeze response. You're nothing if not predictable. I'll have to push you then," he says in a tone tinged with regret, like I'm ruining this special moment for him.

The petulance in his voice fans the flame growing inside me.

He grips my upper arms with steady hands and backs me toward the window. Behind him, the axe lies forgotten. Behind me, through the open window, the storm rages.

"Wait," I blurt.

He stops but digs his fingers more firmly into my arms. "What?"

I point toward the knife with my chin. "Can't I cut my wrists instead? I don't want to jump."

He narrows his eyes and studies me. In return, I widen mine in a plea.

For an instant, I think he's going to say yes and hand me the kitchen knife. I envision plunging it into his sternum.

Then he laughs. "Not a chance. While you bleeding out from stab wounds *would* be the most fitting end, I can't risk my fingerprints being found on the knife."

Even when I'm facing near-certain death and have nothing to lose, this man who knows my every fear and shame, doesn't consider for a moment that I might turn the knife on him. And his willingness to underestimate is the one thing that can save me now.

I just need a chance. Some way to grab the knife. Or the poker. Or the axe. Or to lunge at him and scrape at his eyes with my fingernails. Something, anything, to fight back. To save myself.

I fill my lungs with air, bounce on my heels, and get ready to make my move. And then, an explosive crack rings out, filling the small room. We both startle, and his grip loosens. He whips his head around toward the sound as it echoes off the wall.

A gunshot?

It doesn't matter what it is. It's my chance.

I yank myself free and dive to the floor, scrabbling for the broken glass. My hand closes around the biggest shard I can find. I grab it and pop to my feet, raw instinct driving me forward.

As he turns back toward me, I lurch at him and plunge the glass deep into his neck. His eyes go wide with surprise, not pain—not yet, at least.

"Fascinating," he chokes out, blood bubbling at his lips. "You broke free of freeze." He sounds almost proud.

His knees buckle. I stumble back, as he crumples to the floor, the glass still protruding from his neck. He reaches for me with trembling hands.

I watch him, unblinkingly, until, at last, his fingers twitch and still for good. The sound of sirens breaks through the steady beat of the rain outside. I peer out the window and see the flash of lights as a police SUV careens into view.

It's over. I've saved myself. I want to fall to my knees and sob with relief. But a thought intrudes. *Alex.*

I step over Dr. Wilde's body and run down the stairs.

Alex

. . .

When the recoil slammed through my left shoulder it reverberated in my broken collarbone and torn right shoulder. My vision whited out with pain. I have no idea how much time has passed.

Now, I force my eyes open to the sound of footsteps on the attic stairs and my chest clenches. Is it Emily—or *him*? I pull myself further into the closet, scrabble for the gun.

Outside, faint sirens grow louder, until they're screaming in the driveway.

"Em?" I croak, but my voice is only a hoarse whisper.

"Alex?" Emily's voice calls out, clear and loud. "Where are you? It's over."

It's over. It's finally over. Salty tears pour down my cheeks.

Still clutching the firearm, I drag myself across the bedroom. She comes into view in the foyer. Blood dots her hands and arms. Her face is a white sheet, her hair a tangled mess around her face. But she's alive.

I'm alive.

We're alive.

She jerks her chin at the gun. "You saved us. The gunshot distracted him long enough for me to—. It's over."

I see in her face what she's not saying.

"How? The knife?"

She shakes her head. "Piece of broken glass."

I crack a weak smile. "You dug your way out of the tower."

Another shake of her head, her red hair bobbing. "*We* dug *our* way out."

She steps over the threshold and sinks to the floor beside me. I grip her icy hand with my good one. That's how the first responders find us. Huddled together on the floor, holding hands.

part iv. happily never after

The tower in which Maid Maleen had been imprisoned remained standing for a long time, and when
the children passed by it they sang,

> "Kling, klang, gloria.
> Who sits within this tower?
> A King's daughter, she sits within,
> A sight of her I cannot win,
> The wall it will not break,
> The stone cannot be pierced."

—*Maid Maleen,* as retold by the Brothers
Grimm

Maleen and Ruth crawled out of the rubble of the
tower and blinked up at the bright sky, so long
hidden from them. The gardens outside lay dead

and dry, wilted brown sticks where flowers once grew.

"The trees are silent," Ruth whispered. "No birds sing."

The entire world was silent, Maleen thought. The earth was scarred and parched. The fields were bare. The cobblestone streets outside the wall were empty.

Ruth's face fell. "It seems we've escaped to a new horror, Mae."

Maleen squeezed her friend's hand with her own bruised and bloodied fingers. "Then we'll escape this one, too. We have our knives, after all?"

She raised the knife, now coated in dirt and bent from the impact of the stones.

Ruth smiled, a faint, tired smile that slowly bloomed into a true grin, lighting her face.

We do, indeed." She patted the pocket of her grimy skirt, touching the cool metal concealed within its filthy, silky folds.

Without discussing the matter, the women knew they would go their separate ways now. Bound forever by what they had shared, but ready to move forward in the world alone.

—The Tower, by Emily Rose

thirty-nine

Alex

One month later

I survey the still, empty farmhouse. Spring sunlight streams through windows I kept shuttered for so long. The light illuminates dust motes swirling in the air. I haven't left yet, but the house already feels unlived in, as if it knows its purpose as my fortress is ending. The thought brings a smile rather than the panic I'd expected. It's served its purpose—both good and bad.

It kept me hidden away from my past, but it also kept me hidden away from my present. No more.

On the kitchen counter, I place the key on top of the brief, unsigned note I've left for the new owner:

Here's to escaping our towers. The garden blooms in late April, and the best blackberries grow along the north fence. The house has its own heartbeat; learn to listen for it.

My fingers brush the rough edge where I tore the page from my notebook. Emily will make this place her own, turn it into something other than a hiding place. She's already transformed the cabin into her writing studio, and she swears the ghosts of Maleen and Ruth linger in the farmhouse attic and wave to her from the window.

I'll be glad to leave my ghosts behind when I leave. I'm ready to undertake the slow process of stitching myself back together, piece by piece.

The door opens and the spring breeze drifts in, carrying the loamy aroma of thawing earth and new growth. Robert's smiling face, as familiar as my own, appears in the open doorway, backlit by the morning sun. The scar on my collarbone twinges as I turn, a souvenir of that night, like the spiderweb of cracks still visible in the attic window.

"Ready to go?"

His grin broadens, the skin around his eyes crinkling. He's beyond thrilled that I've decided to join him for the remainder of his final posting—even if the events that prompted me to do so are grim. And he's used up all his leave so we can take a whirlwind trip first.

He's all in on the trip, but he wanted me to see a therapist first. Talk to someone. But once I told him the man who tried to kill me and Emily *was* a psychotherapist, he stopped asking. Instead, he holds me on the nights I wake up shaking.

All my memories from the original attack have returned. And they're rough. Coupled with my recovery from the fall, it's been a rocky ride.

But I don't want to waste any more time on either of the two experiences. I don't want to close myself up. And I don't want to talk. I want to, finally, live. To walk out into the sunshine and reveal myself.

I grin back and grab my bucket list notebook, its pages nearly full now. "Ready."

I step out onto the porch gingerly, still favoring my newly healed ankle, and place my hand inside his, rubbing the callous on his thumb with my finger.

I take one final long look at the farmhouse, then turn toward the cabin perched on the rise to study it for a moment. This property provided me with security, protection, and safety for years. Or at least the illusion of these things.

It was the psychotherapist who'd led Tristan to me.

Wilde had rented the cabin earlier in the year. In his archived booking email, he said he needed solitude to work on his research. Was it a coincidence that he chose my property? Or had Tate somehow tracked me down and pointed the doctor in my direction? With both of them dead, I'll never know. But what I do know is hiding didn't save me in the end.

I remind myself that I don't need to hide anymore. I've set myself free.

Robert nuzzles my cheek. "We should head out. We have a long flight."

"A long adventure," I respond.

We walk down the steps to the waiting car at my halting pace. I don't look back a second time.

forty

Three months later

The fairy lights strung along the eaves that overhang the farmhouse porch cast a warm glow. Hundreds more of the tiny twinkling white lights wind through the verdant, blooming trees. The summer air is redolent with the scent of flowers and buzzes with the tinkle of glasses and the low hum of conversation. The sun hangs low in the sky, but hasn't yet dipped behind the purple mountain.

I planned my book release party for the summer solstice for this very reason—the day will be long, and so will the celebration. I lean against the railing and survey the gathering spilling out from under the white tent to the wide lawn.

Sam and Jillian cross the yard to join me on the porch. Jillian's long tiered maxi skirt swirls around her ankles. My agent hands me a flute of prosecco as he mounts the stairs.

"Here's where you've been hiding," Sam says.

"Not hiding. Just taking it all in," I promise.

He raises his glass in an impromptu toast. "To breaking out of towers—and hitting the bestseller list."

Jillian squeezes my arm. "And to think you almost missed your deadline," she teases gently.

We had a long, boozy lunch on Sam's dime after I turned in my book. And whether from the wine or her easy manner, I poured out the whole story about why I struggled to write this book—and why it's the most necessary piece I've ever written. She understood, as writers do, and confided that she started writing romance after becoming a widow at twenty-two, awash in a sea of grief. It turns out opening up to someone, letting them know me and knowing them in return, doesn't make me vulnerable. It makes me powerful. Whole. I owe this realization, and so much more, to Alex.

My gaze drifts over the lawn and I spot a familiar figure hovering on the edge of the celebration in the tent. I excuse myself and head down the stairs, pausing to smile at the late evening sun lighting up the cabin windows.

My writing studio is set up in the cabin, although some days I work in the farmhouse kitchen. I feel close to Alex when I'm there—in between her pithy emails and our infrequent phone calls. A beautiful arrangement of orange roses and white lilies sits on the porch—a congratulatory bouquet from her and Robert, sent from somewhere in Southeast Asia.

By the time I reach my inherited herb garden, Tristan's broken free from the party. He stands alone, looking down at the overabundance of riotous basil. I come to a stop beside him and hesitate for an awkward moment, trying to decide how to start this conversation.

He turns toward me, one hand in the pocket of his linen pants and the other clutching a fluted glass.

"Nice turnout," he says.

As I study my estranged husband, I silently thank him for breaking the ice for both of us. He looks tired. But not haggard, not like he did in the aftermath of all that happened. He has the lazy smile I know so well and the same warm eyes. The light tan is new, and I wonder if he's started running again.

"I'm glad you came," I tell him.

It's true, I realize with a start.

"I wouldn't miss it." He clicks his glass against mine. "I read the book. It's your best work, Em."

My smile is so wide my cheeks ache. "Thanks. I'm

surprised you found the time. I thought you were working overtime on ... the case."

"I was. But we've officially closed the investigation," he says quietly. "Dr. Wilde's notes helped us connect everything. All the attacks, going back to Alex. Wilde documented everything."

My smile slips away. "Everything? Even the way Tate pulled him into his world, ensnaring him?"

Tristan and I understand our psychotherapist was a damaged person, but we also agree that he was, in a way, one of Tate's victims.

"Especially that. He was studying himself by the end. Taking notes on his state of mind in the barn where he hid to watch you and Alex. When he ran out of space in his notebook, he dictated detailed records on the satellite phone they found on him."

"How's the townhouse?" I ask. It's an obvious subject change, but I don't want to dwell on Dr. Wilde.

"Empty," he answers simply. "I miss you. So do Ty and Lashina." He hurries to add, "But I understand why you need time."

He does, I know. "Tell them I say hi."

"I will. You working on anything? Or just basking in the glow of all the effusive reviews of *The Tower*?"

I point my chin toward my writing studio. "I'm starting a new book. A thriller this time."

His eyes widen. "About what happened?"

"About women who save themselves. And each other."

I meet his eyes. "About how protection can become its own kind of prison."

He flinches but holds my gaze. "Emily, I—"

"I know why you did it," I cut him off gently. "I know you love me. I know everything you did was an effort to keep me safe." I pause, choosing my words with care. "But you kept me in the dark. In my own tower. And I need to know who I am when I'm standing in the light on my own."

"Do you think you'll ever be able to forgive me?"

That's the question, isn't it? Can I forgive him? I don't know. What I do know is forgiveness isn't a binary event, but a winding path. There are days when I ache from missing him, and I'm sure I'll find my way back to him. And there are days when the betrayal cuts as raw and deep as any physical wound, and I don't know how I'll ever trust him again. More than any of this, though, I know I need to forgive myself before I can move forward—with or without Tristan.

I look out over the property Alex has entrusted to me —my fresh start. I'm changing it from a fortress to a sanctuary alive with creation and possibility. And I'm listening for the heart of the house, eating the blackberries that burst with flavor. I've even brought her pollinator garden back to life. I have so much here. But not everything.

Then again, I never had everything. I thought I did. But I didn't. I had a caretaker, but not a partner; a lover, but not a friend; a relationship, but not a union.

After an eternity, I turn back to my husband. "I still love you, Tristan. That hasn't changed. But there were so many secrets between us, walls we never broke down. I need to figure out who I am and what I want when those walls aren't there anymore. I need to see myself clearly before I can see us clearly."

He nods, his expression pained but not surprised. "I understand," he says roughly. "I want that for you, too, Em. Even if it means I have to let you go for a while—or forever."

"Thank you."

I need to walk this winding path alone for now. I need to tend to my own healing before I can begin to mend what's broken between us. Tristan and I have both spent so long trying to protect each other and save each other. It's time we learn to save ourselves.

He leans in close and for a moment, I'm transported back to a thousand other summer nights we've shared.

"But I hope it's not forever," he breathes.

The spicy scent of his cologne, the glint in his eyes as he murmurs in my ear, the electric thrill that pulses through me at his proximity. It would be so easy—too easy—to fall back into his arms, find solace in his strength like I have so many times before.

I remind myself I have my own strength. Leaning on Tristan was a habit, but not a healthy one. If we have any chance at a real future together, we need to break free of our old patterns. We both need to learn to stand on our own.

I force myself to take a small step back, putting a whisper of distance between us. A shadow crosses his face, but he doesn't push.

"I'll give you as much time and space as you need," he vows. "I'm not going anywhere. When you're ready, if you're ever ready, I'll be here."

I nod, not trusting myself to speak around the lump gathering in my throat. I let my fingers rest on his arm briefly, a silent recognition of the story we've shared and everything still unwritten. Then I turn away and head toward the tent where my guests are gathered to hear me to read a passage from *The Tower*.

As I walk, I breathe in the honeysuckle-scented air and soak in the warmth of the breeze that caresses my arms. I begin to hum softly along with the buzz of the bees hovering in the purple sage and raise my face to the glow and twinkle of the fairy lights that drip from the trees. When I step under the white canopy, my mind is still, my heartbeat is steady, and my footing is sure.

I'm ready to tell my story, even though it has no ending.

author's note

Publishing this book is one of the scariest things I've done in a long time. Writing it? That was cathartic. But putting it out into the world? Terrifying.

I've written more than fifty books. I *know*. I can't believe it either. So you might think I'd be over the fear by now. But that top-of-the-roller-coaster, stomach-tightening dread mixed with exhilaration? I don't think that ever goes away. (For the record, I abhor roller coasters.)

As a reader, a writer, and a person, I love digging into the human psyche, so psychological thrillers hold a lot of appeal for me. I find unreliable narrators less appealing. It's as basic as this: I don't choose to spend my limited free time with liars, sociopaths, and psychopaths. But what about narrators who are unreliable because their memories are missing, or they're traumatized or trying to protect someone? Suddenly, I'm interested.

So at the outset, I knew the narrators might be flawed and damaged, but they'd be people I was willing to spend hundreds of hours getting to know. When I conceived of Emily as a writer with an anxiety disorder and a deadline, I knew her book in progress would be a fairy tale retelling featuring a self-rescuing princess. I settled on *Maid Maleen* and began to research its themes. That led me to a journal article by Katherine Langrish titled *Maid Maleen: A fairy-tale study of trauma*, in *Gramarye*, Issue 12 (Winter 2017), which, in turn, led me to Langrish's fascinating website, Seven Miles of Steel Thistle (well worth checking out). And the story fell into place.

This book is both a natural evolution of my writing and a new and different creature. It's also probably the most honest thing I've ever written. Like Emily, I know what it means to be trapped by anxiety, to build walls that feel protective but become prisons. This book grew out of my own hard-won journey from isolation to connection. Sometimes freeing ourselves looks more like digging at a stone wall with a dull spoon than a bold gesture. But we get there all the same.

I write to make sense of the bleakness in our world—but also to find the beauty in that ugliness. If you read fantasy novels, you may be familiar with the terms *grim-dark* and *noblebright*, two distinct approaches in the genre. In 2017, the writer Alexandra Rowland coined a third: *hopepunk*. You can find several essays online discussing the ethos of hopepunk (and if you can't, email me and I'll send you links).

As it applies to my (admittedly non-fantasy) books, it's the idea that kindness, connection, and resistance matter, even—no, *especially*—in the face of darkness. I believe we have to be resilient, optimistic, and brave despite the odds and despite our fears. I believe we rescue ourselves and each other. Our weapons are empathy, concern, and hope.

That may sound soft, but it feels radical. Words have power. Stories can shine a light in the darkness—and lead us to build a community rooted in authentic kindness, care, and courage. The journey to get there will be frightening, dangerous, and demand great sacrifice and bravery. But in the end, we—and the world—will be better for it.

That's what I wanted for Emily and Alex in *Cut Off from Sky and Earth*.

And that's what I want for you and me, too.

acknowledgments

Thank you to everyone in my personal life who supported me when I wrestled with writing (and then publishing) this book instead of sticking to my multiple ongoing series.

To my husband, David—my first reader, impassioned cheerleader, and deliverer of reality checks. Even when I waver about my work, he's steadfast.

To my children:

Adam, for enthusiastically encouraging me to get this book out into the world—and for assessing my shiny plans and ideas with an eye toward business reality;

Jack, for our wide-ranging conversations about ergodic and metaleptic literature, which convinced me I hadn't bitten off more than I could chew;

and Sara, for being my break bestie, always ready to join me on a coffee date or trip to the library.

Thank you, too, to my siblings. My brother, Trevor, was a thoughtful, insightful brainstorming partner as I worked through how I wanted to get this book into your hands. My sister, Theresa, kept me focused and energized through our near-daily check-ins, texts, and calls—yes, with regard to writing, but also with regard to other important things, like eating and showering.

I also owe professional thanks to Jack for using his artistic talent to bring my cover vision to life, and to David for overseeing the process.

Trevor put on his editing hat to join Louis Maconi in polishing this book. As always, I'm grateful for Trevor and Lou's outstanding editing, proofreading, and keen attention to detail.

And finally, thank you to my readers, who were nothing but patient and supportive as I worked on this side project in secret—even though it meant a longer wait between series books.

Thank you for making space in your life for my stories.

discussion questions

1. Emily writes about two women trapped in a tower, yet finds herself living in one. How does her relationship with Tristan both protect and imprison her? At what point does protection become control?

2. Both Emily and Alex have experience with violence, but they respond differently—Emily by seeking safety, Alex by withdrawing from the world. How do their survival strategies shape who they become? What does their evolving relationship reveal about healing?

3. The novel explores how trauma distorts memory and perception. How do Emily's and Alex's recollections of their experiences shift over time? What role does truth—remembered, reconstructed, or repressed—play in their healing?

4. The story of *Maid Maleen* and Emily's retelling, *The Tower,* weave through the novel. In what ways do Emily and Alex parallel Maleen and Ruth? Are they closer to the characters in the original or to the characters in Emily's retelling? In what ways do both Emily and Alex become their own rescuers?

5. The novel takes its title from a line in the fairy tale: "Meat and drink for the seven years were carried into the tower, and then she and her waiting-woman were led into it and walled up, and thus cut off from the sky and from the earth." How are Emily and Alex—literally and metaphorically—cut off throughout the novel? What does it mean for them to reconnect with the world, with each other, and with themselves?

6. Tristan lies to Emily about his identity and past, insisting it's to protect her. Can deception ever be justified in the name of love? Do you agree with Emily's choice to leave him—not out of anger, but to rediscover who she is without him?

7. Like Emily and Alex, Tristan struggles to deal with his traumatic past. What parallels do you see between Tristan and his mother Tara and Emily and Alex? What lessons do you think Tara and Tristan could take from Emily and Alex's reclaiming of their stories?

8. Alex's memory comes back in broken images during the climax of the story while Emily's is triggered by the scent of sandalwood and Tristan's is tied to the weather. Have you ever uncovered a long-buried memory in a

surprising or unexpected way? What do you think this phenomenon might mean for the way we process experiences?

9. Melissa F. Miller's author's note draws a connection between this novel and the fantasy subgenre known as *hopepunk*, rooted in the belief that kindness, connection, and resistance matter, especially in the face of darkness. How do Emily and Alex embody this philosophy? Do you find this approach more or less compelling than darker psychological thrillers?

10. In the author's note, Miller writes, "Sometimes freeing ourselves looks more like digging at a stone wall with a dull spoon than a bold gesture." How does this image resonate with Emily's arc? Can you think of times in your own life when liberation came gradually, rather than all at once?

11. The novel argues that we save ourselves and each other through empathy, concern, and hope. How do Emily and Alex do this? How does Tristan fit into this dynamic? Where do you see mutual rescue versus individual strength? What does this suggest about the power of connection?

about the author

Melissa F. Miller is a multi-time *USA Today* bestselling author of mystery, thriller, suspense, and romance novels. A former complex commercial litigator, Melissa graduated from the University of Pennsylvania with a BA in medieval literature and creative writing (poetry), and earned her JD, *cum laude*, from the Duquesne University School of Law.

After fifteen years, she traded the practice of law for the art of storytelling, drawing on her legal background and love of research to craft fast-paced, twisty books for readers who believe light drives out darkness, love is brave, and kind is strong. Her stories feature strong, resilient characters who confront serious (and sometimes dark) issues with heart.

Melissa is a member of Sisters in Crime, International Thriller Writers, and Novelists, Inc. When she's not writing, you can find her tending her garden, practicing yoga, or drinking coffee. She lives outside Harrisburg, Pennsylvania, with her family and their rescue cat and dog. (The cat's in charge.)

She'd love to welcome you to her online reader community, The Neighborhood.